Liaisons

Look out for other Black Lace short fiction collections

Liaisons
A Collection of Erotic Encounters
From Black Lace
Edited by Lindsay Gordon

BL

This book is a work of fiction.
In real life, make sure you practise safe, sane and
consensual sex.

Published by Black Lace 2009

2 4 6 8 10 9 7 5 3 1

Roadside Rescue © Janine Ashbless; Table for Three © A.D.R. Forte; My Tutor ©
Primula Bond; Advanced Corsetry © Justine Elyot; Men © Charlotte Stein; Junking
© Alison Tyler; Perfect Timing © Kristina Wright; Archeogasms © K D Grace;
Wednesdays and Tuesdays © Sommer Marsden; The Woodsman © Charlotte Stein;
Glamour © Carrie Williams; Under the Big Top © Mae Nixon; A Stroll Down
Adultery Alley © Portia Da Costa

First published in Great Britain in 2009 by
Black Lace,
Virgin Books,
Random House, 20 Vauxhall Bridge Road,
London SW1V 2SA

www.blacklace.co.uk/www.virginbooks.com/www.rbooks.co.uk

Addresses for companies within The Random House Group Limited can be found at:
www.randomhouse.co.uk/offices.htm

The Random House Group Limited Reg. No. 954009

Distributed in the USA by Macmillan, 175 Fifth Avenue, New York, NY 10010, USA

A CIP catalogue record for this book is available from the British Library

ISBN 9780352345165

The Random House Group Limited supports The Forest Stewardship Council [FSC], the
leading international forest certification organisation. All our titles that are printed on
Greenpeace approved FSC certified paper carry the FSC logo.
Our paper procurement policy can be found at www.rbooks.co.uk/environment

Typeset by Palimpsest Book Production Ltd, Grangemouth, Stirlingshire FK3 8XG

Printed and bound in Great Britain by CPI Bookmarque, Croydon CR0 4TD

Contents

Roadside Rescue

Janine Ashbless

Absolutely bloody typical.

Of course her car had chosen to break down on the emptiest road in Scotland, on an afternoon when it was lashing with rain. Of course it would be on this day of all days. And of course there'd been no reception on her mobile phone, just one bar flickering fitfully on the digital display.

Sarah's first reaction had been rage: the sort of helpless rage that was unpleasantly close to tears. She'd slammed the steering wheel with her hands and sworn at the car and then at the rain and then at God, if he happened to be listening. But, after that, she'd got a grip on herself. There'd been no other vehicles in sight and she didn't remember passing one in twenty miles. She'd had to make contact with the outside world somehow.

And of course she hadn't brought waterproofs: she'd expected to spend the whole weekend indoors, either in bed or in the hotel restaurant. She did have an umbrella in the glove box but when she'd got out of the car, leaving the emergency lights flashing, she'd quickly discovered that it wasn't going to help much. The wind had been coming across the rolling moor-top in petulant gusts, nearly snapping the ribs of the umbrella as she clutched it low over her head, flattening the little white tufts of bog cotton to the ground and driving the rain nearly horizontally. Her dress – her lovely flirty rose-print dress that she knew Mervyn would like so much, and take such pleasure in stripping from her – had been soaked through in less than a minute.

Gritting her teeth, she'd turned towards a rocky crag that was the nearest bit of high ground and had set off through the coarse grass. Icy peat-brown water had closed over her ankles at once as she negotiated the roadside ditch, and she'd howled inwardly at the thought of how much she'd paid for the pretty summer sandals she was now ruining.

But she'd made it. After ten minutes she'd reached the top of the hillock and found two bars' worth of phone connection, enough to ring out. She'd thought of dialling Mervyn but she'd only managed to get through to his voicemail when she stopped at the garage outside Glasgow, so she'd rung her break-down service instead. And the operator had promised a recovery vehicle within an hour.

He was quite a bit faster than that, actually. Sarah was safely back in the car but still wallowing in her fury and panic when she saw the flashing orange lights in her rear-view mirror; suddenly all the bad stuff went away and she was so relieved she could have cried, though she was instantly ashamed of her weakness. The truck pulled up just ahead of her car and parked with lights still shimmering, and a figure in bulky yellow waterproofs paced to her passenger door and knocked.

'You all right?' he asked, bending to look in the lowered window. Under his hood he had a disarming smile, but the gust of wind-driven rain made her recoil.

'Yes. Just cold.' Her dress was plastered to her legs like a second skin. She'd thought about pulling on the change of clothing she'd brought, but that would have left her with nothing dry to wear later. She couldn't believe how chilly the rain was – not like July at all. Why on earth had they chosen Scotland to meet?

'On your own?'

'Afraid so.'

'Well, you've not picked the best week to be holidaying. Pop the bonnet will you, and I'll take a look. If you want to go sit in my cab the engine's on. It'll be warmer.'

He disappeared behind the raised bonnet and Sarah braced herself to face the weather. She felt she ought to talk to him about engine symptoms, but the wind nearly knocked her sideways as she got out and she couldn't even look into the sharp-edged rain. She gave up on any thought of toughing it out, and scurried for the flat-bedded garage truck parked on the verge ahead. The vehicle was so tall she had to climb up onto its broad back seat, from where she could see the repairman stooped over her car's engine. The rain made his fluorescent clothing flare and wobble through the glass.

What if he couldn't fix it quickly? she asked herself. What would Mervyn do if she were late? He could be so impatient sometimes. And if she was really late he might think something terrible had happened. Would he call the police? Would he dare? She needed to get to a phone.

The mechanic came back over and braced the cab door open against the wind. 'You've got a blown cylinder. I'm going to put your car on the back and take you into town. OK?'

Sarah nodded, and rain showered off her hair.

'There's a towel behind your seat there, if you like.'

'Will it take long to fix? The cylinder?'

His eyebrows rose. 'Well, if you're lucky and we've got the parts in we'll maybe get it done tomorrow. After that you'll have to wait until Monday.'

'Tomorrow?' She was aware she was keeping him standing in the rain but she couldn't help the squeak of protest.

'You got somewhere you need to be in a hurry?'

'Fort William. I'm supposed to be there tonight!'

He shook his head. 'No chance. Not in that car, anyway.'

'Well – is there a taxi?'

'Not around here.' The bang of the door cut off the cold draught.

Tomorrow? They'd only booked two nights in the hotel; that was all Mervyn could get away for. It was all going to be ruined. She imagined him sitting in the hotel bar, his tumbler of single malt on the table before him, his fingers drumming on the polished wood as he waited and waited and she didn't turn up. He'd be furious, in his cold polite way. It was all a complete mess.

Sarah felt an unexpected flicker of anger. It wasn't enough that she'd had to go through this, she was going to get the blame too. Mervyn would extract some sort of forfeit. He'd withhold something that she wanted just to make his point.

Sighing, she shrugged off the picture and found the towel behind her seat, along with a sleeping bag. The towel wasn't laundry-fresh; as she rumpled her hair she could smell a faint masculine aroma, disturbing yet oddly comforting. She kept an eye out through the window as she rubbed her thighs and arms, lifting her skirt, then pulled down her top to mop her chest. Her nipples were poking through the wet cotton of her bra rather obviously and she pressed them with the palm of her hand in a vain attempt to quell their impertinence. Her thighs were itching from the cold and she scratched at them, feeling a rash flare on her pale skin.

The rescueman was lowering the back of the truck, attaching a winch to her car, then using a hydraulic control to draw the smaller vehicle up the ramp onto the truck bed. The orange truck lights throbbed steadily, twinkling in the raindrops that crawled down the glass. He worked quickly, efficiently, strapping the car down with long canvas bands. She liked that. She liked his broad shoulders. She liked the smell of him on her skin, and that made a little worm of guilt squirm inside her. She squashed it flat.

With everything secured he returned to the cab and jumped into the driver's seat in front of her, hastily stripping off his waterproofs. Underneath he wore a white sweater and worn jeans, and the rain had got through to them too in patches. 'Pass the towel,' he said, twisting to look at her.

She handed it over. 'Sorry, it's a bit damp.'

His eyes flicked up and down her. Blue eyes, and the beginning of nice lines in his face. He probably wasn't even aware that he'd done it, she thought, but she knew he'd taken in the way her wet dress clung to her, and she blushed, smiling. He hesitated before speaking, but she did not seize the chance to look away and break the moment.

'Oh, I can cope with a little damp.' His humour was gentle. 'Wouldn't be living up here if I couldn't, would I now?'

'I suppose not.' She could feel herself glowing. His gaze dropped to her wet breasts and this time he was clearly conscious of where his eyes were resting. 'But you'll be wanting a hotel room now.'

She didn't know what to say. He caught his lip in his teeth and waited.

'OK,' she managed.

The tentative flicker in his eye died down. 'Since you'll be staying overnight, I guess.'

'Uh-huh.'

'And we don't want you catching your death.'

The moment – the something that might have been, the barely definable suggestion of possibility – passed and he turned away. Sarah watched as he dried off with the towel, rumpling his hair to dark spikes. The back of his neck was weathered brown, his broad hands ingrained with old oil. Her heart was suddenly thudding in her chest. She had to say something, had to keep him talking, because she could feel Mervyn's disapproval looming at the back of her head and, if she let the conversation lapse, it would come crashing in on her.

'You know I've only got basic membership,' she admitted. 'I'm only entitled to roadside assistance, not recovery to a garage.'

He glanced briefly over his shoulder. 'Well I'm not leaving you here, am I? We can sort it out later. Unless there's another garage you'd rather be calling?'

'No.'

'Well then.'

At that moment she saw her fingers touch the back of his neck. They'd moved entirely without conscious direction and, though he was the one who jumped, she was damn sure he was no more surprised than she was. His skin felt silky-warm.

'Those are cold!' He laughed to cover the precarious moment.

'Sorry,' she whispered, feeling the prickle of his nape hairs under her exploring fingertips. His heat was irresistible. 'I really could do with somewhere to warm them up.'

'Oh?' He took a deep breath. 'Well, you know, I can think of somewhere ...'

'Go on then.' She had no idea where this daring was coming from, but it seemed to be determined to press on, wilfully ignoring Mervyn's thunderous glare.

'Well ... You mean that?'

'Yes.'

He was galvanised. He scrambled over the back of the seats, sitting in the notch between the headrests – the cab was just tall enough – staring at her, his breath suddenly loud down his nose. His lower lip was caught once more in his teeth, making his smile lopsided and wary. He still didn't look like he believed what she was offering until she reached up and laid her hands on his thighs, framing the bulge of his crotch. He put his hands on hers then, stroking her fingers and up her wrists, his fingertips callused, his touch increasingly firm. She undid his belt, slipping the top button of his jeans then working down the fly over what was a growing bulge. He had to help her pull out the burgeoning length of his cock, which quickly swayed impressively erect. His shaft surged and thickened even as she ran her fingers down his length for the first time. She could smell the washing-powder perfume of fresh clothes on the heat of his skin.

He was definitely on the substantial side.

'God, yes,' he said in an undertone as she tipped forwards to take his blunt and eager bell in her mouth, tasting his salt: there was nothing floral about that. He felt hot on her cold lips. He wrapped his fingers in her wet hair, quite gently, pressing her down on his cock. She took it all the way to the back of her mouth and held it there, squeezing, until he groaned with pleasure.

Because that was how Mervyn liked it too.

It was a wonderful cock, Sarah thought. She gave it the licking and sucking it deserved, until he was perfectly hard. She was good at sucking dick – Mervyn had told her that. She knew she could keep doing this until the stranger came in her mouth, and then she could walk away almost innocent. But the unknown rebel twisted in her guts and she pulled off. 'What's your name?' she asked softly.

He looked mesmerised. 'Gavin.' His cock swayed, its wet length glistening.

'Hey, Gavin.' She reached into her cleavage, finding the little package nestled there, warm from her body heat. 'Put this on.'

And, as he tore the pack and skinned on the rubber, she turned and flipped up her skirt, presenting her pale thighs with their red scratch lines, and the round firm gift of her bum. When he tugged her panties down and touched her slash he found a hot and slippery wetness that was nothing to do with the rain. He pushed his wonderful cock home into that wet, as tight as a piston in its sleeve, and gripped her bum with his oily hands as he began to work her. She braced her arms on the back of the seat, taking him all the way. He's thicker than I'm used to, she admitted, as he stretched her wide. That pressure, the way he made her insides yield to his bulk and his force – that was something she desperately needed, she realised now. She could feel her interior surge of arousal, a glacial shifting, and she pushed back against him, her gasps coming quick and sharp.

And, God, he was sweet. He even leaned in over her to touch her clit and drive her to her climax while his thick cock pumped her pussy, so that she came first, panting and squealing – and then he came too, shooting his cream into her tight grip.

Behind her eyes Mervyn's disapproving face disintegrated in an explosion of light.

In her hotel room that night Sarah sat on the edge of her bed and wondered what the hell she'd been thinking of. She'd never tried such a thing in her life before – so what had made her jump a recoveryman like that? Sure, he wasn't unattractive, but she'd been on her way to visit someone else. Was that it then? After weeks of anticipation, was it being unable to cope with being frustrated at the last moment?

It wasn't just weeks, she reminded herself. It was nearly three months since she'd last been able to meet with Mervyn. And then it had been a night at the theatre – two tickets bought separately – and a furtive against-the-wall shuffle in the Ladies' during the second act.

She recalled that passionate struggle wistfully, but the picture blurred and was ousted by a more recent memory: Gavin shafting her doggy-style on the back seat of the truck cab. His grunts of pleasure as he powered his way into her. His hard thighs and thick cock.

Her phone rang.

Sarah knew who it was before she picked up. She'd left a message on his voicemail as soon as she could, and later rung the hotel reception at Fort William to leave another apology and a backup message: I'm stranded overnight seventy miles south of you.

'Sarah.'

'Mervyn – are you OK? Did you get my message?'

'Yes. Where are you now?'

'I had to take a hotel room.' She hurriedly explained about the car and finished with, 'Are you coming to pick me up?'

'I don't think so. That would hardly be wise.' He was always very careful about traceability was Mervyn. He'd never so much as given her a lift to the station. Sarah felt her shoulders sag.

'Well what are we going to do?'

'You can drive up tomorrow. And I'm going to wait here – I'm sure I can find something to keep me amused.'

She felt the hurt flex inside her. 'Are you sure? That'll only be one night we have together then.' Even if Gavin did get the car fixed quickly, she added to herself. If it wasn't until Monday she'd have blown the whole weekend for nothing, plus she would have to take a day's leave from work.

'It'll have to do, if you can't manage to keep your car road-worthy. Are you in your room at the moment?'

'Yes.' She was reeling a little from the clipped accusation.

'Alone?'

'Of course.'

'Go and look out of the window.'

She stood and went to open the curtains. 'What am I looking for?'

'What can you see out there?'

'Not much – it's dark.'

'And your room light is on?'

'Uh-uh.'

'Good. What's out there by daylight?'

'The main road through the village.' Gavin had described it as a town but it was really no more than a village with a castle, a tiny museum, and a single hotel. 'It goes along the water ... We're on a sea loch here, I think. It's calm out there. No beach or anything.'

'Excellent. So anyone out there can see into your lit window?'

She shivered. 'I guess.'

'Touch your breast.'

She held her breath.

'Sarah?'

'Yes?'

'Are you doing it?'

'Mervyn ...'

'I want you to touch your breast, slowly. Squeeze it.'

An inner trickle of warmth told her how much she was in thrall to his voice. 'OK,' she breathed, and cupped the warm curve of her right breast in her free hand. 'I'm doing it.'

'Rub your hand all over it. Play with your nipple.'

The familiar ache of excitement was running like a tide through her body. 'Yes,' she said.

'Is it hard? Tell me how you're doing it.'

It was hard like a bullet. 'Yes, it is. I'm pinching it between my finger and thumb and twisting it. Like you do to me.'

'And do you like that?'

She couldn't keep her voice quite even. 'It makes me want to feel your mouth on my breasts.'

'On your what?'

'My breasts.'

'Oh no. You don't use prissy words like that. *Breasts* and *pussy* are for good girls. You're not a good girl, are you, Sarah?'

'No,' she whispered.

'No. You're a dirty girl, aren't you? I know that. Ever since that day you stayed behind after my lecture for a little extra tuition. Wanting me to fuck you. It's not allowed, is it? But that didn't stop you. In your short skirt and tight blouse, wiggling your pert little body at me. Begging me to touch you.'

Sarah shut her eyes. It was all true; hers had been a crazy all-consuming crush on the handsome older man. 'Yes.'

'So don't tell me about your *breasts*, dirty girl. What is it that you're touching for me?'

She was on familiar ground. 'My titties. I'm touching my titties and thinking about the way you suck them.'

His stifled groan was audible. 'Then get them out for everyone to see, Sarah. Do that now.'

With a whimper she slipped the top buttons of her blouse and laid it open over her breasts. She wasn't even wearing her bra; that garment was still hanging over a radiator to dry. 'I've got them out. I'm touching my bare titties for you, Mervyn.'

'That's right. And anyone looking up at that window can see them now, can't they?'

'Yes.'

'And what else will they want to see?'

'No,' she groaned. 'Please.'

'Say it.'

'My ... pussy.'

'Your twat, girl. Your dirty cunt.'

She took a deeper breath. 'My cunt.'

'Are you wearing a skirt, Sarah?'

'Yes.'

'Tuck it up then. Pull down your knickers. Show them. Touch yourself. Tits and twat.' His voice was sounding croaky.

'Please ...'

'Do it now.'

'Yes.' She obeyed, easing her panties down her thighs.

'Have you got your hand right in your snatch, dirty girl?'

'Yes. Oh, yes.'

'Let me hear it.'

She lowered the phone to her crotch to let him hear the moist little noises her fingers were making in her slick flesh. He did not speak for some moments.

'Now tell me what you're doing.'

'I'm fucking myself. I've got one leg up on the window sill and I'm sticking my fingers in my cunt and stroking the juices all over my clit. I'm all wet, Merv. I'm all wet and slippery and my titties are wobbling and I'm going to come soon.'

'Good. Let me hear you. Let me hear you come, you dirty girl. Touching yourself where everyone can see you, like a real whore. Standing there with your tits on show, playing with yourself.'

She drowned his voice with her own, babbling as she slithered into orgasm. She thought she heard his staccato grunts, but couldn't be sure because, as her moans died away, the connection went dead and she was suddenly alone in her hotel room, with her cheeks burning and the muted TV flickering. She let out a long breath then, almost like a sob.

That was the second time today she'd betrayed Mervyn. She'd pleasured herself just as he'd demanded, but she hadn't done it in public view. When he'd first told her to touch her nipple she'd moved quietly away from the window and put her back to the wall. The confusing thing was, she didn't understand why.

The garage looked closed when Sarah approached it at 5 p.m. the next day, her suitcase rumbling behind her on the pavement flagging. The big wooden double doors were shut, but there was a light on in the window of the reception office, so she pushed the door open and heard a bell ring deeper within the building. She had to clench her teeth against an inner wash of embarrassment. How was she going to be able to look him in the eye?

Gavin stepped out from an inner door and smiled at her. 'Hey.' He was wearing a blue boiler suit and from under the rolled-up sleeves his forearms protruded, grey with oil to the wrists.

'Hello.' OK – so she did look him in the face, and the warmth in his blue eyes made her tingle. She spoke quickly to cover her confusion. 'Is it all done?'

'I told you it would be, didn't I?'

'It's just I'm cutting it so fine if there's to be anything left of the weekend ...'

'Oh aye.' He tilted his head ruefully. 'And we're supposed to be on a half day today. I sent the other guys home and stayed on myself.'

'Oh.' Sarah didn't know where to look. 'I am really grateful, you know.'

'No worries.' He nodded at the door behind her. 'Just lock that and come on through to the back, then.'

'What?' she said in a small voice.

He raised his eyebrows. 'To get your car. It's in the workshop. I can't leave the office unattended.' A flick of his eyes indicated the till and Sarah had to admit he had a point. This was excruciating, she thought. But she dropped the latch of the Yale lock and followed him through, trundling her case behind her.

Act like an adult, she told herself. You just fucked him, that's all.

The garage workshop was big enough to hold maybe half a dozen cars, but there were only two there at the moment, including hers. Sarah glanced around, suppressing a little shiver; it was rather cool in here and she was back in her floral dress, which was dry once more but didn't provide much insulation. She noted racks of new tyres and the two inspection pits with their hydraulic ramps to lift vehicles overhead, batteries and toolboxes and coils of wire rope and electric leads. The room smelled of oil and filed metal. There was a calendar on one wall that she thought relatively tasteful. Well, it could have been worse.

'Hold on a sec.' Gavin went over to a workbench, dipped his hands into a bucket of gel that was an alarmingly lurid shade of green, and scrubbed them clean in the sink. 'I'll just get your invoice printed out.' Wiping his hands on a paper towel he stabbed a few keys on the nearby computer. 'Luckily we had compatible engine parts in. It'll run, though I've got to say it doesn't look good long-term: I'd be in the market for a new car if I were you.'

'Oh.' Sarah sagged a bit.

'And, seriously, you're not looking after it right. Do you want to see what I drained out of your oil sump?' He brought her a metal pan with inches of liquid in the bottom, viscid and pitch black. 'When was the last time you had it serviced? The oil and filters changed?'

'I don't remember.'

'You can't just keep running an engine on this crap forever, you know.' His smile softened his serious words. 'You've got to give it a bit of TLC or the crud just builds up and wears the working parts out or seizes things solid.'

'Yeah, I know. Sorry.'

'It's just about looking after yourself. I mean, there are much worse places to have a sudden engine failure than a back road in Scotland.'

'Much worse,' she admitted, and fire sparked in his eyes as they both wordlessly acknowledged what had happened the previous day. Sarah felt the heat in her cheeks. Gavin cleared his throat. Putting the oil tray aside he turned back to the printer.

'You gave me a good mark on my customer service form, I hope?' he asked over his shoulder.

She answered his warm grin with her own, rather shyer. 'I gave you an honest appraisal.'

'Oh,' he said shaking his head. 'That's scary. Marks out of ten, eh?'

'You didn't do too badly.'

He chuckled. 'Well, this is the bill for the repair work.' He pushed a computer printout towards her. 'I've only charged you for parts, not labour.'

Her smile faded. 'Why?'

'Well, you know ...'

'Do you think that's why I did it?' Her voice was sharp suddenly, startling even her. He stood back, looking serious.

'No. I just ...'

'That's sort of insulting, don't you think?'

'So why *did* you do it?' His voice was calm, his eyes searching. It took the wind out of her sails.

'I ... don't know. I just –'

'You just ... ?'

'It just happened.'

He reached out and caught her by the waist, pulling her up against him.

'What are you doing?' she protested weakly.

'It just happened,' he whispered, kissing her. She gave up on the idea of protesting, even though he was pressing her clean dress to his grimy overalls, because under those protective clothes he was all muscle and eagerness. They kissed for a dizzying moment in which she felt like the ground was falling away and he was the only thing holding her up. His body was so solid she felt like she was liquid in contrast. His hand slid to her bottom, cupping her cheek, caressing its roundness voluptuously. It was a hand with a mission of exploration: she realised that as it slid round to her thigh. He'd just worked out she was wearing a tiny little thong that didn't cover her bottom.

'Is that for me?' he chuckled, as they broke for air.

Sarah shrank a little in his arms. 'No,' she admitted.

Gavin's ardour cooled as he read her expression. He let her go and stood back, looking thoughtful. 'Who is he then?'

'Ah . . .' She shook her head. 'He's . . . We've been together five years now – well, sort of. Since I was at university.' When Gavin waited patiently she felt obliged to go on, though the words seemed dry and harsh in her throat. 'He was my lecturer, my tutor, there. We started seeing each other. It had to be secret, of course. And we still see each other when we can; it's just not that easy for him to get away. He's head of department now . . .'

'I see.'

'I love him.' She'd expected the confession to be passionate when it was finally uttered but, she thought with alarm, it sounded only pathetic.

'He's married, isn't he?'

Sarah's face felt like it was crumpling and she fought to keep it smooth as she explained, 'He can't leave his wife: she's got MS and she depends on him.'

Gavin's eyebrows rose.

'Don't look at me like that,' she said hoarsely.

'Like what?'

'Like you know something and I don't. He loves me. I love him.' She stopped suddenly, because other words were forcing themselves up her throat. She tasted them, rolling them about on her tongue, shocked even as she released them: 'He's the only man I've ever been with.'

Until you.

He shook his head, swearing under his breath. 'Looks like it's more than your car that needs attention,' he muttered as he took hold of her. He bore her back step by step to a bench, pinning her up against the scarred wood to kiss her. Sarah tried to formulate some protest but his lips kept getting in the way of her breath and every time his mouth moved on hers, her words dissolved in the wet heat. His kisses were deep and wild, nothing like Mervyn's, was her only coherent thought – though in fact Mervyn barely kissed her at all. Then for long moments she couldn't think at all, only feel, only submit. When he pulled away at last she was breathless and shaken and her body felt like it didn't belong to her; it felt like it had made some decision without her and she was left to keep up as best she could.

Gavin's hand closed over her left wrist, pinning it gently to his chest. He reached behind her to the bench and brought forth a length of webbing strap. Quietly he knotted it about her wrist.

'What ... ?' she whispered, surfacing from a whirlpool of sensation.

'It's OK. I just want to get a proper look at you.' Trailing the strap, he pulled her into the middle of the workshop. There was a hoist there for lifting cars, already raised over head height, though no vehicle sat on it. He threw a loop of the strap over a metal strut and pulled on it to raise her arm over her head.

'Gavin!' She started to squirm, suddenly nervous. He quieted her with a kiss, gentle and lingering.

'Don't be scared, Sarah,' he murmured. 'You have to trust me.'

How could she trust him – a man she hardly knew? How could she not – when his hand was moving on her breasts like that, making her melt with pleasure, and when his eyes were full of such warm promise? He'd done nothing since they'd met but give her what she needed, she realised. So she stopped resisting, and he kissed her again to reward her before tying the webbing about her other wrist. Then he stepped back. She was standing with both arms raised loosely above her head, her expression charged with fear and need. Gavin bent to take up the hem of her dress and pulled it slowly right over her head, over her elbows, over the strap, settling it over the metal hoist where he let it hang out of the way. He smiled as he looked down at her. The bra and knickers were a matching set, white sprigged with little red flowers.

'Very pretty.'

Sarah shivered, aware once more how cool the air was here, longing for his warmth against her. But he stepped away, briefly, in order to thumb the control of the hydraulic hoist. With a hum and a rattle it rose in the air, lifting her arms out over her head, then pulling them taut, then lifting her on her toes with her whole body stretched. As Sarah's eyes flew wide open Gavin brought the machinery to a stop. There was such a look of pleasure and anticipation in his face that she squirmed in her bonds, feeling the warmth seep into her panties as she writhed her thighs together, making him breathe hard down his nose. He pulled open all the poppers of his overalls and retied the garment around his hips without once taking his eyes off her. Underneath he was wearing a plain white T-shirt, which he pulled off with a single careless motion and dropped on the floor. Sarah saw for the first time the full muscle of his bare chest and shoulders and the flow of dark chest hair over the contours of his skin, and she quivered, thinking he was like his machinery: strong and hard and made for a physical purpose. The blue fabric was tented at his crotch.

Then he closed in again to run his hands all over her, making her skin shiver and dance. 'He doesn't deserve you,' he whispered, reaching round to her back to unhook her bra, loosing her breasts to hang like teardrop pendants, her areolae puckering in the chill. He worked the flimsy garment up her arms and knotted it about her wrists, and as he did it her stiffening nipples rubbed against his bare chest and she whimpered with arousal. 'All in good time,' he chided, settling his hands on her breasts and teasing her nipples. Then he relented: 'Mind, this looks like a good time to me.'

Sinking to his knees he put his mouth to her breasts, one at a time, back and forth, licking the stiff points and the soft orbs and the breastbone between, sucking and tugging and chewing on her sensitive nipples until she squealed with delight, her breasts slippery with his spit and swelling pinker, rasped by his stubble, while he groaned with pleasure into her flesh. His hands delved between her thighs, squeezing the gusset of her knickers and the ripening flesh beneath, exploring the shapes and the depths of her sex, up between her bum cheeks, down to massage her burning mound, pulling her gusset aside to plunder her slippery split.

'Yes!' she gasped.

'Really?' He pulled away from her nipple. 'You're sure you don't want this then?' Yanking down her knickers, he pulled her bodily forwards, wrapping her legs about his shoulders as he sat back on his heels, burying his face in her muff. His mouth closed over her clit and she squealed out loud, writhing on him. She was partly hanging off the hoist and partly sitting on his hands and wholly helpless, a prisoner of his tongue and his mouth and the swelling white-hot need in her that raged towards release, coming out in a spitting, shrieking explosion. Her cries of 'Yes!' sounded like pure fury.

Gavin set her back down and stood, wiping his mouth. He wasn't smiling now; he had retreated to some inner place. His eyes might be blue but they burned. Turning to the workbench he sank his left hand into the bowl of filthy oil. 'I'm going to get you dirty before I get you clean,' he warned, fingers dripping on the floor as he circled her, sizing up every inch. Flushed and quivering from aftershock, Sarah could only groan. He splatted a black handprint on her pink breast, on the white globe of her bum cheek, on her belly. He wiped his fingers over her nipple, filthying her. He found an oily rag and flicked it across her thighs, leaving grey stains and making her squeak with shock. Then he stood back, admiring his work, the pale canvas of her body so debauched with the evidence of his touch. 'Not quite yet,' he muttered to himself.

He went in search of the finishing touch. When he returned with a plastic bottle and twisted off the cap, she saw that it was more motor oil – not used and filthy this time, but brand new. He tipped the bottle lovingly over her right shoulder, watching as the thick golden liquid spilled down the slope of her breast to piddle off her swollen nipple in an arc, and slide like syrup in a wave down her curves. Sarah pulled uselessly against her bonds and ground her hips and moaned.

Gavin took her face gently in his dirty hand and kissed her one last time, simply dropping the oil bottle at their feet. 'You're far too good for him,' he whispered.

Fumbling in the folds of his overalls and the cotton briefs that she glimpsed beneath, he uncovered his big cock which stood like metal, the ruddy glans glistening with readiness as if it had been oiled. Then he reached into his pocket and produced a condom packet. 'Tear,' he said, presenting it to her lips. She gripped the plastic in her teeth and they tugged together, popping the little disc of latex from its package. She watched as he smoothed it onto his erection with his clean hand, like he was anointing himself. Then he stepped round to her rear. He gripped her from behind, running one hand up and down her torso and over her breasts, through the clean oil and the dirty, squeezing her slippery flesh as his cock pressed eagerly into the juicy folds of her pussy, seeking its entrance. Then he lifted her off her feet, tilting her arse into him, and impaled her sex with powerful thrusts.

'Oh, God, yes!' Sarah cried, hauling down with her arms, kicking the air with her heels. He took some of her weight but with the oil down her front his grip was almost frictionless and her body felt like it was melting in his hands. She couldn't push back against him so she just had to let him have his way, thrust after thrust, mauling her slippery flesh with his big hands, filling her to the brim – and then to bursting. In that cold garage her cries echoed from the walls. Her flesh gave up its orgasm; a bone-wrenching, kicking, struggling thing that nearly dislocated her shoulders, and left her dissolving loose-limbed in his grasp as he groaned and emptied himself into her.

After he'd meticulously cleaned and dried her, and left a mountain of blue paper towels overflowing the bin, she paid the repair bill.

'It's still a few hours north to Fort William,' said Gavin thoughtfully. 'You could stay here tonight instead.'

'That's OK.' She smiled at him and reached up to touch his cheek, brushing her thumb across his lip in happy remembrance of the kisses he'd planted on every part of her body.

'Well.' He looked a little disappointed, but resigned. 'Have a safe journey then. I'll let you out.'

He went to unbolt the big wooden doors and Sarah climbed

into her car, readjusting the driver's seat to her leg length. She watched him as she buckled her seat belt. He'd done so much more for her than rescue her at the roadside, she thought, and she touched her handbag absently. Inside was the garage invoice, complete with telephone number.

Starting the engine, she eased out into the Scottish evening. It was drizzling again. Gavin bent to her open window. 'Are you sure you're OK then, Sarah?'

'Yes.' She looked him in the eye. 'Yes. I'm sure. I really am. Thank you. I mean it.'

'OK.' He brushed her cheek briefly with his finger, then stood back. She drove out onto the street, took a deep breath and then, lifting her hand in a wave, she turned and set off: not right to Fort William but left towards England, and home.

Janine Ashbless is the author of the Black Lace novels *Divine Torment, Burning Bright* and *Wildwood*. She has two single author collections of erotica, *Cruel Enchantment* and *Dark Enchantment*, also published by Black Lace. Her paranormal erotic novellas are included in the Black Lace collections *Magic and Desire* and *Enchanted*.

Table for Three

A.D.R. Forte

He looks so damned hot in those black slacks. I picked them out for him. He loves them, saves them for special occasions.

Tonight he's wearing them for her.

I watch them. They're slow dancing in the living room, his hands around her waist, hers around his neck. He's a good dancer. That's how I first noticed. That was the bait.

During a California-style Carnaval party, among the orgy of mindless drunken gyration, he alone was dancing – actually dancing. Sweet, seductive boy with a tight ass doing the merengue, making me sweat just by looking at the motion of his hands and his hips, and I couldn't take my eyes off him.

I got him down on the beach alone. Or so I thought. Until he unzipped my shorts and pushed me back against the sand and I felt his mouth on my hard cock. Then I realised I was the one being seduced. Always have been with him.

They've stopped dancing now. She's watching him with that intense, hungry gaze – I know it well. I've seen it on my own face too many times. He leans into her, and their lips touch. His hands slide up her legs, raising her skirt to her hips.

Groin to groin, they kiss, and I know she's feeling the weight and the heat of his erection against her flesh. She's got that sinking, melting feeling in her stomach that wants and wants and wants. When too much is still not enough.

I know the way she lusts after him. Pretty girl, do I ever know how you feel right now.

After the first night on the beach I tried not to fall. I'd been burned too many times, too many ways. I'd had enough of the game. I told him. He didn't argue; he didn't commiserate. I remember sitting at the breakfast table and watching him stand up and strip. I watched him walk out to the mini lanai outside the kitchen and stand there, stroking his magnificent cock to full length. His face in profile as he squinted against the bright glare of the morning sun on the water.

I watched him turn and spread his legs, hands on the railing as he bent over and pushed that perfect ass towards me. I'd walked outside and caressed his cheeks, squeezing them hard to watch the skin pale and then redden.

'I don't have protection out here,' I'd said. And after no answer, 'Or lube.'

He didn't move, and we'd stood silent and aching in the morning sun, a battle of wills. I lost, of course. I remember kneeling, the wood of the deck burning under my knees while I spread his cheeks, licking and laving his hole, feeling him tense and arch back against my tongue. I still know the first moment my cock touched his skin and the jolt of desire like pain through my body. Beyond lust.

Beyond just another fuck.

I can still close my eyes and hear his breath coming short and rough, trying not to show pain when I pushed into him. Even though I was trying not to hurt him, trying to control the sudden hungry recklessness, I was as thoughtless with need as a horny teenager again. So aroused by the idea of his submission, I couldn't think. Couldn't do anything but be a slave to my dick.

All it took was one fuck and I belonged to him. Caught, tied up, compromised in every way. His.

Now I'm watching him in the arms of a girl, because he wants to know what it's like. Just once.

'You've never?' I asked when he told me about it one Saturday morning, lying lazy and sated across my torso, one head propped on his hand, the other stroking my chest.

'Never.'

And I found it hard to believe. Hard to think women could have kept their hands off him. I imagined him as a twenty-something: that dark hair long and tousled, those wide, dark eyes sultry and soft with youth. But then he laughed at me and gave instead the picture of a pale, shy nerd hiding behind glasses and oversized college sweaters.

'I wanted girls then. I wanted boys too. But I never dared ...'

Him? My delicate Lucifer? I shook my head and laughed, unable to comprehend anything but the beautiful man lying across my hips, but I agreed to his ploy. I've never been able to deny him much.

He told me all about her: the one he already knew would be the one. The elegant, little suits she wore to work, her pearl earrings, the way he never saw a panty line under her tailored trousers. His words painted her for me: bright, sexy, confident. Daring enough to fulfil his fantasies, smart enough to handle it. Sugar and spice and all things nice.

I saw her for myself the first time tonight: all laughter and glossy, dark hair uncurling in the wind off the ocean. And, of course, I was jealous. Never mind that I'd agreed to it all. I felt the hot angry little sting behind my ears. How dare she touch his arm? How dare she smile at him that way?

I told myself I needed to get over my own baggage: the wife and the divorce and the seemingly endless string of boys who took my money and crashed my sports cars and fucked around in my bed. But it still stung, and I stewed and seethed until dinner time when I held her chair out for her, when her hip just barely grazed my arm as she sat.

The paranoid voice in my head fell silent under her dark-blue gaze, and I sat down too. Powerless to run, to distance myself, to pretend I wasn't so aware of them: a pretty girl and a gorgeous boy. And God only knows what I ate – if I ate – because my brain was mush. I drank too much wine on a too-empty stomach while he told her stories about us and she laughed and leaned towards him. I stared at the pale curves of her tits shadowed by black silk and felt myself get hard.

He leaned over to her in turn, his fingers brushed her wrist, and my hard-on responded. I watched the narrow gold chain he always wore – the one I'd given him on our anniversary two years ago – dangle forwards to catch the light and sparkle . . . and dazzle me.

After dinner, I saw my chance. I ran. I bolted outside to the lanai with a glass of brandy, reminding myself that I'd only signed up to watch.

And I'm regretting it now as I look at them move in each other's arms.

He has her braced against the wall. She hasn't bothered with panties under the elegant little black dress that's hiked up around her waist as he kisses her. Only thigh-high stockings with lace at the tops. How fitting that she would unknowingly have exploited my one weakness when it comes to women. Only the woman he could have chosen . . .

I can feel fate in the kiss of damp ocean breeze on the back of my neck.

His hand moves over the bare skin between her stocking and her bunched dress. His fingers glide along the ridge of her hip, following it inwards; searching. I bite my lip.

I want to guide his fingers into her softness, show him how to make her cry out with pleasure while I kiss his neck.

Distracting and aiding, being both teacher and whore. But he's doing well enough on his own: one hand between her legs, pushing the dress down from her shoulder with the other. He bares one full, curvy tit. Bends to capture her nipple with his lips.

She closes her eyes. I can tell because her head is turned to the side, lips parted as she runs her fingers through his hair. My dick aches, straining to be touched, sucked, caressed. I know the feel of his mouth. I can imagine it as he teases her nipple. His tongue dancing around and around the sensitive tip; lips tightening suddenly, painfully, a jolt of pleasure through her skin. I see her fingers close into a fist, her head arch back. I smile. I can imagine how she tastes, the texture of her nipple rough on my tongue ...

I'm caught between the gaze of one and the touch of the other. I didn't think it would be like this. I don't know what I thought. Perhaps I was a little drunk with flattery that Michael had flirted with me at last, after all the months I watched him while pretending not to. Thinking that if only, if only he weren't playing for the other team ... the things I could do.

Perhaps I was a little flustered, feeling that somehow he'd seen into my deepest, dirtiest thoughts. The ones I had about him while lying on my bed with nothing but the radio on, and my prettiest pink rabbit vibe humming between my legs. Thinking about what he looked like naked while I pressed the bunny nose hard into my clit. Wondering about the size of the dick I wanted to feel inside me so bad, I sometimes believed I'd do anything just to have it. Anything at all.

But when he asked, when he actually suggested it – this insane, crazy, sexy idea – I scolded myself. I told myself not to be a fool. At the worst it would be utter embarrassment, faux pas, drama. Things neither Michael nor I could afford if we still wanted to keep our careers. At best, all I could hope for was some awkwardness and the likelihood that the other – his unknown, mysterious significant other – wouldn't really want to watch. Who would?

Who in their right mind would be able to stand the idea of sharing Michael, far less watching? No. The only reason his lover had agreed to me at all was because you can't say 'No' to Michael, not when he turns those eyes on you and turns up the heat in that smile. I know why *I* gave in. I figured it had to be the same for *him*.

Until I actually saw them side by side. Am I sick for thinking father and son? Even though they're so different: one light and one dark; the blonde, muscled California tan beside the brunette, fair-skinned sensuality. Am I even sicker for the way it made my nipples tighten to imagine them touching each other? For the thought that I wanted him to watch Michael fucking me.

Do I want to make him jealous?

I saw the way his eyes lingered, knowing. He isn't any stranger to a woman's body. I'd stake good money on the fact he knows exactly what he likes, and I wonder if he likes what he sees now. I know that Michael does.

My dress is in a puddle at my feet and Michael runs both his hands down my naked torso, shoulders to thighs, fingers pulling my nipples taut, then releasing them to bounce upwards while his hands continue on down. His cock – the hard delicious cock that's been pressing into my thigh as he pleasures me – tents his stylish pants. I see the lust in his eyes and it makes me squirm with delight. Oh, the aphrodisiac that is power. Every straight girl's fantasy of turning a gorgeous boi – and here it is. Standing right before me.

But it's more. It's something I don't recognise in his gaze, but every inch of me knows it, understands it even if my mind doesn't. I want to please that demand; I want to give everything in me up to it.

'I can't wait to fuck you,' he says.

I blush. The heat travels from my face to my breasts to my clit. I slide one hand between my legs, spread my lips with my fingers and brush my clit with the pad on one finger. Little short bursts with each flick of my finger. Little short hits of endorphins to my brain like a drug. Time slows down.

Slower and slower, the faster my finger moves. A paradox of measured breaths and frantic heartbeats. He watches me, his lover watches me, and I tease myself, touch myself for them both. Who is this girl in stockings and heels, slutting herself out for a pair of gay men?

I don't know, but I know her desire. I feel it hotter and hotter in my chest. I feel the lazy, deliberate kisses on her neck, the hands on her chest, kneading her breasts, tugging at her nipples. The heavy absence of feeling as he pauses now and then to watch, fascinated as my fingers bring me closer. Faster and faster. My fingers and my heartbeat, his heartbeat, the only things that race while everything else is frozen.

Waiting. My hips arch upwards, tensed. Tight. 'Oh, God.'

He parts my thighs, pushes them wider apart, baring my pleasure to his curiosity. Breath is stifled in my throat, my clit spasming under trembling hands. He kisses me, mouth on mine, palm cupping my pussy, fingers toying with the wetness of my slit. Catching and holding my fluttering orgasm until the last pulse of pleasure fades into shivering arousal that still demands more …

God, she's beautiful. Women in their clothes and make-up and guile are attractive, desirable, intriguing. Beauty is what remains when something strong like passion strips all the rest of the bullshit away. If they have it. And she does.

They're a beautiful pair. The breeze is turning cold at my back, pre-come soaks into the fabric of my slacks, but I don't move. I watch.

He takes off his shirt. She tucks her hair behind her ears and runs her hands over his shoulders. I smile. I see the business-woman, the vixen. He drops the shirt on the floor, turns to her, hands suddenly possessive on her hips. I see my beloved seducer. I have to change position, refold my arms while I steadfastly ignore my dick.

Even though she's kissing her way down his chest. Taking her time as if she truly enjoys each little mouthful of his skin when she sucks on it. I believe she does. There's nothing fake to her, nothing done just for his benefit – or mine. I've seen her gaze stray this way. She knows that I'm watching.

She unbuttons his pants and, although I can't see her face, I see her hands caressing his ass as she pushes the soft black fabric downwards. He isn't wearing a damn thing under them of course. A pair of sluts, both of them.

He stands before her naked and she strokes, massages his cheeks. By now of course, she's sucking his dick. My dick quivers with jealousy and envy and lust. I know every inch of his skin that she explores, the tight space between his cheeks where her fingers glide like elegant predators.

I have to take a deep breath and turn away. I only signed up to watch. Nothing else.

But something warns me. I turn to see her getting to her feet, circling around him as he braces his hands on the wall and leans forwards. A posture I know so well. My mouth goes dry. She moves to the side and her ass fills my vision now. Softness instead of muscle. Feminine jiggle with each motion that my confused, distressed body responds to hungrily. Wanting it.

She slaps his ass and I groan aloud. I give in. My hands

unfasten my zipper, search blindly for my only instrument of release while I watch her sweet ass shake every time she hits his. I watch his fair skin turn red. My hand moves in time to her rhythm.

Up. She slaps him. Down. She smoothes his flesh, cups his balls. Up. She slaps him again.

He moans, twisting his perfect derrière from side to side. My dick pleads with me. I imagine taking him when she's finished with her punishment, when his gorgeous ass burns to the touch, red as fire. Wetness runs down my fingers and I still my hand, panting, willing the desire to sink, to wait. I don't want it to be over yet.

Fascinated, I watch her hands move: now higher on his ass, now lower. Harder slaps. She pauses, rubs her hand over his cheeks and up his back. She leans into him, pussy and tits crushed against his back and asks him something. He answers. He laughs.

Over the whistle and crash of ocean and wind I hear the warmth of their voices, but without words. Frustrated, my teeth savage my lower lip while her fingers probe him, fucking him. I grit my teeth and my hand pumps hard against my flesh. Who knew jealousy could be such a turn-on? But then, tonight, I feel I'm learning things I never knew.

Who said you can't teach an old dog new tricks?

She's whispering to him again. He straightens suddenly, smiling as he turns and catches both her wrists. Laughing, she lets him push her back against the wall, hands held above her head. Her tits look gorgeous stretched like that. I long to run my hands across them, testing the hardness of her nipples. Just like I long to rub my dick between the cleft of his reddened ass.

She looks up, looks right at me. He turns, still holding her in place, my angel – devil prince with his barbarian captive princess. For an instant their gazes meet mine. Without knowing it, without meaning it, I feel myself nod. Just once.

He turns away; she looks down into his face, her lips parted, pretty face reflecting the anticipation, the desire that I can't see on his. She spreads her legs, standing on tiptoes in her heels to give him access. And he pushes into her. Her head goes back; her eyes close. I release the breath I don't know I've been holding.

Straining, thrusting, their bodies join. My hand moves with steady, certain rhythm now, driving towards the inevitable, final scene of this act. I hear her cries, sharp and breathy, punctuating the song of the breeze in my ears. His body slams into hers; his ass squeezed tight. Her tits bounce with each thrust. In the indoor light I see their skin shining with sweat.

I feel the ice of my own sweat ruining the lining of this jacket. I feel the constriction in my balls heralding the fact that soon I'll ruin these slacks too. With a vicious smile, feeling like some perverted father-god, I let go of conscious thought. I give in to the blank ecstasy of release . . .

I wake up in Michael's arms, the smell of our sex and his body filling my senses before I even open my eyes. It makes me smile, despite the twinge of pain in my clit as I move to extricate myself from the bed.

Last night fills my mind. The shower: we spent an hour there alone – maybe more than that – I can't put time around it now. I think of how he rubbed the soap over my breasts and my pussy and my shoulders and belly. I think of watching him rinse it away in sections, bit by bit, the sight of the suds sliding down my own naked body more erotic than anything he could have done to me with his own hands.

I stand at the window and look out at the busy ocean, its voice muffled behind glass.

Water cascading around us, he'd smiled. He pinched my puckered nipples, rolling them between his fingers until I moaned and squirmed and begged him. Until I felt the wetness between my thighs that had nothing to do with water. Then he turned the spray of the shower between my legs and let the stinging pressure savage me into coming again and again and again. And when he lifted the spray to fall harmlessly on my belly and asked me if I'd had enough, when – panting – I swore I had, he called me his sweet liar and brought me over again.

Will I let him do anything to me? I think I know the answer to that. My body does.

Wincing and smiling, I steal the shirt lying over a chair at the foot of the bed and drape it over my head. I've lain beside Michael; I've breathed his breath. He's held me and kissed me and I've felt his body tremble along mine. It's warm and sweet there with him in the bed, where he possesses me.

But there's still a part of this unfinished.

I open the bedroom door and listen. Silence but for the ever-present sound of the sea outside. I walk on bare feet down the hall to the kitchen, shivering a little in the morning chill, following some instinct that pulls me. The sound of the surf grows louder; rumbling.

I find him sitting at the kitchen table, coffee cup in hand.

He looks up at me hovering in the doorway and I realise – something in his eyes tells me – that the shirt I'm wearing belongs to him. I've slept in his bed. I've held his lover all night. I want to ask where he's been, but I can't find any words.

'Coffee?' he asks me at last.

I just nod.

We aren't the same people who met last night before dinner. He doesn't get up to pour me a mug of coffee. He simply holds out his own, and I come to stand beside him, take the mug in both hands and inhale the powerful, aromatic brew.

'Brazilian?' I ask.

He smiles. 'Yes. Dark roast,' he tells me. The good stuff. No bullshit espresso in this kitchen. I take a sip and we both listen to the surf roar pure fury for a minute before it subsides into its steady, grumpy thrashing again. I hand the mug back to him and he puts it on the table.

We aren't strangers.

He pushes the chair back from the table and turns to face me. I stand between his knees while he releases the few buttons of the shirt, lets the oversized garment slide off my shoulders. His fingers stroke my nipples; the dusting of curls between my legs.

'I thought I'd given up on women,' he says. His finger slides between my lips, probes the tender flesh and I draw a sharp breath, bite my lip hard. He smiles. 'Michael get rough?'

'I let him.'

He laughs and slides the finger past my painful clit into my cunt wet with morning arousal. I close my eyes as my tired, over-stimulated flesh responds – yet again – to a knowing, sensual touch. Briefly I think that in all my life it's never been this way, not with a single one of my so-called straight lovers. I wonder what the hell has happened to me in one night. And can I ever go back now?

'But then . . .' he says and, with my eyes closed, I listen to the gentle rumble of his voice as his finger moves behind my pelvic bone, coaxing my hips into movement too '. . . I thought I'd given up on a lot before him.'

Oh so did I. So did I.

'And now you,' he says. He grinds his finger into my softness and I open my eyes, give a little cry half of pain. His eyes – the colour of sun-touched morning water – are focused on my face. I'm trembling, my pussy clenching helplessly around his finger in an effort to prolong the sweet, unbearable rocking.

'Are you gonna take him away from me, pretty girl?' he asks me, and I hear the sadness, the anger in his voice. I squeeze my eyes shut, open them again.

Once – before last night – I would have sunk behind the cold, calm voice of reason. Before last night I would have said, 'It's just one night. An experiment.' I would have lied to him, to Michael, to my own conscience.

Now, I let myself fall into that unforgiving, demanding blue.

'Are you gonna send me away?' I counter. My voice almost, not quite, breaks from the pressure of my racing heart.

He swallows. The pressure of his fingers inside me makes my legs shake, my head swim. I'm falling. No. God, I've already fallen. And hard.

'No.' And his voice is low and rough. 'I can't send you away.'

Her scent and the scent of the coffee mingle in my brain: earthy, heady, druglike. From the corner of my vision, I see movement, see him pause in the doorway, yawning. Naked as God made him ... or as a god. Still caressing, teasing her, I look past her and meet his gaze. He takes in the sight of us and then he smiles.

I slide my fingers from between her legs as he comes around the side of the table and she moans a little with disappointment. But only until his hand touches her lower back and his lips brush hers.

'Did you both start without me?'

'Yes,' she replies with a smile.

'You're late,' I add.

I stand and lift my fingers to his lips. He licks the taste of her from them before I wrap my fingers around the base of his neck and pull his mouth to mine. His lips are already bruised from her kisses last night, and I bruise him a little more. When I'm done, his breath comes fast and shallow. His lips are red.

She moves behind him, and peers at me over his shoulder, a smile playing about her lips. I return it. I can't resist her either, with her evening-sky eyes and her mischief.

But I decide that there are worse fates than this ...

We move in symmetry, orbiting each other. Touching when we get too close, when we fall into each other's gravity. Drawn in by a core of desire that ties us up, binds us together. I'm not sure how I belong here. Or why. I just accept it.

I'm standing behind Michael. He's on his knees. I stroke his lover's cock and bring it to his mouth. I tell him to suck it. I call him a slut.

I know he'll punish me for it soon enough, and the thought turns me liquid hot inside. I watch, fascinated by his mouth sliding along the shaft, by the glisten of saliva-wet skin. It excites me to see him like this: obedient. To see us dominating him, because the truth is that he really owns us. He tames us, traps us and plays with us, and we use him, punish him in return. I guess that's the game.

His lover pushes him away at last. We wait, unsure of the next move: we're making the rules up as we go. Improvising. Cheating a little for advantage ... I know Michael is: his hands stray to his cock and he makes no move to hide it.

His lover smiles. 'I want to watch you fuck her ... and I want to fuck you.'

Michael smiles because he knows he's won. I have another moment of doubt, thinking that I'm incidental, just a novelty. Or maybe a necessary evil. But, as Michael rises and turns to me, as I see desire, dark and light, in the way both of them look at me, I forget uncertainty. I only know need: the burn kindled so slowly, so subtly that it takes me by surprise.

My heart speeds up to a frantic pitter-patter, pitter-patter. The blood pounds in my head. Michael puts both hands on my waist and kisses me. The taste of a man's kiss flavoured by another man's cock makes my stomach clench with excitement. Makes my clit throb. This is forbidden and terrible and I'm shameful for loving it, for wanting them both.

'I'm a bad girl,' I hear my voice saying as he releases me from the kiss, as he moves me back up against the table, pressing my ass to the edge so that I scrabble up to plant myself on the top.

'Yes,' he whispers, voice husky and distracted with lust. 'I like you like this.'

As he spreads my legs so far apart I wince. Worried, I check for the coffee cup and the saucer but they're gone. It's only me on the table, spread wide, my feet resting on air. So wet I feel a trickle of liquid over the crack of my ass. Michael's finger finds it. He rubs the bud of my entrance, probing a little into tender flesh. I shiver.

'Should I stop?' he asks.

I look over his shoulder into eyes the colour of the restless sea outside. I know what he wants. He runs his hands down Michael's shoulders; his chest pressed to Michael's back. His hand moves over Michael's, pressing into me again. I struggle to find a mouthful of air. To nod. To tell them, 'Yes. I consent.'

I feel Michael's finger slide into me and I close my eyes against the whisper of pain that burns up in the desire that overwhelms it. He fucks my ass slowly with one finger. Then two. I feel another touch, just as male, just as devastating, on my clit. I don't open my eyes. I concentrate on breathing, on the agonising pleasure between my legs.

Michael moans and then I do look. His face is red, his fingers curl a little in me, tensing. I see his lover's hand stroking his cock with the same rhythm that's making my clit quiver and tighten.

'Are you ready for him?' he asks. And I nod, mute. Too far gone with nerves and lust and too drunk on the unthinkable to manage words. Seconds pass, or is it years between the burning emptiness of their fingers leaving me and the cool, slick caress of lube.

My fingers grip the edge of the table. My shoulders are arched with tension, my lower back tied in knots.

I can't, can't, can't. But I want it, oh, God, I want it. I want Michael's cock hard against my opening. I want the sob in my throat, the pain that's not pain.

'Fight me,' I hear him say. 'Push back.'

Automatically I do what he says, never mind that my brain is telling me it doesn't make sense, and I feel him sliding inside of me. I feel the lust breaking away from pain. Feel my hips moving up, ass off the table, fucking. Vicious and hungry, I've left all inhibitions behind. I'm his, theirs.

I complete the triangle, the triad, the triskelion: sacred three.

I'm almost there when Michael stops, hilt deep in me, and I protest in wordless moans, but his fingers only tighten on my thighs. I watch his face as he holds his breath. He's filled in turn. And I know. Oh I know how it feels while I watch him bite his lower lip. That wanting. The sinking, going under, the tremor in his chest and stomach. The high of submitting. And the pleasure rising and rising as the rhythm builds again.

My teeth mirror his, sinking into my lower lip. Harder and harder. I taste blood and I think I can't take any more, but I'm so close. I need it. I need it so badly. I see my torment reflected in Michael's face, in his lover's face. We're all falling together. Doesn't matter now who's on top. Nothing matters but the end.

The release.

Heat rushes up my body, heat explodes between my legs. Pulsing on and on and on. I hear myself scream.

I feel Michael's cock spasm, I hear them both moan. I look into Michael's eyes. Not really thinking, because I can't think, but I don't need my brain to get it. I know.

Shaking so much I can barely move. I tell my overwrought muscles to relax. I close my eyes, lean back and let my head rest on the cool, hard table. Wood under my head. The thought makes me laugh a little; I'm giddy.

'She likes it,' he whispers to Michael, in a breathless voice. I hear them laugh.

It's over. But it's just begun.

A.D.R. Forte has written numerous short stories for Black Lace collections.

My Tutor

Primula Bond

Does once a year count as infidelity? How can it? The moment is so fleeting, like an eclipse or an equinox, like one of those festivals that spring out of the calendar before you're ready. Even though it's regular as clockwork, every single year, it still hits you between the eyes. The dreamed-of, long-awaited carnival celebrated with such fever, such intoxication, such wild dancing, that everyone wonders, hidden under their real and imaginary masks, how the fuck we cope with our happy mundane lives back home.

Every summer my heart lurches to see it's only a week away, two days, a day, one hour, till I take the journey again. Anyone would think I was travelling across the globe. It's only an hour to Oxford, but it couldn't be further away from home. From the present. I wave to my family from the train, hiding my blushing cheeks, the new lingerie in my bag, and then I'm gone.

And everything changes when I get there. I change. I take so much more care with mascara, lipstick, my *maquillage*, even though before the night is through my face will be kissed and licked until the mask is smudged and smeared and wiped away.

I take the key from the porter and hurry across the quad to my guest room. All chintz and carpets, even a double bed, so different from the scruffy single room I slept in when it all began.

That's on another staircase, in another quad, and I can never go back there, because the reflection in this unfamiliar mirror is twenty years older.

Baron was furious. As always he had his back turned. He was smoking and leaning like the caricature of an Oxford tutor against his mantelpiece. 'Browning, Bella. I asked you for an essay on death and Browning.' He tossed my essay aside, the handwritten pages fluttering hopelessly into the dry grate. 'Not a regurgitated A level question on the madness of Ophelia.'

Hot, stupid tears were making my eyes water. 'I've been up all night crying. Sorry.'

'Fucking marvellous. Finals in a week and you're acting like a schoolgirl. And not in a good way.'

There was an ambiguous silence. I think he was trying to make a joke, but I was far too nervous to get it. I didn't know him so well then. I tried to open my book with trembling hands, burning up with embarrassment. I'd heard Baron swore at his students, and everyone hated him for it, but it had never happened to me. Maybe because usually we were tutored in pairs, but coming up to Finals he was taking us individually. Oh yes. He took me individually all right . . .

I looked at his shoes. Highly polished brown brogues, tapping impatiently. I could imagine his brutal fingers twisting those thin laces into shape every morning. Or maybe, in the old days, gripping a cane and whipping it down on some poor student's bare bottom. My stomach knotted tighter. I couldn't tell if it was a kind of hectic, Ophelia-like excitement or because I just felt horribly thick. John Baron was a world renowned expert on Victorian poetry, Robert Browning in particular. And me? I wondered what the hell I was doing here. Sometimes the entire gamut of English literature may as well have been written in Swahili.

'Some post-grad rugby player dumped you?'

My breath caught with surprise. Where were the barked questions, the impossible list of sources and research and revision to complete by next week?

'What makes you think he's a rugby player?'

The shoes stopped tapping. I froze as Baron stepped over the surprisingly luxuriant Persian carpet and perched on the sofa arm furthest from me. My biro snapped in half, bleeding blue ink over my denim skirt, and I tried to dab at it with my snotty tissue.

'Because you're like all their groupies. Blonde, buxom. Gagging for it.' Baron crossed one long leg over the other, took a drag and blew smoke out noisily. What brilliant props we all had when we smoked. 'Guy's an idiot.'

'How do you know it's Guy?' I looked up, blushing even more furiously. 'How do you always know everything?'

He had his tweed-sleeved arms crossed, cigar smouldering between his fingers, and he was staring at me. He never stared at his students. He always looked at their work, his books, the mantelpiece, finally the door. I realise now that he was an awkward academic. But we just thought that he was middle-aged, abrupt and scary. So the first time I saw his eyes under the longish tawny hair I was stunned. They were like a lion's. Hazel, and flecked with gold.

'I meant guy, as in man. So I'm right, am I?' He tapped the cigar ash into a saucer and actually smiled. 'Gorgeous girl like you. He's *definitely* a fucking idiot.'

Our shared laughter was sudden and intoxicating, but I was so exhausted and hot and weakened by the softness in Baron's voice that I burst into tears again.

'Bella, time's nearly up.' He leapt up and marched about the carpet, gesticulating towards the window. 'The bar will be open for lunch. The Cornish pasties are always tasty.'

I shook my head and cried even harder. Now I'd got over the embarrassment, crying felt fantastic. A relief. Weeping in Baron's study, where no one else could get to me, tears and snot dripping all over my short skirt and my tights, my hysterics a valid excuse to forget the bloody tutorial and my useless essay.

'Not hungry?' Baron sighed, and I heard the pop of a cork. 'What happened, then, to make you bawl your eyes out all night? What did that Guy do to you?'

Outside it was, as usual in Oxford, raining. Inside it was warm. I could smell smoke, lavender and polish. And deep red wine. Baron twiddled a delicate crystal glass in front of me, then pressed it into my hand. I preferred lager, but still. I took a big gulp and the red wine went straight to my head.

'He wasn't doing it to me. That's the whole problem,' I whimpered. 'He was doing it to Ingrid Smorgsen.'

Baron's eyebrows shot up, and he sat down at the far end of the Chesterfield. I looked at his eyes again. And now at his mouth, blowing out another plume of smoke. A sensuous lower lip, full and reddened by the wine. Very white teeth.

'He was fucking her?'

'Not just him. Rob was there, too.' I pushed my thighs together, remembering what I'd seen. The three bodies, a mass of naked limbs jerking violently about on the floor. Breasts. Cocks. Bottoms. Ingrid's mouth, opening wide, her tongue and long throat. Christ, the shock. And the rush of horrified excitement as I watched them through Guy's ground-floor window. The same excitement rushing through me now, but stronger, because Baron was listening and watching me. 'They were both doing her.'

'You poor baby.' Baron paused, and sat down beside me, but not too close. 'What did you see, Bella Donna?'

He laid one arm along the back of the sofa.

'Guy was behind her, holding her hips, her bottom all pinched up and red in his hands like it must really hurt.' Nausea rushed through me. 'Christ, it makes me feel sick – his cock going right in, his butt pulling back, then banging in and out. He was taking her like a dog.'

'And Rob? What was he doing?'

It was so quiet in there. The clock ticked, tocked, ticked, on the mantelpiece. One of the pages of my essay slipped out from the grate onto the hearth.

'I can't tell my mates. They'll either laugh or think it's revolting. But I've got to tell someone.'

'Of course you must. I'm a grown-up, Bella. I'm good at keeping secrets.' He laughed softly. A gorgeous, low, sexy laugh I'd never heard before. 'I've a few scandals of my own, you know.'

I looked at his knees, crossed comfortably, his hand resting on the sofa seat beside me, rocking the wine about in the ridiculously delicate glass. I leaned back and closed my eyes.

'It still makes me feel sick. But Rob was in front of her, holding his cock in one hand, her hair in the other, and he was stuffing it into her mouth. She sucked it in, looked like she was going to bite it, her head kept jerking forwards where Guy was shoving her from behind, and then she started sucking Rob's cock like it was a lollipop, she closed her eyes and groaned and she really enjoyed it, even though Guy was going at her from behind, scraping her knees red raw across the floor. I keep seeing his bottom pumping back and forth into her like some kind of zoo animal – he's my boyfriend, for God's sake!'

I staggered to my feet, doubled over now with nausea. But my knees gave way. Baron's hand encircled my wrist and he pulled me gently back down again.

'Not any more, he isn't.'

I leaned against his tweed jacket and his arm was round me now. I was shaking as if I was ill. He pulled me closer. My head was tucked under his chin. I could see dark spikes of stubble pricking through his skin and I could smell a kind of citrusy cologne.

'The boys were laughing at each other, over her head, as if she was a piece of meat. Do you think they laugh like that about me? I should have gone away, shouldn't I? But I was rooted to the spot, my legs wouldn't move, the way they were doing it, poking at her like animals, I couldn't help watching until they all started going really fast and shouting and screaming. I saw their cocks slipping in and out of her mouth and her bottom, all shiny and wet –'

'It can be good doing it that way, if you do it right.'

His remark didn't register until much much later. Years later. I was gabbling now. 'I couldn't breathe, then that look came over their faces, you know, when guys are about to come and their faces go red and kind of bulge in that hideous way and they shut you out –'

'Young guys like them, maybe, who think they're studs – no fucking *finesse*.' Baron's voice rumbled below my ear where I was lying on his chest. My heart was pounding in time with his. 'I wouldn't shut you out.'

I was twenty. I know now that he was forty-five, but that was the moment he went from older man to charming lover. There was my jerk of a boyfriend hung like a donkey but still a brute. And there were Baron's arms, his voice, the life he'd already led, so calm, so strong. So full of promise. I said nothing.

'It's time I exercised my rights over you.'

'*Droit de seigneur*, do you mean?'

'Ah, so you remember my medieval tutorials?' He laughed and my skin prickled. 'No. I meant my *droit de* tutor, if there is such a thing. A modern version. Nowadays you have the choice to refuse, which those poor wenches didn't. But I'll take advantage of you anyway.'

The laugh was rumbling up from his chest again. The excitement building inside me, pressed close to his big warm body, stopped me speaking.

'You'll be struck off!' I squeaked, trying to pull away. My short skirt rucked up even higher, and we both looked at my long legs. The wine slopped over my ink-stained fingers as I put the glass down on the table. The confusion was rushing back, making me hot again.

Baron took my hand and licked the wine off my fingers, one by one, and I heard myself whimpering again to feel his long wet tongue on my skin. I licked my lips and watched my fingers sliding into his warm wet mouth.

'That's doctors, or judges, who get struck off. But sure, it's forbidden.' He really was like a lion. Even his hair, golden and swept back, was like a mane. And the way he waited. For answers. For dazzling displays of intelligence. And now? For a kiss? For the right moment to seduce me? For me to do it for him, undo my blouse, show him my breasts, right here in broad daylight? Open my legs?

His eyes flashed as if he could read my mind and, under my scratchy black tights, I felt my pussy twitch. 'You going to tell?'

I shook my head and really that's how it happened. My fingers, wet from his saliva, were caught in his thick hair. His face was close as he wiped the remaining moisture from under my eyes. All so gentle. His breath was on my face. I could smell faint cigar smoke and eau de cologne. My lips slid against his, and then he was biting my mouth. I was so shocked I couldn't breathe. My tutor! Nearly as old as my dad! But we fitted, like gloves. How come this felt so horny?

His hands were so calm and warm, stroking my face, my hair, and then he kissed me. You always know the point of no return, don't you? That was my moment to stop it, but no way. It was my time to wait, and I let him. I wanted to know what it would feel like and it was magic. Very soft, the scrape of his stubble on my chin, but the warmth and wetness of his mouth, his tongue trailing round the tender lining of my lips, so that it tickled and made me shiver. He kissed me harder, parting my lips so that his tongue was inside, tasting of red wine, and I sucked on it.

I realised I was struggling to breathe, suffocated by the sudden ferocious desire rocketing through me. He was heavy lying on top of me. It was intoxicating, but it was also squeezing the life out of me. I twisted under him, and I realised my tights and my knickers were wet.

'Where are you going to, my pretty maid?' he enquired, reaching to undo the buttons on my shirt. Guy's shirt, actually.

I gasped and wriggled as his nails scraped my skin, my own fingers digging into the leather seat. 'Anyone could barge in looking for you.'

'Who cares? They'll either run a mile or else stay for the show, if they've any taste. That doesn't bother you, does it?' He could tell I was still tense. 'It's a bit late to come over all shy with me, Bella.'

He pushed my shirt off my shoulders. I could feel the warmth of the fire on my skin. I felt so young and beautiful as he looked at me, traced my collarbones, trailed his fingers over my breasts. Guy loved my breasts. He used to knead them like dough, roughly, until the pain became delicious, then snuffle at them like a puppy. I used to try to slip a nipple into his mouth, aching for him to suck it, take some more time, but by then his permanently stiff cock was at bursting point and he couldn't wait. Like it was when I saw him with Ingrid. Thick and hard and thrusting up another girl's cunt ...

I groaned, crazily turned on by the thought of Ingrid's bottom opened up, her cunt filling with Guy's cock, her mouth sucking on Rob's hard-on. I couldn't help comparing the two guys, wondering what this older man's cock would be like, how it would feel, how big it would be.

'You OK with this, Bella? Because I want you like hell, and I don't think I can stop.'

In response to my thoughts, his words, his touches, I arched my back, pushing my breasts towards Baron.

He smiled, running his tongue across his lip. He lifted my shirt away so that my skin prickled with excitement. Does he have a big cock? I wondered. The way he's looking at me, holding my shirt open like unwrapping a parcel, my breasts bulging out of the too-small, cheap bra, he had a way of looking all admiring, hungry, like he's not had it for years, not seen anything so gorgeous as me in years, though I'd heard so many stories about him and other female students. Just then I felt like a prize. A fresh young prize. The power and sexiness were like a head rush.

'You're beautiful, Bella,' he said. 'Those boys have no idea –'

'Bet you say that to all the girls,' I giggled, then went cold. How stupid, how young that sounded.

He smiled, pulling my shirt right off and throwing it to the floor. 'Only the ones I want to fuck.'

'That's supposed to make me feel special? How many other girls?'

He smiled, and ran his fingers over my breasts. 'Just enjoying talking dirty, Bella. You're here, and you're now.'

I struggled to my elbows, scrabbled about for my shirt. 'This is like another bloody tutorial. I don't understand a word you're saying.'

He pushed me back down and in one movement ripped off my skirt, tights and knickers. 'Relax, darling. You don't need to think about anything. Just let me enjoy your luscious body. You know it's luscious?'

I squirmed again, trying to close my thighs over my luxuriantly hairy pussy. Waxing wasn't the fashion then, though we all tidied our bushes up if we were in for a hot night. I wonder how many men cared then, or care now? It's the cunt they're after, isn't it? My nipples pricked up, burning and hard. We both looked at them, tight red nuts like beacons telling the world I was horny. Desire snaked straight down to my cunt and my legs loosened, opening a little.

Baron reached out to touch my nipples, then looked again at me. I smiled. It felt like a slow, seductress's smile, even though I was so young, because I felt so delicious. Any resistance had ebbed right away. Lust and desire had rushed right in.

Baron leaned over me and kissed me again, long, slow, wetter and harder this time, then suddenly hoisted me onto his knee. The daylight coming through the window was harsh and bright now. My breasts, tumbling heavily into his hands, felt exposed as if I was on stage. I was straddling his knee, my bare pussy rubbing against the fabric of his trousers. I must be leaving a sticky smear there. I started to rock slightly, desperate to relieve the building, burning pressure.

He put one arm round my waist to stop me moving. He caught one bouncing breast with his other hand, and pulled it towards his face. I leaned back on his thighs, pushing my breasts hard against his mouth, desperate for him to suckle me. One hand reached between my legs and my fingers started to poke and prod desperately inside my warm, wet pussy lips.

'You really are wasted on boys your age, Bella. Have you any idea how sexy it is, watching you finger yourself like that?'

I tossed my hair back, opened my legs further, pushed my fingers in harder to feel my wet cunt sucking on them.

'You're making me feel sexy, Baron.' I barely recognised myself. My voice was cracked, and husky, and saying his unfamiliar name.

His golden eyes rested on my face, then he looked down. I shifted to part my legs a little more, and edged my fingers further into the auburn curls. I held my breath to stop myself gasping out loud as they grazed the hidden clit.

'In that case, I'm going to keep you here all afternoon. And you're going to come back to my room again, and again, and we're going to go on doing this.'

The potent mix of awe and desire was crushing me.

'Doing what, exactly?'

'This, exactly.' He started fondling my breasts, and pulling me towards him he bit hard on one nipple, then turned to the other, biting and sucking it, sending shocks of desire straight down to my cunt. 'Even after you've graduated.'

I pushed myself hard against his face, grabbing his hair and angling my nipples brazenly into his mouth, scraping them against his teeth, pulling back, muffling his cheeks and ears with the warm mounds as if to drown him.

'You think so, do you? You don't think I'll leave this place, run away, get married, never look back?'

I rose up on my knees. My moist pussy stuck to his trousers for a minute, the tiny curls caught on the fabric, tugging the tender skin before letting go. I wanted to be higher up than him, feel his head burrowing in between my breasts. He was hurting me now, biting and nibbling as my nipples stretched taut like arrows, hard yet sensitive, feeling the pain yet relishing the pleasure. My hips started automatically to gyrate, answering the messages sent down there from my tits.

'It's called a liaison, Bella. It'll keep us alive. You'll come back to me, and I'm going to have you, year after year. Just you wait and see.'

I wriggled my buttocks backwards, still leaning hard against his face. His cock was hard underneath me, edging between my bare buttocks. I scrabbled for his zip. I felt him tense and for a moment his mouth relaxed on my nipple, but I got my hand firmly inside his trousers, pulled them down his hips until my fingers landed on his waiting prick. It was a quiet, stunning moment of ownership. My tutor's cock.

'And the other girls you talk dirty to? The other nubile young students?' I challenged him, egged on by the sudden vision I had of him having sex with other girls, here on this sofa, writhing on the Persian carpet, licking red wine off their breasts, taking out his cock and thrusting it inside them . . .

His cock jumped in my hand as if to remind me it was there. I tilted my pelvis in answer, offering my eager sex, holding the rounded end of him and guiding it until it rested just inside me. My whole body felt like one pulsating pussy.

'They're not here now, are they?'

'You wait, Baron.' I pushed my nipple hard into his mouth again and squealed as his teeth closed round it and he started to suck, filling me with hot desire and a soaring confidence. 'I'll be the best.'

Instead of waiting, relishing the suspense, I let myself drop, driving myself onto his cock. He kept his mouth and fingers on my nipples, rubbing and pinching, biting and sucking, the sensations shooting up me, making my head light with pleasure, shooting down me, making my cunt tighten with impatience.

He gripped my hips and started to guide my rhythm, pushing his cock further and further up me. I couldn't believe how big it was, how hard, much bigger and harder than Guy's. Christ, what a surprise! What a bonus! I laughed to myself. Baron was doing *me* a favour, not the other way round.

Then we were growling and swearing, tearing at each other like enemies, bucking furiously against each other. I gripped him with my thighs, thrusting my hips against him, cramming him in, grinding right down to the very base so that he filled me with all those solid inches of rock-hard, thrusting cock.

Each time we pulled back and slammed against each other we became more violent, and I screamed out loud as I felt the impending orgasm flick on inside me. I couldn't hold on much longer. I wanted to show Baron that I might not be the best student he'd ever tutored, but the best he'd ever fucked. That was my challenge. Not getting a degree, not dissecting Chaucer. Fucking my handsome tutor until he never got me out of his head.

The college clock chimed twice. Way past lunchtime. At the same time footsteps pattered across the wet quad and up the stone staircase towards Baron's room.

We were grunting and rocking hard now, my hair flying, the excitement rising as he bit and sucked my nipples, dug his fingers into my hips to keep me locked against him. I wanted it to keep going as long as possible. Forever, preferably. On the other hand, I couldn't stop the inevitable. I opened my eyes and watched him, and at the same time he lifted his mouth from my breast and looked at me, and we fucked each other harder still.

Someone knocked at the door.

'Who? Who?' I hissed, wanting to scream with excitement. His eyes flicked to the door and back to me and he gave a monumental thrust.

'It's Ingrid,' he growled, accelerating us both towards the climax rushing nearer. 'How about that, Bella Donna? It's Ingrid, come for her tutorial!'

His head fell back against the sofa and he stared at me, but his eyes stayed focused and bright as he started to shoot up me. I rode him for all I was worth, moaning in my own exquisite pain as I started to come, and as I started to come I milked it, making it sound unmistakable, moaning louder, wilder, so that Ingrid could hear. Then I leaned over and kissed him again, licked his lips, flicked my tongue over his teeth, sucked his tongue as it slipped into my mouth. He strained up against me, his mouth warm and fixed on mine, and I felt him pumping his juice into me. I squeezed every drop and held it there. I didn't want it to ebb away, because then it would be gone for good.

There was another sharp rapping at the door, and we jerked apart.

'Come in, Ingrid!'

We stared at each other, trying not to laugh. I gripped him inside me as hard as I could. His gorgeous cock twitched once, twice, then started to slip out. I twisted away from him to yank my skirt on. As I wrapped my shirt round me, not bothering to button it, and turned back to him, a shaft of watery sunlight came through the window.

Ingrid started to open the door. I just watched him zip his trousers over his big cock and smiled.

Our mingled juices dripped down the insides of my bare legs as I zipped my skirt. My nipples were sore and throbbing, poking against Guy's cotton shirt. I was going to walk past Ingrid, across the quad, into the library, smelling of Baron's spunk.

'Ah, there you are, Ingrid!' he cried, walking calmly towards the mantelpiece. One run of his fingers through his hair and he looked just the same.

Me? Ingrid could see it, smell it, the minute she walked in. I looked totally, thoroughly shagged. I stood aside for her to step nervously over to the sofa, watching her waggle her pert bottom in tight white jeans. The same bottom my ex boyfriend had rammed himself up a few hours ago.

Baron winked at me, right there in front of her, and said calmly, 'Oh, Bella. Don't forget to take your knickers with you.'

In the Fellows' Garden they're already gathered, champagne in hand, and I heat up with pleasure as old faces above black bow ties turn, see me arrive and light up.

'Bella, you look just the same, even after twenty years!'

I laugh, ridiculously gratified. Glance around for him. 'That's down to my surgeon!'

'Don't be daft!'

'Serious!' I concentrate, stop myself peering rudely over their shoulders. They were my best friends. Although, of course, I never told them. 'He's brilliant with Botox. And you don't think my hair is still naturally this red, do you?'

'Whatever,' says Rebecca, tugging at her wiry grey ponytail. 'You look a million dollars.'

The gong goes for dinner. Where the fuck is he? That's what this is all about, you see. For one night, in this college, in these clothes, with these people, with this man, I'm twenty years younger again.

'Who are we trying to kid?' Seb has appeared by my elbow, as he does every year. As he did the very first day I arrived, sweating and nervous, as a fresher, and carried my bags up to my room. My spindly bespectacled admirer, sender of valentines, provider of tissues, opener of champagne. I turn to look at him and blush with surprise. He's changed. He's bigger, and broader, now, his eyes are sharper and bluer, more direct, his glasses exactly suit him. His suit hangs on him as cool as Bryan Ferry. 'We're all middle-aged now.'

'My God, Seb, you look so good! Look at you! I hardly recognise – that cool haircut!'

'Been the same for quite a few years now, Bella.' He rubs the greying stubble across his head and grins, still boyish but sexy now. So sexy. 'You just never noticed.'

'Darling Seb,' I say, closing my eyes as he pulls me into his chest, holding me for a couple of beats longer than friendship, the time it takes to feel his heartbeat. To want more. He kisses my face, his mouth a touch closer than friendship. 'You seen Baron?'

He pushes me away. 'Haven't you heard? Baron's retired.'

'Gone to the Outer Hebrides, like he always said he would!' chimes in Rebecca. 'You know, I always had a crush on him.'

They start to walk across the quad towards the hall.

I dawdle, staring up at Baron's blank windows.

A year after we graduated we were all back for a reunion dinner. An invitation was handed to us when we checked in to come to Baron's study for sherry.

'Look at you, all grown-up. Except as usual, Bella, you're late,' Baron said, standing by the mantelpiece and holding out a glass. 'Guy, Ingrid, Rebecca, the others, they've all been, drunk me nearly dry, and gone again.'

I crossed my legs, my expensive sheath dress riding up my bare thighs, self-conscious as hell. I hadn't given Baron a thought in the last year. I'd dressed like this to tease my old flame, Guy, not him. Show everyone how sophisticated I'd become in one short year. I wanted to show Ingrid that I was more beautiful than her. I even wanted to make sure poor Seb would still love me.

But now I was back on that leather sofa and all I could think of was Baron and that last tutorial a year ago, me sliding up and down Baron's enormous cock while he nuzzled my breasts.

'Fuck, and there's the bell for dinner,' I said, draining my sherry in one. Baron watched me. Looked at my legs and my high heels. My cunt went tight, and I got hot. 'I'd better get down to hall then.'

'You can be five minutes late, because tonight I'm saying grace,' Baron said, in front of me now and unpinning my hair. His fingers on my neck made me shudder with excitement. He kissed me, then unzipped his trousers. 'And now you're going to wrap those beautiful red lips around my cock.'

So I took his hard cock into my mouth and sucked him off so hard and so fast that my jaw ached all that weekend.

The following year I was later still for the sherry.

'Guy and Ingrid are engaged,' Baron told me, unzipping my dress and edging his fingers up between my legs. 'Imagine that. Do you think we should tell all the guests at their wedding, when she's all in virginal white and he's the big hero, what you saw? What they got up to when they were students? Do you think they still do it like a couple of farm animals? Her blonde hair swinging about, those big tits dangling. God, those tits were great, Guy pulling her backside open to get inside that wet crack.'

'And here was me thinking you only spoke in poetry!' I laughed and gasped, rocking against his fingers as they poked inside me. 'They'll take Rob along on honeymoon, won't they, so that she can get down on all fours and suck his cock and Guy can watch Rob pumping it, shooting into her mouth while he takes her like a dog.'

'She was good. You know I had her in the first year? She could barely speak English then, let alone read or write it, but she had such amazing tits and she thought that this was what you did, fucked with your English tutor, so it didn't matter. But she'll never be as good as you.' Baron groaned and massaged his crotch while he pushed his fingers harder, more urgently, up my tight cunt. 'So you're not upset by the idea of those two, then?'

'It turns me on, Baron. I'm even grown-up enough to be turned on by the thought of you fucking her,' I gasped, pulling away from him and lying down on the floor. 'So maybe they try it another way. Guy takes her up the arse, and Rob fucks her cunt,' I said, opening my legs and fingering myself, the climax already bunched up crazy and ready. 'I've never done it, but I heard it's possible.'

'Bella, I'm shocked!' Baron grinned, taking out his cock and weighing it in his hands. 'I never thought you could be so dirty!'

'I'm just sorry I wasn't there to join in with you and Ingrid.' I pulled him on top of me, my back scraping on the Persian carpet, and pushed his face onto my wet pussy. He parted my lips hesitantly, looked at the sweet frills inside. I tangled my fingers in his hair and shoved his face in, and felt his tongue lapping at last, sucking and licking at my clit until I came.

'Now you'll be tasting my pussy juice all evening,' I laughed softly, walking ahead of him into hall. 'Chef will be pissed off.'

After about five years of these liaisons, in fact the June I got married, we added the frisson of rushing back to his room for a post-dinner fuck as well as the sherry fuck, so that dinner itself would be an elongated agony of polite tittle-tattle over duck *a l'orange* while my pussy clenched impatiently, and I slowly licked summer pudding off my spoon and tried to catch those tawny eyes while he conversed solemnly at the high table.

We never phoned, never emailed in between. Never thought about who else we'd had. And we barely talked when we met. There wasn't time. But each year we developed secret signals which made the laughter and lust bubble inside as I tried to swallow meringue, bite into Stilton. Me tugging my right earring meant I wanted him to suck my breasts first. My left earring meant he was to lick my cunt. His were simple. Twiddling his left cuff link meant he wanted me on top. Right cuff link meant missionary.

But there was one position we never tried.

'I'm not sure I'll be back, Seb,' I say, shivering out in the moonlight. 'I'm done here.'

He does his thing of lighting two cigarettes and handing one to me. The others are waiting for us in the cellar bar.

'We all knew, Bella. You were like a bitch on heat. And Baron? Christ, every June the man thought he'd died and gone to heaven. But there were others, you know. In January, April, August ...'

My heart thuds. The whole thing flashes before my eyes, all those drinks, dinners, signals, the calendar secretly marked, packing and preparing, the journey here, my eyes flicking to seek him out, taking the stairs to his study two at a time. He's gone, but I've got a hungry pussy here that's been waiting all year to be filled.

'He could have told me he was leaving.'

'He's done here, too.' Seb shrugs. 'But I'm not.' He takes out a key. 'June comes round every year, right?'

Talk about signals. I look at the key, glinting in the lamplight. He's wanted to fuck me for twenty years. Still does. And, God, he's gorgeous. Why did I never see it? He starts to walk across the quad, through the archway to his staircase.

I take my shoes off, and follow him.

'I want you to take me like a dog, Seb.'

**Primula Bond is the author of the Black Lace novels *Club Crème*
and *Country Pleasures*, and of the Nexus novel *Behind the
Curtain*.**

Advanced Corsetry

Justine Elyot

I fell into this business unintentionally. I started out as an enthusiastic amateur, became a connoisseur and now I am proud to call myself a master – or mistress, I suppose – corsetière. If you ever want to talk busks, fan-lacing, whalebone, or the respective merits of under and over-bust models, I could be your woman.

Of course, should you choose to engage me in conversation on this subject, I must warn you that certain assumptions may be made regarding your personal preferences. These days we get our share of trendy young things surfing the wave of the burlesque revival, but our traditional customer has more personal reasons for favouring this most retro-chic of foundation garments.

Few people are better placed than I to appreciate the allure of the corset; her restrictive embrace, her provocative display of the finer feminine features, her fetishistic cross-lacing. You cannot ever forget you are wearing one; like an insatiable lover, she demands your full attention.

This is why I often find myself measuring and fitting women who want a little more than the traditional ribboned satin or silk. I have requests for custom-made pieces in rubber, latex or leather; others require additional features, such as delicate chains crossing the breasts, or linking the front and back of the garment between the thighs. One customer even emailed me to request that I add a harnesslike leather construction connecting the panels, which could run between the thighs and up the cleft of the buttocks, and to which could be attached various phallic objects. I wish she could have summoned the nerve to request this of me face to face; I always had a feeling we might have hit it off.

I thought then that I had heard every outré suggestion possible: corsets for fetish balls, corsets for waist restriction, corsets for the bedroom, corsets for lovers of Victorian kink.

As it turned out, however, things could, and did, get more decadent still.

My clients had occasionally come with friends, or even lovers – the intention being to canvass an additional opinion on what suited best, or perhaps to add a little titillation to the experience.

The couple I saw on that memorable afternoon were a different proposition entirely.

When I arrived in the small waiting area outside my atelier, she was sitting, hands folded demurely, while he stood scanning the photographs and framed magazine clippings on the wall. At first, there seemed nothing of especial note about them; indeed, they were rather less showy in their style and fashion taste than many I see. This in itself seems noteworthy in retrospect; at the time I simply cocked an admiring eyebrow at his Italian suit and her immaculate haircut and invited them into my fitting room.

At first I was taken aback when my initial 'what can I do for you?' spiel, addressed to the lady, was responded to by the man. He appeared at least twenty years older than her and, for a bizarre moment, I wondered if he were her father. It was a relief when he used the words 'my wife' in his reply, and I presumed the more exotic dynamic of Dominant and

Submissive – a bread-and-butter breed of customer, though I usually only interview one of the two.

Instantly her silence became fascinating to me and, throughout the man's lengthy discourse regarding their wants and tastes, I kept my eye on her. She was somewhere in her 20s, though conservatively dressed for her age in a blouse of ecru silk, the high neck adorned with what is incongruously termed a 'pussy-bow'. A knee-length tweed skirt and low courts completed the ensemble; she was hardly the pink-haired, rubber-skirted brigade I generally tend to en route to the Fetish Ball.

Her head remained bowed, our eyes never met, and I found myself wondering whether her doggedly maintained silence conveyed weakness or strength.

When the time came for her to have her measurements taken, she stood unbidden and planted herself in the centre of the room, chin up and shoulders back, awaiting instruction.

'You will need to remove your blouse and skirt, Mrs Fox,' I told her, affecting intense concentration on my tape-measure while she unbuttoned and cast off her outer layers of clothing. I was struck by two things once the clothes were neatly folded: the 1950s styling of her underwear, which was a flesh-coloured bra and girdle with old-fashioned metal suspender snaps; and the understated magnificence of her body, all luscious curves and creamy skin.

'Surely you will need her naked?' said her husband, standing behind her with his arms folded. 'To get the true measure of her, I mean.'

'I ... do not usually insist ...' I told him, though my throat dried at his suggestion. I longed to see what was held in by that severe girdle, cut so tantalisingly high and yet retaining the letter, if not the spirit, of modesty.

'I think in this instance ...?' His voice trailed away, questioningly.

I nodded, caught up in his scheme, made complicit by the slightly menacing smile he flashed in my direction. 'If you could just slip out of your underthings for me, Mrs Fox,' I said, my voice much lower now.

Even then, she did not look up or speak. Almost casually, she turned to present the clasp of her bra to me. I unhooked it briskly and took it from her, touching her shoulder to indicate that she should face me once more. Beautiful tits, high and firm with strawberry-pink areolae, were my reward. I caught myself fidgeting with the tape-measure again while she struggled and wriggled out of the tight girdle and, although I am noted for my composure, I found I could not look at her husband for fear of blushing.

Besides, a feast for my eyes was before me: the legs were not model-perfect, but they tapered nicely; the thighs were milky and a well-tended cluster of golden brown fleece curled between and above them. Unusual, I thought, that he doesn't make her shave; I had understood it was de rigeur these days.

'Could you raise your arms above your head for me, please?'

I moved around behind her, placing one end of my measure in the small of her back, risking a swift glance down at the curve of her arse (perfection) before returning in front to run my smooth tape across her breasts. The coldness of it perked her nipples up more so they stood stiffly, and, without even thinking about it, I pulled the tape a little tauter and rubbed it slightly back and forth. She bit her lip, and I had to exhale briefly, watching her rock on the balls of her feet and clench her fists. She felt that. Again, her husband sent that flicker of a smile in my direction, emboldening me.

Keeping the tape firmly held in one hand, I scribbled down her measurements on my desk pad, pulling slightly at her numerated tether while I did so. I had to admire her poise and grace; she did not stumble in the least.

Passing swiftly through the duller terrain of under-bust and waist, I came to another favoured spot – her hips. 'Let's keep this smooth – you have just a little pot belly here,' I clucked at her.

Her husband laughed and said, 'Yes, she does, doesn't she.' Her cheeks flamed, but she kept her eyes fixed to the floor and made no other response.

'The corset will hold that in for you; nobody will know it is there,' I said reassuringly, working hard at keeping my hand steady when I laid my length of plastic-coated fabric across the upper slope of her buttocks. Then I took a measurement I often eschew – the broadest part of her bottom and around the upper thigh. I had to kneel to check the measurement, my nose no more than an inch from her triangle of fuzzy hair, and the smell of her was, for a moment, almost too evocative. I took a lungful of it, to keep and bring out in my bed that night, thinking of other white thighs parted and welcoming, other crimson lips glistening at me. It had been so long.

But I am a professional, and I rolled my tape back up, wrote down my figures and turned to the gentleman, ready to enact business.

He held up a hand. 'Don't put your tape away yet,' he suggested. 'I think we may want something in the way of a garter or stocking top – perhaps you could measure the circumference of her thighs. Just at the very top, perhaps – as high as you can comfortably go.'

I stifled a smile. 'Certainly, Sir. Madam, may I ask you to stand with your feet a little apart.' The very tops of her thighs were tightly encircled, just below the crease of her bottom. It was impossible to perform this task without brushing my hand against her muff, and so very easy to rest it gently between the slightly opened lips of her vulva. Good Lord, she was dripping. I pushed my knuckles discreetly upwards, garnering a good coating of her juices, before completing my task. My tape also harvested a little of her lubrication.

It was all I could do not to put my hand to my nose and take a deep breath while I trotted out final arrangements for our fitting at top speed. I wanted them out, door locked, feet up on the desk, skirt hitched, hand inside knickers, post-haste.

For the rest of that week, every spare minute was consumed by thoughts of her. Did she ever speak? What did her voice sound like? In the heat of sex, would she make a noise? Was she silent even at the moment of climax? Had her husband enforced a speaking ban, or was it voluntary? I remembered the humidity between her thighs, the sticky, wanting smell of her. Was she a willing participant in this, or was I her unwitting tormentor?

I hoped to find out the answers to all of these questions and more regarding the exact feel and taste of her at our next meeting – though I expected the latter queries to remain unanswered. I constructed her corset – red satin, with black velvet running the length of the bones – with greater care than I usually expend. How perfectly it would frame her, covering her middle to expose more fully the tempting expanses above and below. I laced the eyelets lovingly, seeing the criss-cross pattern traverse her back from tailbone to bustline in my mind's eye.

The day of our fitting arrived at last; she was again respectably dressed in a boxy Jackie O-inspired skirt suit. When I passed the corset across the desk to her, she fingered it tenderly, catching her breath and shooting me my first eye contact – a cringing gratitude.

'Do you think it will do?' I asked her, smiling.

'I'm sure it will be just right,' replied her husband, taking it from her and holding it up in front of him. 'Once we've added our little extras.'

'Extras?'

'Let's have her try it on first, then we can discuss the adjustments I have in mind.'

He left it to me to issue the order to undress. My mind raced while I watched her perfectly polished nails wrestle with the large buttons of her jacket. Adjustments. Extras. Memories of the customised corset the lady had requested by email flashed through my mind. Was something along those lines required here? I rather hoped so.

How obediently she divested herself of her clothes, folding them neatly and piling them on the nearby chair, unsnapping her suspender clips, rolling down her stockings, tackling the hooks and eyes of her front-fastening basque and then standing quietly naked, head bowed as always, hands clasped modestly over her pubic triangle. She was not fully naked, though, for there was a plain silver torc around her neck, which fastened with a tiny chain at the back. Almost like a collar, of a very discreet kind.

She complied patiently with my every request while I settled the corset in under her bust and commenced the task of lacing it.

'How tight do you want it?' I asked, addressing my question unthinkingly to her husband.

'Well, now, I think we decided that we don't want it so tight that her breathing was affected. Tight enough to ensure that she is constantly aware of it, I suppose.'

'I understand completely.' I pulled hard at the laces, enjoying her gasps, and the first sound to come from her throat – a tiny mewl. 'So you have a voice,' I said briskly, and she fidgeted uncomfortably. One hand moved to cover her right buttock and I noticed for the first time a tiny mark there, dark red, almost a bruise but not quite.

'Don't cover it, or I shall tell the lady how you came by it,' said her husband in a warning tone. 'You are to behave yourself for Miss Frost, remember.'

Her hand moved away and once more her bare bum was on full display, mark and all. Now that the corset was laced, it swelled and undulated magnificently, crying out for attention.

'Now, how's that?' I asked, clapping my hands together with satisfaction at the beautiful picture she made, nude but for her severely cinched waist and silver collar.

'Exquisite,' commented her husband. 'Almost exactly what we wanted. Give us a twirl, love.'

She pirouetted obediently, then struck a number of suggested poses – hands on hips, one leg on a chair, bent at the waist. 'Perhaps you would like to photograph her for a private catalogue?' he suggested and, when I demurred, he said, 'Do you mind if I do?' and took a number of pictures on his mobile phone.

'Almost exactly?' I quoted him when he had finished, holding my notepad and pen in my hand as if ready to dash off a list of new requirements.

'Yes.' He lowered his voice. 'I have been led to understand that you can provide modifications to order. Is this correct?'

I nodded expressionlessly. 'Quite correct. I am discreet and prepared to cater for even the most unusual tastes. If you could tell me what you have in mind ...'

He produced a piece of crumpled paper from his breast pocket – a blueprint of sorts – and handed it over.

'Fascinating,' I commented, looking up at his lovely little submissive, still standing in corset and collar in the centre of the room. 'I shall have to think how I can make this work ... So these ... ?'

'Chains, linking the top of the corset to her ... necklet. Crossing the breasts, with a nipple clamp in the centre of each cross. I envisage sterling silver, perhaps even white gold, for the clamps. Would you be able to source something like this?'

'I'm sure I know an outlet or two. And then these straps below ... ?'

'Yes, thin straps – about a centimetre in width – of black leather, attached to each side of the front panel, crossing her thighs diagonally and meeting in the centre. As you see, they would pass underneath and between her legs, and up the cleft of her arse.'

The word 'arse' was oddly jarring; perverse as our conversation was, it had the feel of polite dinner-party chat.

'Yes, I see, and there are these small metal loops around the ... anus and the ... er ...'

'Yes, they don't have to be metal, though. I will leave that to you. The idea is that a vibrator or dildo can be screwed into each ring and inserted into my wife when she is wearing the corset. The part of the strap that passes between her lips should also have a patch of some reasonably rough or coarse fabric stitched on that will rub against her clit when she walks. Our aim is that she will be in a state of permanent sexual stimulation, though I would prefer that she cannot quite achieve satisfaction. So the fabric will need to be just a little too rough to be comfortable, and the penetrative objects just long enough to enter, but not so long as to provide relief. What do you think? We can go elsewhere ...'

'No need for that,' I said quietly, though I must admit I had been rendered momentarily speechless by what he had said. Speechless and extremely aroused. I wondered how she felt about it all; she had maintained her statuesque pose throughout.

Head bowed, hands clasped.

'I will need to take additional measurements.'

'As you wish.'

I stood directly in front of my subject, unwinding the tape-measure very quickly so she could hear the light swish of it, such an efficient sound.

'Your nipples first, I think. Are they quite hard enough?' I turned to her husband.

'Perhaps they need to be a little harder,' he agreed.

The pad of my thumb described a light circle over both tips until her chest began to buck and heave a little. I applied my finishing touch – a firm pinch to each – then wound my tape around the pair, pulling it as hard as I could get away with, looking for a grimace or, better, a sound. I got the grimace; the sound did not come.

'Small but not too small,' I noted. 'There will be a standardised size of clamps for them.'

'Oh, I'm aware of that.'

'Now, to the matter of the rings. What size of penetrative object were you considering?'

'Big enough to be noticeable. If you could perhaps measure both holes and then order rings for perhaps half a centimetre larger all round. She will need to be stretched a little.'

'I understand. Well, shall we start down here? I think, my dear, I will need you to bend over. Could you put your hands on that footstool just there and spread your legs as much as you can. That's ... just the job, dear.'

The whole spread was wide open and willing, from the swollen ruby of her clitoris to the brown bud peeking at me from between her cheeks. I felt like a gourmet at a feast, unsure of which dish to sample first.

I started at the top, or rather, the bottom.

'Perhaps if you use your fingers? To get an idea of what she can comfortably take?'

I acceded to her husband's request, snapping on a pair of thin latex gloves, and took a jar of lubricant he had produced from his trouser pocket. I smeared it liberally around the entrance of her pucker, greasing it up and pressing my thumb against the ring. 'Don't clench.'

My gloved index finger snaked slowly and surprisingly easily beyond her sphincter. I twisted it around in there for a minute until she began to squirm, then introduced a second finger. She began to whimper a little, so I went for the third, ramming them up repeatedly as far as I could and pressing down on her little red mark with my other hand. 'Yes,' I said, now having to work at controlling my own breathing. 'If I measure the width of these three fingers, that should be sufficient.'

I took off the glove and wound the tape around my fingers, enjoying the residual warmth from the invasion of her most private space. I thought about putting a fresh pair of gloves on for the next part of my measuring mission, but the prospect of all that hot, wet, yielding flesh against mine was too much to resist.

One finger was sucked into the tight, slick cave of her cunt, two were better, scissoring and prodding at the sides, feeling for the bump of her G-spot, finding it and rubbing it. And then, yes, she definitely moaned; her walls quivered, and I added a third finger. I could feel the suction; she was pulling me in and I was tempted to stay, but I realised that this was not on today's agenda, so I pulled out with a luscious squelch and added the figures to the list.

'She's extremely receptive,' I remarked to her husband.

'She's a slut,' he said, and the smallest of sighs escaped his wife's lips.

That night I thought about Ruby for the first time in years.

I thought about how she had loved to be on display, how

she would contrive to show off her suspenders even in polite company, how she would goad me into meting out discipline, how she would beg to be shared.

And that had been the sticking point. I had been unable to share her.

Mr Fox, it seemed, had no such scruple. Sharing his wife would be my first taste of that particular brand of honey in almost a decade. But was she like Ruby, or was she just doing it to please her husband? Perhaps I should just take her gushing pussy as a silent consent. Yes, perhaps I would do that.

Production of the Foxs' custom corset was a complicated job, involving much research and negotiation with some of the BDSM toy suppliers, but I looked upon it as a labour of lust.

When I was eventually able to stroke the leather nether harness, poking a finger or two through its rings, I called my deviant couple to invite them for a final fitting. On the manne-quin, the contraption looked devilishly wicked and alluring and I could not seem to stop experimenting with tightening and adjusting its fixtures. The two specially made dildoes – thick, but not quite long enough to go far – stood on my desk like sentinels ready to greet her when she walked through the door.

She saw them straightaway, flinched and then turned to the mannequin.

With her eyes, she asked her husband's permission to touch and examine her new garment, and she stood before it, running her elegant fingers over the smooth silk and the expensive leather, moving closer in to gape at the shining silver nipple clamps.

'You've done a wonderful job,' commented Mr Fox. 'My wife will get a lot of pleasure from this. And so will I.'

Mention of his wife's pleasure struck me instantly as a subtle green light. I smiled at him and nodded. 'The pleasure was all mine. I do enjoy these projects.'

'Good. Should we move on to the fitting?'

Without having to be asked, my model tugged at the ties of her wrap dress until it fell open, exposing her bra. She slipped off the skyscraper heels she was wearing, but her husband shook his head, and she put them back on again. She had only to shrug off the dress, unclip her bra and step out of her knickers today, and it was scant minutes before she stood in front of us in nothing but hold-up stockings, high heels and that silver collar.

Having removed the corset from the mannequin, I prepared to transfer it to Mrs Fox – a complex operation, involving much unlacing and unclipping. First I tied the main body of the corset tightly, but not too tightly, reining her in until the required hourglass was moulded. The straps at the front hung down between her thighs, but I left them there and began work on the thin chains that were to cross her breasts.

I clipped each chain to her collar, so that silver Xs adorned the pert little tits, then I went to work on attaching the nipple clamps. One notch, then two; the nipples crimsoned and stood out like tiny beacons. How lickable they looked, and the discomfort indicated by her gritted teeth was not putting me off in the least.

Nonetheless, it was time to move downwards, to fix the leather straps, passing them down between her thighs to hook them up at the base of her spine.

'Open your legs; this needs to pass between your pussy lips,' I told her, keeping my voice dispassionate. I manipulated the strap until it sat inside her labia, pressing directly against her clitoris. I lined up the ring with her vaginal entrance, then pulled the strap upwards between her bottom cheeks, performing the same alignment exercise over her hidden rosette.

'Is that tight enough, do you think?' I asked Mr Fox, tensing the strap as much as I could.

'That seems just about right,' he opined. 'Let me check.' He pinched and felt his way around the new features, nodding approval as he did so. 'She certainly won't be able to forget she is wearing it. Even less so when the extras are added.'

'Shall we try them out?'

'Oh, yes, I think so.'

I picked up the thicker of the dildoes, relaxed the strap enough to screw it into place in its ring and then ordered Mrs Fox to bend over on the desk with her legs as wide as possible.

'Is she wet enough to take this straight in?' I wondered aloud.

'Why don't you test her with a finger?' suggested her husband.

I took him up on it, giving her clit a good workout before pushing two fingers into the soaked void. She was wet enough all right, wiggling her bum frantically and trying to pull me in further. Oh no, she was not getting that yet.

'She's saturated,' I noted, laughing to Mr Fox. 'I don't often see a customer as satisfied as this!'

He laughed back at me. 'Not satisfied yet. Not until permission is granted, at least.'

'I quite understand. Now, let's stretch that dripping little quim, shall we?' I pushed the dildo inside in one swift move; her hips rotated, desperate to suck it in further, but she would get no more than the four inches of smooth black silicone.

Now I was too involved in my work to think about donning gloves; I affixed the anal plug to its ring and lubricated her clenching and unclenching arsehole with some of the copious juices of her pussy. I took my time with this operation, keeping the cheeks spread wide while I worked, talking to her in a low voice as one would to a skittish horse, for she was trying to hump the dildo in her cunt like a woman possessed.

'Keep it nice and relaxed, dear,' I whispered. 'It will stretch you, and you will feel it, but it won't fill you; no, you mustn't have that satisfaction without your husband's permission, must you, my dear? I do wonder where you will be wearing this lovely thing; I'm sure no amount of cover-up would hide the obvious fact that your holes are filled and your nipples as swollen as overripe cherries. I expect you'll draw quite a lot of attention wherever you go. I like those heels, my dear; they do thrust out your bum quite helpfully – look how ready you are now. Now, keep still, dear girl, and don't tense those muscles.'

I pushed the dildo against the tight little pucker, easing it in, keeping a tight hold of her spread cheeks in case she panicked, though I suspected she was well used to this method of penetration. She took it without protest, grunting quietly and rocking back and forth, until it was fully seated.

All that remained for me to do was to tighten the straps so that neither dildo could possibly be dislodged and leave her to accustom herself to the sensation.

'Well, that's ... very nice,' said Mr Fox, and I had to agree with him. The slightly protuberant flange of the anal dildo separated her cheeks pleasingly, and her pussy lips swelled out at either side of the invasive strap. Now I was tempted to take up Mr Fox's offer of a photography session, but he interrupted my train of thought, ordering his lady to, 'Walk across the room for us. No tottering on those heels.'

Mrs Fox straightened, straining to keep her posture dignified and refined, but, from the moment she took her first waddling step, it was obvious that dignity and refinement would not characterise her gait in this garment. Unable to close her thighs, and highly conscious of her penetrated bottom hole, she had to bow her legs slightly in order to get anywhere. Keeping her head down, she shuffled across the room, working hard at keeping upright on those vertiginous five-inch heels, coming to a halt at the full-length mirror.

'Lovely. Now get on your hands and knees and crawl back.'

She dropped to all fours and began to creep towards us. Oh Lord, I had never seen anything so exquisite as this beautiful, silent, submissive woman in her depraved garb, crawling in my direction, embodying all my sublimated fantasies together.

'Would you excuse me for a moment?' Mr Fox picked the strangest moment to leave the room, just as his wife had arrived at my feet.

'Oh ...' I glanced after him, mildly concerned, then turned my attention to the woman on the floor. Without looking up at me, she crouched over and kissed the toe of each of my patent-leather court shoes.

Then she spoke. 'Mistress,' she said. Her voice was low, almost a groan.

'I beg your pardon?'

'Please forgive me,' she murmured, her lips still so close that her breath misted the shiny shoes. 'I have not been quite ... honest with you.'

I reached down and hauled her into a standing position by the elbow. 'What do you mean?' I snapped, horrible visions of myself and her in the Sunday scandal rags springing into my head.

'No, no, there's no harm done, I hope!' she beseeched. 'I'm sorry. Let me tell you the truth and I hope you can forgive me. Please?'

I nodded and went to sit behind my desk, indicating that she should remain standing. When my mind was at rest, then so could her body be.

'I ... the thing is ... I've spent months wondering how to set up a meeting like this. I've thought and thought about it, but I'm quite shy.'

She looked at me questioningly.

'Go on,' I said.

'That man – Mr Fox, or whatever – is not my husband. He's a friend of mine. He agreed to do this for me. The thing is, you've probably forgotten, but I came in once with a girlfriend. She wanted a rubber one. I just ... I suppose I became a little bit obsessed with you. Your manner – it's very mistressish, you know, and I really like that ... I longed to come in and get fitted myself, but I was just too shy. I couldn't face it. I fantasised about it all the time, though, and discussed it with my friends on the net until they got quite sick of hearing about it. It was me that emailed you about the corset design, thinking that, at least if I had the corset ... but it wasn't the same. I knew I had to come in myself, but there was no way I could ask for this on my own behalf. Ralph agreed to help me. I know him quite well, from the internet and a couple of parties. I was pretty sure I could trust him.'

She stopped for a second, her darkly lipsticked mouth half open, as if it had run out of steam.

'You wanted me to dominate you while fitting a corset?' I asked for clarification.

'Oh yes. And afterwards, of course. But I do love corsets. The fabrics; the restraint; the frills and finishing touches. They are so erotic to me.'

I half smiled at her. 'Well, I certainly agree with you there.'

I stood up and positioned myself in front of her. Even on her heels she was a few inches shorter than me. I wrenched up her chin and put my lips against her ear.

'I don't know your name, little girl, but I do know your game, and it's an exceptionally dangerous one.'

She moaned, pushing her face against me, trying to divert my lips on to hers. I wouldn't have it.

'What about your friend Ralph? Do you want to involve him in this game now?'

'I want him to watch. He wants to watch.' She half sobbed, her body gyrating again in an effort to get some pleasure from its stubby intruders.

'Where is he now?'

'He said he'd wait by the stairs.'

'Then you'd better go and fetch him.'

I released her chin and turned her towards the door, setting her on her way with a stinging slap to her bum.

Off she waddled, returning five minutes later with her mildly embarrassed-looking friend.

'Ah, you're back,' I said. 'I have a favour to ask of you. In my desk drawer you will find a selection of full-length dildoes. I would like you to replace those in Miss here's harness with two larger examples. Then, while she is busy using her tongue to satisfy me, I want you to make sure that she is feeling the full benefit of the replacements. Do you think you can do that?'

'I'm sure I can,' he said smoothly, rummaging in the drawer while my little admirer stood trembling with arousal at the side of the desk.

'Good. Bend over then, girl, and wait for him to saddle you up.'

I watched while the shorter objects were removed and long,

thick rubber intruders took their place. She whimpered a little when the anal plug was halfway in, but Ralph was not one to allow that kind of thing to put him off, and he slid it slowly to the hilt, tightening the strap in place once more. Now she was barely able to walk at all, but, at my command, she knelt in front of me.

I leant back against the desk, steadying myself. I did not want that imposter Ralph to get a good eyeful of my cunt, so this would require some delicacy.

'Now I want you to push my skirt up just enough so that your tongue is able to reach my quim. Can you do that?'

'I'll try, Ma'am,' she said, pushing her head under the tweed and up to my stocking tops. I rarely wear knickers when I am corseted myself, so she had no obstructions to encounter. The rumpled skirt rested on top of her head, and there was no way Ralph could see anything forbidden to him.

'Good girl,' I crooned. 'Now, Ralph, get down on your knees behind her and work that arse and pussy hard. Come on then, girl, get to it.' I reached down and tweaked a clamped nipple; she squealed and her tongue darted out, hitting the spot perfectly.

What a hungry little mouth she had, devouring my liquid heat, running the tip of her tongue around my clit in luxurious circles, waiting for it to swell to unbearable proportions before sliding her lips over and breathing on it, lapping at it, sucking on it. Tiny yelps issued from her throat, vibrating over my whole sex, in time with Ralph's diligent pull-and-pushing on the deep-set dildoes.

'You can't imagine what you look like, can you, you little trollop? Kneeling here being fucked in both holes while you eat pussy as if your life depended on it. I don't think I've ever seen a slut to compare with you. I'd love to introduce you to my friends.'

A long, starved moan buzzed between my thighs; I signalled Ralph to slow down. I didn't want her coming just yet. Noticing the man's bulging trousers, I gave him permission to masturbate, pulling her head closer to my crotch, mashing her mouth up against my clit, using my other hand to twiddle with her sore little nipples.

'Next time you pull a stunt like this, young lady, I'll spank your arse for you,' I promised her. She sighed, her tongue in a frenzy now, her bottom wiggling furiously, while her whole body worked at relieving itself on the twin phalluses.

The three peaks came in rapid series, one rising as another fell. First Ralph roared and splashed his seed all over her bum and thighs, then, as it dripped downwards, she caught the perfect configuration of dildo and nerve ending and howled on to my clit, triggering my own explosion.

For a few minutes, the three of us were slumped together like felled skittles, panting and enjoying the stars that circled our heads.

Ralph was the first to tuck himself in and button himself up, leaving my naughty little customer to fall sideways. I wiped my thighs with a tissue and patted down my skirt, thinking that now was the time for private catalogue photography.

She was flushed and sweating, her mouth glistening with my spendings, her bottom and thighs sticky with Ralph's spunk. Her cheeks were still rudely thrust apart by the large dildo, and the strap still cut into the middle of her cunt lips. Her nipples were more like cherry stones than cherries now and one high heeled shoe hung off her heel. She looked a mess; a gorgeous dirty feast of a mess.

'We need photographs,' I told Ralph, and he nodded.

Her name, it turned out, was Jess. Her modelling and catalogue work for me is much admired in corsetry circles these days.

And if you gain my trust, and ask me very, very respectfully, I might just show you my private collection.

'Advanced Corsetry' is Justine Elyot's first short story for Black Lace. Her collection, *On Demand*, is published in December 2009.

Men

Charlotte Stein

I've made this list for you, my love, because you always wanted to know and I never told you. I was afraid you would be jealous and secretly angry in that smiling way you had, and then even more time would have been shaved off the time we had together.

But I've made it for you now, in a fit of strange pique of the sort you were always fond of. The men I've had, and loved, and in the order they came about.

Number One:

He was a bartender in some town that had a name I couldn't pronounce, and he had sleepy hooded eyes and was long and languid and sensual. His hair was as thick and glossy and as black as the ink I'm writing this with.

I was young and awkward and, when he said things to me like *se me hace agua la cola*, I didn't understand and had to look the words up in my little Spanish to English dictionary. Most of them didn't make any sense once translated – the language was thick with euphemisms and veiled meanings – but some of them were fabulously disgusting. And then I would blush all over, inside the roots of my hair and to the soles of my shoes, to think of the lewd and naughty things he had made beautiful in another language. His accent turned all the words into sultry, feathery sorts of things that twisted me inside out.

The heat saturated everything. It slid down the walls and over our bodies and into our pores. It made us slippery against each other as though oiled. It made my hands glide over his glorious honey tea skin and meant that I had to discover him everywhere.

He was just as good, from tip to toe.

We made love too often for heat like that, but he was irresistible to me and I was irresistible to him, apparently. We became insatiable maniacs, drinking gallons of strangely named Latin American juices in between mostly slow, but sometimes frantic, stretches of sinful sex. Sinful because I had never heard of some of the things we did, and it certainly all seemed very wicked to me.

I asked him what the word for wicked was in Spanish, and he said it was *cachonda*. He told me I was *la zorra*, and I would repeat the words back to him until he smiled that delicious smile that made those furrows pretending to be dimples plough their way through his cheeks.

He said that my voice sounded lovely when I spoke to him in his native language – though it wasn't really his native language, just the language that his parents left to him, along with the bar – but that it only sounded lovely in a way that wasn't Spanish at all. 'You've made up a new language,' he told me, 'a new language with your crazy accent and your bizarre pronunciations,' and it was funny because he was the one who made up a new language.

It was called how to be in bed with somebody.

He taught me that you're supposed to take all of your clothes off when you're in bed with somebody, and he did it by taking all of his clothes off first. He did it while I was getting something that seemed like lemonade, and as matter-of-factly as someone signing their name. I then drank the not-lemonade down as though it were vodka. It seemed as though something needed drinking, upon seeing a suddenly naked man.

I remember thinking: I can't believe I'm about to have sex with this unimaginable man. Even though, in hindsight, the whole night had been leading up to having sex. Tequila shots and licking things off each other's hands and the sucking of various fruits in dirty dirty ways. We'd practically kissed around a slice of something that might have been mango, and he had put his hand high up on my sticky-with-the-heat thigh, and looked at me with those hooded eyes.

What more did I want?

Nakedness, I wanted nakedness. I'm glad that it took nakedness. But then, of course, he insisted on my nakedness. He did it slyly, though, like a thief stealing my clothes. The first time I kept my dress on, and then the second time at some point in the middle of the darkest night, with rain slapping up against the shutters, he stole my blouse. And then in the morning, my skirt was unwound like peeling off a bandage to reveal the invisible girl underneath.

Though there was nothing invisible about me when I was with him. He made me feel viscerally, solidly real, made of flesh and bone and nerves. I could feel my whole body surrounding him and surrounded by him, and my self-consciousness fluttered away as though it had never existed. I barely even saw it go. He was bold and unabashed about his body; why should I have been any different?

I remember watching us in the spotted mirror on the wall: that long sloping line of his body; the curve of his back sliding into the delicious plump bow of his ass; and the way he curled his hips into me slowly, so slowly. The way my legs spread for him, with complete uncaring all-over-the-placeness.

He would come in late from the bar, creep up the rickety

staircase in the rickety old building I lived in, and I would hide behind the door and then jump on him as he came into the bedroom. I would hook my legs around his waist and weigh him down like an anchor, down down down to the bed. He never said no, and was always strong enough not to be weighed down by me.

But somehow I dragged him on to the bed anyway.

He was the first man ever to go down on me, and he did it without a word. No asking, no hesitation, no warning. He did it as though making casual conversation, though admittedly the conversation was about sensuous sexual erotic things. And I can't imagine how any casual conversation could really be about sensuous sexual erotic things: 'So, you seen the weather in your pussy today? My cock says it feels like rain.'

I'm not sure it works. But his tongue worked very well against my clit. So did his kisses, which he placed all over my sex as though it was as pretty and kissable as my mouth. He said things to that effect, too, that translated badly. Though I was loathe to have him say them in English, because somehow it wasn't as sexy.

He told me that I made him sink, and found little flowers on his way home that smelt of things strange and exotic, and put them in my hair. I still have those little flowers, dried and pressed in between the pages of books that we read together. I can still smell his strange cigarettes, making heavy mysterious clouds in the air. I can still feel his hands on me, drawing down over my hips and then between my legs, caressing my face while he caressed my pussy.

He had a thousand words for my naughty bits and they all made me so tense with excitement and arousal that I could just have come from hearing him say 'I love being inside your pussy' in a different language. I learnt words like 'again' and 'hard' and 'soft' and 'wet' quickly, and made him speak them to me more and more frequently because my body loved the exotic.

'You're just fetishising the foreign,' he told me, with those scything dimples in his cheeks, and I laughed at him, calling him my Latino love god, my samba-dancing, passion-obsessed smoulderer. That he couldn't dance and didn't really know much about being Mexican beyond the language made it funnier, and sexier, and sweeter: we were both fumbling in the dark towards ourselves.

I liked it when he was mysterious and written in a different language, but I liked it better when he was him.

Number Two:

Oh yes, Number Two was The Fireman.

Number Two was tall and as big as a horse and delightfully rumpled, perpetually like he'd just got out of bed because, well, he had.

I used to make him wear nothing but those big trousers they have with the braces, and strip for me real slow so I could lick with my eyes the tattoos on his arms, and the long stripe of his back and that lovely crisp hair on his lovely big chest.

He wasn't macho at all in the bedroom, and was only too happy to be my little plaything, my stripper whose shtick was *being a fireman*. We saw a guy do something very similar at Hot Dudes, giggling and drinking sweet cocktails – he wasn't threatened.

'I'm the real deal, baby,' he whispered in my ear. 'I'm gonna rescue you from all that burning up you've been doing.'

But he just made me burn higher, and harder. Where One had taught me to be uninhibited without words, Two taught me how to tell him what I wanted. All my secret fires just waiting for him to put them out.

He seemed like the sort of man who should have been straight down the line and simple, but he was only too happy to be in spirals and complicated.

I would put on his trousers, with the braces that went perfectly over my breasts like restraints – like some sort of crazy bondage girl – and save him from trees and burning buildings and from being trapped inside his clothes. I liked best to put him in peril, and upon rescuing him from the burning building – or 'wardrobe' – I would take a big pair of important-looking scissors and slide them under whatever tight clothing he happened to be wearing.

He liked the cold against his skin, just slipping beneath the elastic of those tiny Spiderman underpants he had. I liked the visual of the silver against the taut muscles of his upper arms. He would giggle in that gruff dirty way he had, and squirm impatiently, and sigh when I told him that, in order to heal the terrible burns he'd endured, I'd have to lick him everywhere.

I would put an ice cube in my mouth to make it extra cold, and when I lapped at all his hot places he'd tell me how much he loved my little icy tongue. There were places he couldn't stand for me to tickle wetly, but he'd stand it anyway because he loved trying to bear it. I would lick his sensitive nipples until he shivered and then I'd bite, and then lick, and then bite, until he croaked out for me: 'Oh, you slay me, you crazy wicked girl. You really do me over, I swear.'

I kept his big boots on when I fucked him.

He'd keep them on too, for me. Sometimes he would come home, half in his uniform looking like a cartoon hero from a kids' TV show, still soot-streaked in places so that he left little track marks all over me. He painted patterns on my belly, little sun spokes around my belly button, clouds on my breasts. Flames all over me.

'Oh, you're on fire,' he'd say. 'Quick, I'd better put you out.'

And then he would blow on me; he'd lick his fingers and wet my nipples and blow on them, or blow on my clit, or the sensitive places like my inner elbow or the line between my thigh and my pussy. Or, if we were in the shower, he'd tell me that he should get the hose, and the hose – or 'shower head' – would find its way between my legs to douse the flames. Little needles of sensation all over my clit until I was nice and creamy – even through the water of the shower – so that he could lift me up and fuck me against the slick, tiled wall.

He liked to get me so slippery, and so swollen, that, when he finally decided to fuck me, the feel of his cock shoving into my cunt would make me moan loud and long, even if friends were staying over, or his elderly aunt was in the next room.

'Shhhh,' he'd say, 'shhhh,' but he'd be laughing as he said it.

He was a real giggler, my fireman. He giggled when I slid down the pole at his station in just my underwear, and when I leaned against the truck and said: 'Come and put my fire out, Fireman. I'm burning up, baby, and only you can cool me off.'

Though he never really did his job properly, and set me alight instead.

Number Three:

Number Three was the naughtiest thing I've ever done. He was not allowed. I should have been a better person, etc.

But I wasn't a better person. Numero Uno and Mr Two had made me a naughty girl, damn them to hell, so I became a naughty girl at work too.

There was this patient, you see, this patient who had spent a lot of time in hospital. He had a tumour close to his spine and, though it had been removed and everything was fine – it was fine, it was really OK – he still had trouble walking. And me being a physiotherapist, I had to help him walk better.

It seemed that I helped him do other things better too. Or maybe he helped me, I don't know. He was a rascal, that one. He was a bad, bad boy. I had to be that bad just to keep up with him. I had to be cheeky and flirty and probably risked my job.

Oh, very inappropriate.

'But, oh, who cares, it's us,' he said, as he slid a cheeky hand up the skirt I never wore to work before he was there.

God, he was so handsome. He knew he was handsome even when he was sick and weary and struggling, those big dark eyes always undressing me as he called me Doctor Hottie. Paging Doctor Hottie, Doctor Hottie to the bedroom.

'Kiss it, and make me feel better. Give me a sponge bath, doc, and make me feel better.' 'Hey, I really need something more curvy to hold onto when I walk for you today. Do you have anything in mind?'

He started off with the parallel bars. He ended up with his hands on my hips. My hips make great walking aids apparently. Other things on me make great walking aids too, such as my breasts, which when flashed make a complaining patient walk another five steps.

He told me: 'I'd walk barefoot across a burning desert for those breasts. On broken legs. With only a can of Mountain Dew to quench my thirst. It's a real shame we can't do all of this semi-naked.'

I told him that I didn't think my boss would approve of promising nakedness to patients, but he just laughed at me and said that I shouldn't pretend I wasn't into that. Getting caught by my boss. Bad girls love getting caught being all unprofessional by their bosses.

He said he'd seen me looking at one of my handsome colleagues, Jason or James or something J that he couldn't recall, and that he knew I was the type to accost him in a cupboard somewhere or in the elevator like some bad hospital soap opera, and he got a kiss from me for that.

'No,' I told him. 'No, never. Never Jason or James or whatever.'

I'd like to say that I didn't fall in love with him because he was sick, but I don't think that's exactly true. Seeing a man like him – strong and vital and achingly handsome – being vulnerable made me weak at the knees and weak in my heart, and I loved him desperately for it. I loved him for being strong even as he was vulnerable, and I wanted him more, much more than One or Two.

I wanted him *because* of that, and because it was forbidden. 'Tell me it's forbidden,' he would say to me, and then find a way under my top to my always electrified skin, as I did something innocuous like fluff his pillow.

'It's forbidden,' I'd reply, as he smiled slow and syrupy, and said to me that I was his undoing.

'Now you've gone and done it, girl. Now I'm gonna make you pay.'

It had been a long time since One and Two, and even his breath against my cheek was like being woken up inside. And then when coupled with words like: 'Tell me I can still make a girl horny' and 'You're as soft as sin' and 'I dream about that mouth doing what good girls shouldn' t ...' Oh.

Oh, Three. How could you not have known how sexy you still were, how vital and glorious and all the things I've ever wanted in a man? I remember you tasting all strawberry, like hospital jelly, and doing such slight, innocent things that the surroundings made dirty, like sucking my finger instead of a thermometer, and sighing when I brushed the hair from your forehead.

One and Two gave me lessons in anatomy; Three revealed to me a world of subtlety and hidden looks and soft caresses when no one was looking. We made out like teenagers while watching daytime television on his hospital room TV. We held hands and told each other dirty stories and filled out crosswords together with entirely wrong and entirely filthy words. Somehow he turned seven down into *I want to mount you*. I turned twelve across into *pogofuck*.

I think it's the only time I've ever seen a word puzzle give a man an erection.

Number Four:

Number Four was softer and sweeter than all the rest. Something had happened to him, and he couldn't quite do the job he used to do. So he was a musician instead. He wrote songs about girls with big green eyes and black hair, and lips that bewitched him, and a voice that made him himself again.

Oh, he smouldered, my guitar guy. The girls all swooned over him, bought him drinks in the bar he sang at and threw their knickers at his head. He was always self-deprecating about it, and in between songs told them to go and find themselves a younger man, a sexier man, while some rum gal always shouted back that he was plenty sexy enough for her, honey.

He was plenty sexy enough for most of the women in any of his audiences, and they couldn't get enough of his sly smiles and his songs riddled with euphemisms.

But it was me he came home with.

I've never known why. I have no idea why it was me. It's easy when a guy's attractive and no one else seems to notice, but when other girls are hollering about just how good he looks, it's harder. Though, I have to say, I forgot about all of that when he wrote songs with fewer euphemisms in them, just for me.

Fewer euphemisms, and more direct explicit sentences about doing it.

He wrote me rhymes and limericks and ditties. Some were tame:

I've been to Rome and China and France,
But nothing gives me a rise
As the sights and sounds and glorious thrills
Of that place between her thighs.

And some not so tame. Some not tame in any sense at all. Ones that used the real words: cunt and cock and clit. Sometimes rhyming, sometimes not. Always telling me what he really wanted while he sat up there on that smoky tiny stage, and sang songs about driving down long dark tunnels in big cars.

When he was away, I would lounge in our big bed in covers that I hadn't washed so that they would still smell like him, and surround myself in paper covered in his words. I would read the word cock written in his scrawling handwriting, and think about that said same thing sliding into me as slow as butter melting in faint warmth. The sound of his husky voice telling me to turn over so he could see me as he fucked me, but, oh God, I loved feeling him fuck me with my face in the pillow.

'Fuck me,' I'd snap at him. 'Fuck me harder.' But he wasn't like One or Two. He was slow and patient and a fucking tease, and he would draw it out until it was agony. I'd berate him, but he would just laugh and pull me to him and say that I should like being savoured. I should like it and, besides, he wasn't going to do anything else because he knew what it was like to have something taken away from him.

He wanted to savour me, and he did. He would get home from the bar late and still find time to make love to me, and then get by on three hours' sleep so that he could follow me into the shower in the morning. We had different sorts of shower gels and potions, because he liked to spend forever feeling slick and rough and soapy things against my skin.

We'd stay in there until we could barely see for the steam or until the hot water ran out, though it usually took us a while to notice either of those things.

Then we would get out and start all over again. He wanted to start all over again, all of the time. He'd do it until he was exhausted and then fall asleep on my back, or with his cheek resting on my belly or shoulder. He'd do it until he died, and only stopped running himself ragged when I started telling him that he didn't need to do a damned thing to prove himself to me.

He was all man just falling asleep on my belly. He was all man sharing a pizza with me in our bed. He was all man when he was too tired to do me, and all man when he wasn't.

I told him that he was all man while he screwed me sitting in his lap, his hands in the hollows between my hips and my thighs, my back to his front and his face pressed into my throat and my hair. All man, my man, who could just say one word and turn me up too high. He asked me what that one word was and I told him it was his name, and his name turned into 'Oh, baby', and 'Oh, baby' turned into 'Oh, God, oh God.' Praise the Lord for Number Four.

His callused fingers on my clit, his husky voice singing in my ear, his dark eyes like hollows at the centre of the world.

Number Five:
Number Five was my super villain. He had a thing for

dressing up as his favourite comic book character when we had sex, a thing that he didn't tell me about until I screwed it out of him. He dressed up as him for a Halloween party, and I told him how much I liked seeing him be bad in leather, until he caved like a man with a gun to his groin.

He wore a little domino mask that made him look as wicked as the edge of a carving knife, almost as though he was perpetually laughing gleefully about something awful. I think he knew it made him look like that too, and that he looked deliciously macabre. I didn't mind what sort of kink he had when it was as good as that macabre look was.

We had sex while both wearing masks, laughing like super villains who had just killed the hero, and it was like being with Number One: I was made open again, and turned into something new. He was too. He was my playful evil boy, and I was his playful evil gal.

We ruled New York and Mexico and Shanghai and various other places around the globe with iron fists, and made love in impossible and ridiculous places. Sometimes while wearing masks. Mostly just in our civilian clothes.

We had sex at the zoo in a cage of stone animals that periodically made weird recorded sounds. No one was around because it was parade day and late, but I doubt my super villain guy would have cared. He took a picture of me standing in front of a stone rhinoceros and then said: 'Oh, and I guess it's now time for you to take those panties off, you wicked, wicked girl.'

I did. Of course I did. Who knew when the next opportunity to be fucked against a stone rhinoceros would present itself. He was quite a bit taller than me so I had to sort of half perch on its sloping back, but other than that it was as easy as walking, because he was always big and stiff and ready and I was perpetually wet.

Oh, but the best outdoor pursuit we had was in the library. Breckenridge University library. We only went there for my reunion, but after the drinks and floppy sandwiches I showed him the place I spent the most time at, while enjoying the best years of my life. Not with those faces I barely remembered in a bar I never hung out in, but in that old library with the cubicles and desks that still had my name scratched into them.

I showed him the copy of *Love in the Time of Cholera* that still had my handwritten addition: 'One day I'll wait fifty years for someone.' Before he tossed it over his shoulder and launched himself at me like a six-foot three-inch laser guided slab of man flesh.

Mrs Doddy, the seven-thousand-year-old librarian, caught us on the floor half underneath a desk. Apparently she approved of super villains, though, because she just looked at us as we stopped mid-thrust, before leaving us to it. I would say that we feared security but, of course, super villains never fear security. Especially when they're busy giving each other intense orgasms.

The best orgasm I ever had, though, was not in a library, or on a plane, or in some place whose name I can't pronounce, or while against a fire truck, or forbidden and in a hospital bed, or among song lyrics of terrible dirtiness, no. The best orgasm – the best *sex* I ever had – was when he took his mask off.

He sometimes asked me, as we fucked in zoos and libraries and on planes, if I was so easily excited now because of all of these strange and new places we found to make love in, and he never gave me a very super-villainy sort of response when I told him I wasn't. 'No, it isn't the places. It's just you, my darling, you.'

'But you must have fucked around with sexier guys,' was

his retort. 'Hotter guys that made you hotter, real studs who bucked you 'til you could barely walk?'

'Real studs like you,' I said to him. 'Real studs just like you. What more could I want but you? Here, take your mask off and let me look at you.'

And I did look at him, in our cold bedroom. It was cold because the old tree in the backyard had come through the roof a few nights before, and the plastic wasn't covering it right, and it was snowing inside our house. We should have moved downstairs, but he wanted to stay. And in the cool wintry moonlight he looked wicked and gleeful, even without the mask on. He looked sexy and exotic and heroic and vulnerable.

I kissed him long and slow, and then deeper and deeper until it became urgent. I remember the taste of him, not like cigarettes any more but like the cold, and like him. That little agile tongue of his working its way against mine, while his hands found my breasts beneath layers of T-shirts and cardigans.

I remember his hands being warm, much too warm for the cold room, and he whispered in my ear that he had been keeping them underneath his body to make sure they weren't too cold to touch me with. My hands were freezing, so I blew into them before he stopped me. He always liked ice against his skin.

'Except for here,' he told me, and cupped my sex with one big hand. 'Here, I like it when you're burning up.'

I was – he only had to kiss me to make me hotter than the sun. His kisses were wicked and indulgent, and he had no problems liberally spreading them around. At the hollow of my throat, the soft slope of my breasts, the turn of my hip, the plane of my thigh. He kissed me almost everywhere until my pussy became a little juicy pouting mouth, waiting for similar attention there.

But I kept myself on edge, and stopped his kisses when they ventured between my thighs, and gave him some exploration instead. I traced the lines of his twin tattoos – one on each arm – and his scars in the place where his back began to curve. I licked where he liked it best: just underneath his jaw; over his nipples; around the strong curve of his gorgeous cock. I kissed his hips and the strange sinuous muscles that surrounded them, a little less there than they used to be but still sexy. He was always sexy.

Sometimes he knew it. But I liked it just as much when he didn't, and in the dark spaces we occupied together – somewhere just after waking in the middle of the night, perhaps – he would ask me. Am I still sexy to you, am I still a man, to you, am I still?

He was always more than a man, to me. He was everything that a man could or should be, and I was so grateful to have had him. When he made me come around his cock, with his hand gripping my thigh tight and his mouth open over mine, I tried to tell him that he had meant more to me than any man I had ever known. I tried, but all that came out was wordless pleasure, wordless mindless glorious pleasure that I poured into him in thanks, for being my man.

That's my list. I hope you like it, though I doubt you will.

I have that picture of you sitting in the doorway of our new home, still smoking like an ass, that odd look on your face that was partly happy and partly sad. The light is hitting you just right, making you seem dark and deadly and soft and subtle all at the same time, and your feet are bare like they always were. How lovely you are! How lovely you were, my Jonah, my man who was many.

It was always and only you, my Latino love god, my fireman,

my patient, my musician, my super villain. I have only one list of all my men, and all of them are you.

Charlotte Stein has contributed stories to the Black Lace collections *Lust at First Bite* and *Seduction*. Her first single author collection, *The Things That Make Me Give In*, is published in October 2009.

Junking

Alison Tyler

'There's a fine line between "broken in" and "broken down",' Todd snorted. 'Why can't we just buy a new sofa like normal people?'

'Who wants to be normal?' I asked, gazing at the leopard-print lounge in the far corner. Even from a distance, my trained eye noted that the fainting couch was circa the 1890s, with claw feet and a curved mahogany frame. I could easily imagine Todd fucking me on that seductive sofa, one of my treasured petticoats pushed forcefully to my waist, shiny black satin panties ripped aside, stockings and garters askew.

His fist would grip tightly into my dark cherry-cola curls, dragging my head back for a kiss while my hands sought uselessly for purchase on the lion's face adorning the sofa rim. As Todd slammed into me, I'd close my eyes and pretend to be a Victorian maid, caught in a quiet room by the master of the house and fucked royally while the mistress was away. Afterwards, we'd collapse on the couch together, limbs entwined, and whisper dark fantasies about all of the other lovers who might have used the sofa before us. What tales a 140-year-old couch could tell. And why couldn't Todd see what I saw?

'That one's a beauty.'

I turned to see who had spoken, while Todd continued to show every sign that he was ready to flee the packed second-hand store. The stranger was familiar looking. An actor? In L.A.

'Where have I seen him before?' can generally be answered with the name of a soap opera or a pain-relief commercial. But, no, although he was attractive, the man didn't seem the actor type. There was something too real about him. More substance, less show.

I saw Todd eye the man, then stand up straighter, and I had to bite my bottom lip to hide my smile. Both of us had realised simultaneously that Todd was the shorter of the two men. My eye – at the moment trained not on mahogany but men – also noted that the stranger was built lean, no spare meat on his six-foot four-inch frame. Was Todd sucking in his gut, too?

The stranger ran a hand over the back of a chocolate 1960s modulated sofa and, if I were that piece of furniture, I would have started to purr. 'Authentic Naugahyde. They don't make them like that any more.'

'For a reason.' Todd's scowl deepened. 'That thing's uglier than sin.'

'You'd rather have one right out of the showroom?' Dry humour resonated in the stranger's voice. He'd nailed Todd's style in a heartbeat.

'Do you work here?' I recognised Todd's tone from the way he sometimes asked, 'You're going to wear *that*?' when we were getting ready for a party, sending me scurrying back to my closet to replace my first outfit with something less dramatic, more acceptable – taking off the collection of sparkly rhinestone pins adorning my collar, or slipping on standard opaque hosiery rather than fence-net stockings.

The man smiled and I saw the crinkle lines at the corners of his grey eyes, noted the scuff of shadow on his jawline. Suddenly I placed him. He'd outbid me at an auction in a warehouse downtown several months previously, snagging a brass headboard I'd had my eye on. I'd moaned about the loss for a week, but had blocked out the winner's good looks with the sour grapes' sensation of being outbid. Now, I thought about Todd's comment from a moment before. The term 'broken in' perfectly suited this man, from his faded Levis to his well-worn leather belt, which he stroked with his thumb when he saw me watching. Fuck, did he guess what I was thinking when his hand worked the leather? That, in an instant, I'd imagined him bending me over and tanning my ass with the strip of hide? This was a fantasy I'd never confessed even to Todd, and yet I felt unexpectedly naked before the dark-haired man.

A shiver ran from the nape of my neck to the base of my spine, and I had to direct my focus to the nearby trio of nesting tables in order to hide my flush. My fingertips travelled the length of the top table, making curlicues in the thin layer of dust.

'Just a fellow junker,' the man confessed, and Todd immediately turned his back, ending the conversation without another thought. I could see my boyfriend looking for a way out of the store. One Man's Trash was jammed with so many oddly shaped items that there was hardly space to walk. But I caught the man's eye in the ornate mirror on the far wall, saw him watching me, taking in my mod dress, white go-go boots, and the tortoiseshell hair band I'd used to scrape the curls off my face.

Pushed past the edge of his limits of patience, Todd grabbed my hand and dragged me forcefully through the labyrinth of sofas and breakfronts and grandfather clocks out onto the crushed-glass glittery sidewalk of lower Fairfax.

'We tried it your way,' he said. 'Now, let's do it my way.'

How I wished he were talking about fucking rather than furniture. But what would 'my way' be in bed? Rougher than we usually had sex. Dirtier. There'd be a spark of pain involved, a power exchange, a heat that would leave me melting in the centre of the mattress, my body limp and liquid. We'd fuck at 2 a.m., or right after work, or meet in the middle of the day for an illicit liaison between two of his appointments. Anything other than the minty-fresh, lights-off sex Todd and I currently shared on a twice-weekly basis.

The man in the furniture store would have understood. He wouldn't have had a problem getting busy on that sofa, pulling down my knickers, kicking my polished white boots apart. He'd have his belt off in a flash, binding my wrists together over my head, fastening my body to the coat-rack on one wall, whipping me with the cord from one of the 1950s-style lamps.

As I stared through the picture window at the stranger, I let myself be led to Todd's convertible silver BMW, with the rhinestone-studded 'Dentist to the Stars' circling the vanity plate: TM DDS for Dr Todd Mitchell, Doctor of Dental Surgery. I didn't say a single word when he pulled in front of the high-end furniture store on Beverly Boulevard, a place filled with furniture so new that the air smelled only of plastic particles.

The next time I saw the stranger was at the world famous Rose Bowl flea market in Pasadena. Like me, the man was one of the early birds. He appeared aimless, not on an obvious mission, like the couples you'll see out to buy a bookshelf, or a new bunk bed, but walking in a semi-trance, the way I do. That's the only way you'll ever find true treasure. Although today I actually had an agenda.

My best friend Katea and I were officially on the lookout for a coffee table. Todd had won the sofa war, purchased from a saleswoman who looked so freshly scrubbed I thought she must keep her pussy encased in Saran wrap. To even things out, I was allowed to choose the table – but I'd been given a list of rules to follow:

Nothing too dinged up
No 70s styles
Nix on a kidney shape from the 50s
Bamboo was a deal-breaker

If I didn't score today, Todd was going to buy the one he'd had his eye on at the furniture warehouse, anonymous in its ugliness, but one the chirrupy salesgirl had assured him was the height of fashion.

While Katea and I shopped, Todd remained home, ostensibly awaiting the arrival of our new sectional sofa – but also, I knew, avoiding his nightmare of a way to spend a weekend. 'Surrounded by other people's junk? Thank you very much, but no. I'd rather inspect the corners of the condo to see if the maid missed any stray specs.'

He'd said that in a sarcastic tone, yet part of me was sure he actually *would* look to see if she'd remembered to clean the inside of the bathroom cabinets as well as the mirrors on the exterior.

What Todd didn't understand – or could not seem to fathom – was that junking turned me on. The concept of finding a jewel amid the rubble made my heart beat wildly. At least, that's what I told myself as I stared hard at the stranger.

'Look over there,' I said, motioning to Katea.

'You like that lamp?'

'No, the man.'

'I like the lamp,' she said, admiring the sleek silver swanlike neck, suspending the round cantaloupe ball of a lantern like one lone Christmas bauble. Katea shared my passion for vintage – we'd met at a swap meet years before – so shopping with her was dangerous. In a one-of-a-kind world, passions can run strong. Friendships have been destroyed over a tug-of-war for the perfect La-Z-Boy. Luckily for us, we had different tastes.

'But the man, he's the one I saw at One Man's Trash. Do you remember? The one who liked the 60s sofa, while I was mooning over the velvet leopard-print.'

'How on earth could you let a couch like that go?'

'Todd wasn't into it.'

'He's not big on fur,' she smirked. 'He forced you to get rid of your coat, didn't he?'

'It wasn't that he *forced* me . . .' I trailed off, thinking of the three-quarter-length coat with obsidian buttons. Todd had made an offhand remark about the jacket looking like something his grandmother would have worn with an eau du mothball perfume, and I'd tucked the coat into a box for storage.

Katea cocked her head, and then whispered, 'Todd wouldn't be caught dead wearing jeans like that.'

She was right. Todd's $300 jeans lasted only until the first sign of wear. In fact, sometimes he ditched a pair when he simply thought they were *about* to fade, locking onto a hint of gradation in denim colour that nobody but he would notice. The stranger's were threadbare in the knees and seat, but they fitted his toned body to perfection. I would have spent a happy afternoon trading places with those jeans, wrapping myself around this man's body, my skin to his.

Why did this man make me want to change places with inanimate objects – first fantasising about becoming that Nauga sofa, and now dreaming of being turned into a pair of Levis?

He was perusing items in a stall ten feet away, looking at coils of dull silver chains, bundles of rope. I saw his hand reach out to touch a heavy padlock, and I noticed the fact that he didn't wear a ring.

The thought brought me instantly back to Todd, and guilt coloured my cheeks. The two of us had been together for nearly a year, and the month before he'd invited me to move into his condo with him – thus starting the hunt for new furniture. I had been sad to leave my apartment in Hollywood, with the scrolling metalwork on the fire escape outside the window, the black-and-white tiled kitchen, the touches of 40s you couldn't find in most apartments any more. Especially places like Todd's, a sparkling condominium in the recently refurbished heart of downtown L.A.

But I'd been afraid to admit that I'd consider choosing cornicing over a chance at marital bliss. That's the sort of concept that lands you all by yourself in your old age, sharing your cheery yellow Formica table with seventeen cats. At least, that's what I told myself as I tried to accept my new digs. Besides, I'd dated my share of fixer-uppers in the past. Sure, my previous beaus had looked perfect. One had favoured suspenders and Zoot suits. Another had channelled James Dean from his clothes to the silver Spyder he drove. But all had been lacking in one way or another. Liam didn't understand that being exclusive meant not occasionally fucking cute actor boys at the Y. Thad was missing the all-important work ethic. The James Dean lookalike had left me for a girl who resembled Natalie Wood.

Wasn't it time for me to be with a man who had all his parts in working order?

That didn't mean I fell naturally into Todd's universe. Everything here seemed antiseptic to me, which made sense, I supposed, as he was a celebrity dentist. He'd want to project a clean-cut image. But I'm second-hand to the core – the owner of a tiny vintage boutique in the heart of Hollywood – and, as such, we're not the type people would automatically put together. Because of my business, I'm allowed to be creative with the way I dress. My boyfriend traded in his car every two years for a sleeker model, the same way he'd moved from girlfriend to girlfriend before he met me – the bikini model, the airline stewardess. Once I'd learned his history, I was surprised he even sent me a drink at the bar where we met. I had been flattered when he wanted to take me out, and fell more than a little over my head when he started showering me with presents.

'Opposites attract,' Katea said after meeting Todd for the first time. Did she believe we made a good team, or was she waiting for Todd to tire of me and drop me in a bin outside the nearest thrift store? Because, recently, I had begun to think that he liked me in *spite* of my style, that if I were a doll, he'd strip off my clothes and dress me up right, in matchy-matchy clothes like the girl in the furniture store had worn: white on white on white.

'What's he doing with all that rope?' Katea said, shaking me from my reverie.

'I don't know,' I told her, 'but I've got first dibs on the record player.'

We both ran towards the old GE together, my hand touching the turntable first.

'You bought a what?' Todd asked when I arrived home.

'A Wildcat.' I swallowed hard. I hadn't thought ahead, too delighted in my purchase to consider what he might say.

'Is that another word for record player?' He looked incredulous.

'Not just *a* record player, but a *Wildcat*,' I said, talking quickly. 'This one's from about 1974. Built-in speakers. And the arm is automatic. You know, so you can put on the record, and –'

'And –' Todd interrupted me, 'where's the coffee table?'

'You don't understand the first thing about junking,' I teased, trying for light and airy. Who did I think I was? The sing-song hostess from *Trading Spaces*? 'You might go looking for one item, but chances are you'll find six other treasures instead.'

'Don't tell me you bought *six* record players?'

I'd had a Silvertone in my Hollywood apartment – gun-metal grey with built-in speakers – but movers had dropped the box containing the precious player, and I hadn't found a shop able to do the necessary repairs.

'We have a state-of-the-art stereo system.' He pointed to the nearly invisible speakers mounted in the wall, and the furrow in his brow deepened noticeably. He'd seen my record collection, hadn't he? The albums took up two shelves in the closet of the spare bedroom. He'd known I would replace the broken one, hadn't he?

Apparently not.

He didn't move as I started to set up the player in the corner of the room.

'Just wait,' I told him, sprinting up the stairs in search of one of my favourite records. I came back clutching The Police, 'Every Little Thing She Does Is Magic'. I set the record down, placed the needle on the outer groove, and felt Todd watching me as the arm slid right over the record and knocked brutishly against the paper label.

He laughed dismissively, and a weight settled hard in my stomach. But then I remembered. Quickly, I grabbed up my straw bag and dug out my wallet. Feeling Todd's brown eyes on me, I carefully placed a quarter, a dime, and two copper pennies on the top of the needle. When I started up the record player a second time, the machine worked. There was that crinkly whisper at the start, then the sound of Sting belting out one of my all-time favourite songs. Immediately, I felt like I was twelve again, listening to The Police in my bedroom, sprawled on my floral comforter and staring at the posters on the walls. I turned to look at Todd, who didn't have the same lost expression on his face that I felt on mine. He lifted one of his many remotes from the line-up on the mantle. In seconds the exact same song was issuing from the speakers, a few bars behind mine.

'That's been digitally remastered. How can you argue with quality?'

I wanted to ask him the same thing.

'I only have seven bucks on me,' I heard a man nearby say the following weekend. 'Can't we make a deal?'

When relationships start to go south, some people head to the bars. Others seek solace in a stranger's arms. I spent all day Saturday and Sunday at different garage sales, driving to Silver Lake, Venice Beach, or even the Valley if the write-ups in the paper sounded promising.

Todd wasn't waiting at home for me anyway. After losing too many weekends fighting over our very different ways of relaxing we'd decided to take separate but equal days off. Todd would satisfy his needs in the ultimate mall experience, while I went junking. Todd was undoubtedly right at this minute at a Best Buy, pricing out state-of-the-art flat-screen televisions. Or maybe he was at Verizon, drooling over the latest in cell phone technology. If he had finished at those two stores, he'd be buying a Grande Frappuccino at Starbucks to take home with him, where he would spend the rest of Saturday afternoon polishing his glossy appliances and making sure I hadn't left any knick-knacks on the window sills.

I told myself I was working. Scouting for hidden finds for my store. But I was lying. 'Seven dollars, my ass,' I whispered to the stranger, thrilled to see his face once more. 'You've got a twenty tucked into your boot, or my name isn't Fiona.'

He shook his head, but the corners of his lips turned up.

I'd told him my name. I could see that fact register in his chrome-coloured eyes. 'It's here in my wristband,' he said, unzipping the hidden compartment on his thick leather cuff to show me I was right: crisp, folded Jackson. 'For emergencies only.'

I grinned and moved away, losing myself in the tables of odds and ends, but thinking of the way he smelled. Like old leather. Like used bookstores. Like a promise.

My James Dean lookalike had fucked me bent over his convertible. He'd dress me up like a 1950s femme fatale in hot pink jodhpurs and a sleeveless black-and-white checked shirt. Chartreuse chiffon kerchief at the neck, cork-soled espadrilles. He'd pretend he just won a street race, and to the victor went the spoils.

And *I* was the spoils.

We'd fucked after watching *Rebel Without a Cause*. And after watching *Giant*. And *East of Eden*.

The sex had been so good that I'd stayed with him longer than I should have. Even when I knew he was straying, even when I knew his eye had wandered, I'd slip on that outfit and arch my back.

But when I tried to get Todd to do me on his car, he gave me a pained look. 'Just got the Beamer detailed, Fifi,' he said, shaking his head sadly, and not noticing me grimace at his pet name for me. 'I wouldn't want to smudge the sheen.'

I reached for the paper to hide my disappointment, grabbing a pen and starting to circle the promising garage sales for the next week. Hoping against hope that I'd run into my stranger again.

'We've got to stop meeting like this, Fiona,' the stranger said over a tangle of vintage scarves at a church rummage sale in North Hollywood. My hand was on a red silk one, and my heart throbbed at the way my name sounded in his low, rumbling voice. He could blindfold me with the blue one, use the emerald to bind my wrists, the long lilac one on my ankles. He'd start with me face down, and spank me hard with his hand, getting me so wet, so juicy that, when he retied me face up, I would be dripping. He'd slide right in, driving hard, keeping me off balance with the blindfold still in place. I wouldn't know what he was thinking, wouldn't be able to see his eyes.

God, what a vision. And all from simply touching an old-fashioned scarf.

'We do,' I agreed, and then let the statement hang between us.

Until he said, 'Killian. My name's Killian.'

His fingers met mine just as Katea yelled out, 'I think I've found your coffee table!' When I turned to glare at her, the man snagged the collection from out of my grasp and headed towards the cashier at the front of the sale.

'Save some for the rest of us,' she hissed to me.

'Scarves?' I asked dumbly. I wondered if anyone else in the church parking lot had panties on as wet as mine were.

'No, men. Besides, isn't he a bit scruffy for your newly upscale tastes?'

'There's a fine line between "broken in" and "broken down".'

'Which one is Todd?' she teased.

'Neither,' I sighed, wondering if maybe that was our whole problem.

At work, my new record player sat on a shelf by the register, albums lined up underneath. I put on *Empty Bed Blues* and wondered what mess I'd got myself into.

Why would I go for a brand-new model when I was so used to second-hand? Because I'd been burned by one too many fixer-upper types, men I'd snagged at half-off sales, sure I could get replacement parts for them, and who ended up as broken inside as they were out. Shouldn't have been a shock to Katea that I would be interested in trying a boy still wrapped in the box. We were two of a kind in that way, weren't we? Todd had grown tired of the synthetic princesses he'd dated, and I'd become immune to the scruffy men in loose-soled shoes.

Still, my thoughts went again and again to Killian, and more specifically to the items I'd seen him buy: a coil of rope; a packet of fence posts. What was he going to do with that ancient inner tube? Why would he linger so longingly over the barbed wire?

Why did I care?

Opposites attract for a reason. But, while I'd thought that I could ramp up the action in bed with Todd, and he'd thought that he could convince me to peel off at least one layer of sequin-studded vintage, perhaps at heart we were so busy trying to fix one another we'd missed the signs that things weren't ever going to work. An American plug ain't never going to fit a European outlet.

I learned that when I fried my hairdryer in Paris.

Todd didn't agree when I told him I was worried about our future.

'We're the same,' he insisted. 'You take the old and make it beautiful. I take a broken smile and fix it.'

He was trying. He was working to make me see why we connected. But all the smiles he fixed ended up looking exactly the same. I'd peruse the files of his Before and After shots, and feel depressed for the lost gap between two front teeth, for the slightly overlapping canine that now rested perfectly in the exact spot where it should.

I looked around our spotless apartment. Dust-free. Clutter-free. Personality-free.

We were nothing alike.

At the next estate sale in Holmby Hills, I paid little attention to the rows of platform high heels, or the caftans with the intricate beadwork, or even the basket overflowing with Bakelite bangles. Because there he was, as I'd somehow known he'd be. Against all of my intelligence, and with only a care to the most basic animal instincts, I watched from a distance as he hefted a length of silver chains.

He left without making a purchase. I did as well, following his truck – a Ford, as dark red, shiny and well cared for as it must have been on the first day out, fifty years before. Feeling like a new recruit on *Dragnet*, I followed his truck down Sunset Boulevard, through millionaire-land to Melrose, tailing him as best I could. I had a copy of the *LA Weekly* folded on my front seat, with different garage sales and estate sales circled. Did he have the same bible with him?

He must have, because I found myself parking half a block behind him on Rose, in a much lower-class area, but one known for unexpected finds. I walked as inconspicuously as possible to the area of items spread out on sheets on the crisp dried grass, and on card tables on the stained cement driveway, watching as he caressed a leather belt missing its buckle.

My mind did a quick inventory of the items I'd seen him buy, and suddenly I realised what he must be doing. He locked eyes with me, right as I thought: Dungeon. He's outfitting a dungeon. Using only second-hand tools and toys. Items one might never suspect for X-rated activities. My cheeks burned the same red as the deflated India rubber ball lolling on a nearby table.

I turned away, but he caught hold of my wrist and held me.

'I'll show you mine,' Killian said, 'if you'll show me yours.'

'What do you mean?' my voice was husky.

'You want to see the treasures I've found, don't you?'

I nodded. I couldn't help myself.

'I'll show you mine,' he repeated, and now I nodded. We didn't leave just then. He stood in line and paid for his purchases, haggling over the amount for the padlock with no key. Pointing out the fact that the belt was broken, what use could this strip of leather have now that the buckle had broken off?

But I knew. I knew in that heart-racing flash, like I knew in the moment when I pulled the blazer out of the rack at the thrift store that I was holding a Genuine, Made-in-Italy Armani. He was going to use that belt on my ass. Fuck the buckle, he had all he needed in that strip of leather, which the frazzled housewife sold to him for fifty cents.

I followed his Ford to a bungalow on Mesa. Walked through the gate to see that the yard was filled with odds and ends, a roll of wire, a claw-foot tub. Generally, I would have wanted to spend hours poking around, but the man was opening up his garage, and a glint of brass caught my eye.

He'd done precisely what I'd thought. Created a dungeon from spare parts. The Frankenstein of dungeons, in a way, yet beautiful in the starkness. A bit of a bed here, a length of chain there, all refurbished. One man's trash, I thought, as he started to help me out of my jacket.

'A buck fifty,' I told him, 'at a flea market in Athens.'

He slipped off his own leather jacket, and grinned. 'Seventeen, at a little shop in Soho eight years ago.'

He touched the silver links around my throat, the heavy man's Navy ring dangling from the centre. 'The chain was free,' I said softly. 'Broken, but I fixed the clasp. The ring was five dollars. I've had it since high school.'

'Worth more than one hundred now, right?'

I nodded, then ran my fingers over the face of his watch.

'Timex. Was my father's. Engraved on the back with the date I was born.'

I locked eyes with him. This was the reason I collected old items. Because of the stories, or rather because of the *histories*. My pocket watch, in my bag, had belonged to my grandfather. If you popped open the back, there was a faded black-and-white photo taken on my grandparents' honeymoon. Todd had given me a Rolex to replace it, annoyed that I would go digging through my bag whenever I wanted to know the time, not aware of the pleasure that flat circle of gold gave me whenever I held the timepiece in my palm.

With Todd, I always felt as if I were caught in a 30-day trial mode, and I occasionally wanted to remind him that, unlike his brand-new Sony flat screen, I did not come with a money-back warranty. This exchange I was having with the stranger would have horrified him. Todd always liked to tell people what things cost – but only to dazzle them the dollar figure. He'd never have understood bragging about a bargain.

'Your dress.'

'Five fifty,' I started, thinking he wanted me to tell him the price.

'No, I mean, take it off.'

And now I felt those flutters inside. The ones that had been missing for so long. The closest similar sensation I'd felt lately was when I'd snagged something super at a thrift store, finding a jewel among the junk.

'You're the one who snapped up the record player, aren't you?'

I gave him a wicked grin. 'Only needs thirty-seven cents in order to stay balanced.'

'Most people pay a lot more for the same goal. Especially in this town.'

And then we were silent, because we were kissing. His hands on my arms, sliding up to my shoulders, then down to my wrists and tightening. I had on my slip, and my garters and stack-heeled shoes. He was still fully dressed in jeans and a black retro shirt. Polyester with dart points at the collar. Something my English teacher would have worn back when I was in high school, looking geeky and confused by modern fashion. But, on Killian, the shirt looked good.

He looked better out of it, both of us working simultaneously to undress in the garage. Yet, while I peeled off everything, he kept on his jeans and the threadbare concert T-shirt – *Never Mind the Bollocks, Here's the Sex Pistols* – he'd had beneath the long-sleeved shirt. He didn't say a word then, just moved, pushing me up against the makeshift rack, those brass curlicues of the former headboard providing the anchoring for the chain he used on my wrists. He bound me standing up, back towards him, wrists over my head, and I felt the cool metal with my cheek, with my breasts, with my pussy. Felt the cold concrete floor with my bare feet. Felt lost and found in a second, when I heard the music start to play.

Bessie Smith.

On vinyl.

His mouth on my neck, his voice in my ear. 'Just listen to that sound. That magic scratching sound at the start, needle digging into the grooves. Doesn't vinyl always bring you back?'

And I could have come right then, because he'd put into words what I'd tried to show Todd. He'd explained the whole reason, the definition, the purpose. Why I adored surrounding myself with relics from days gone by. But you can go forwards even when you go back. You can dress vintage and have your eye on the future. I could see what the next step was, what awaited me.

Killian could see it, too.

He was on me, then. Stroking my ass and thighs with a length of leather. A belt without a buckle. Whispering to me softly, right up against my ear, 'Do you need a safe word?'

No. No safe word. Because I was turning my back on safety. On all things antiseptic and mouthwash fresh. I was breathing in deep to smell old oil cans and grease and tools and truck parts. Feeling the way I always do when I find a forlorn item at a thrift store or a garage sale. Cradling that discarded sweater or tool or toy and thinking, 'I'll find a new home for you.'

His mouth against my neck, his breath on my ear. 'Give me a safe word, Fiona, so I'll know when to stop.'

But I wouldn't. I couldn't. I shook my head. 'You'll know,' I said, the way I was sure he'd known about me in One Man's Trash, eyes on me instead of on the sofa. The way I was sure he'd known at the Rose Bowl, fingering those heavy silver chains and imagining them holding my wrists tight. The way I was sure this leather belt was intended for my ass.

He didn't fight me. He didn't argue. He stood back and swung, and the fire of the pain flickered through me, but the pleasure cooled me down one beat later. Without speaking, he struck a second time. A third. A fourth. I clenched my thighs together and felt a drop of liquid coat my nether-lips. I hadn't been this turned on in ages, maybe not ever. I wanted him to continue to thrash me, wanted him to peel me down.

'You take it,' he said, and I could tell he was admiring my stance. Even though I couldn't see his face, I knew what he was thinking. That he liked the way I kept my back straight, the way I didn't flinch, letting the pain work through me rather than defeat me. Letting the pain transform me, stripping off my outer layers. Showing off who I really was inside.

I thought of the way the brass headboard had looked at the auction. Realised that this man had retooled the metal, that he'd polished away the roughness, that he'd seen the beauty beneath and brought that pure metal glow to the surface.

Do that to me, I wanted to beg, but I didn't need to. I didn't have to say the words.

He struck again, then again. I felt my teeth nearly piercing the soft flesh of my full lower lip, but I did not cry out.

His hand snuck between my legs. He touched the wetness waiting. Then he pressed against me, so I could feel how hard he was, even through his jeans. So I could see that we were a pair, not mismatched candlesticks like me and Todd – one old and tarnished, one new from Target. But two of a kind. So hard to come by in the world of thrift, where everything has been separated, where items are chipped and repaired poorly with the wrong kind of glue. Killian and I were the same.

He backed off for a moment. He wasn't done.

The belt struck my ass three times in row, hard, and now I rattled my wrists in the chains, hearing the music of metal on metal, aware that my movement didn't bother Killian. He seemed spurred on by the motion, striking harder now, faster. I shut my eyes. I lowered my head. I'd have lines tomorrow. I'd have marks. But I didn't care. There was no past. No future worries.

I was home again. Home once more.

He dropped the belt when I would have begged. When the word was on my lips. He dropped the leather to the cold concrete floor and ripped open his jeans. I felt his cock against me, his skin against the fiery skin of my ass, and then I felt him pressing inside me.

I couldn't remember ever needing to be fucked like that. Wanting, yearning so hard that I almost came from the very first thrust. But I held back, my eyes still shut tight, my whole body welcoming Killian with each stroke.

He fucked me the way I'd imagined from the start. So hard and powerful that my breath caught in my throat, that my heart seemed to pound in my ears. He reached one hand around my waist and set his fingers against the split of my body. His middle finger thrummed against my clit and when he came, I came with him. Lids shut so tightly, I was seeing stars: silver like the metal around my wrists, like the chrome of his eyes.

Laughing to myself that I still didn't know his last name.

'That's got to be a first.'

'What has?'

'You finally escaped from one of those sales empty-handed,' Todd sneered, his hand hovering between the three different remotes decorating the surface of his brand-new coffee table.

I looked at him and thought, You broke my record player. He'd said the movers had dropped the box. But somehow I knew. Somehow I understood. This whole time he'd thought he could wear me down and glue on a fresh surface, the same way he fixed all those broken smiles.

I put my hand in my back pocket, feeling for the stiff paper business card: Killian Curie, Custom Refurbisher – Antiques and furniture. And people.

'I didn't,' I said softly as I made my way up the pristine cream-coloured carpet to the bedroom to pack.

Alison Tyler is the author of the Black Lace and Cheek novels *Learning to Love It, Sticky Fingers, Sweet Thing, Rumours, Strictly Confidential, Something About Workmen, Tiffany Twisted, With or Without You* **and** *Melt with You.*

Perfect Timing

Kristina Wright

She should have called before she drove over to the university. Charlotte tapped her nails on the steering wheel as Henry's phone rang. She hoped he wasn't in a meeting. Or teaching a class. She had been so preoccupied with getting her weekly reports finished and getting out of the library that the thought hadn't crossed her mind to make sure he was available.

Finally, after four rings he answered.

'I'm in the faculty parking lot. Last row by the trees,' she said, by way of a greeting. 'Can you meet me?'

He sighed, but there was a hint amusement in his voice. 'I'm in the middle of student advisement meetings.'

Neither his reluctance nor the overcast sky would deter her. 'Can't you take an early lunch break? Please?'

'You make it difficult for me to refuse,' he said, his voice low and intimate. She imagined him standing in his office, looking out of the window for her car. 'It's hard to think about you down there in the car wearing a dress –'

'Skirt.'

'Wearing a skirt, likely with no panties ...'

'No panties,' she acknowledged.

He sighed again, the resigned sound of a man who knew a woman would not be put off. 'I'll be there in twenty minutes.'

'Hurry. Otherwise, I might have to come up there and seduce you in your office.'

'Been there, done that, love,' he chuckled. 'Probably not the best idea with students coming in and out today.'

'Well then, you should get down here before I'm tempted. I have to get back to the library soon.'

'Yes, ma'am,' he said, obediently.

Charlotte grinned, triumphant. 'I promise I'll make it worth your while.'

'You always do.'

Charlotte closed her phone and rested her head on the seat. Rain threatened at any moment and the wind whipped the blossoms from the trees and shrubs that ringed the campus, scattering them on the wind like spring snowflakes. Birds chased each other from tree to tree, mating season in full swing despite the inclement weather. A fat raindrop plopped on the windshield and Charlotte glanced towards Henry's grey building, debating whether she should pick him up at the kerb. But, no, that might draw attention to them, and the last thing she wanted was an audience. Thankfully, it was spring break and most of the students and faculty weren't on campus.

'April showers bring May flowers,' she whispered as a bushy-tailed brown squirrel pursued another up a tree trunk and raindrops splattered across her field of vision.

She shifted impatiently and pressed the soft fabric of her skirt between her thighs. She was wet already, wet from the anticipation of making love to Henry in the parking lot. She'd had a thirty-minute drive from the library to think about what she would do to him once she got here. It had never really been a question of whether he would join her; he had promised that, whenever she called, he would come. Quite literally, she mused.

The control made her feel a little giddy with feminine power – but it was the anticipation of having Henry buried inside her in mere moments while the rest of the campus went on about their morning that was an arousing, panty-dampening thought. If she had been wearing panties, that is.

Even sooner than he had promised, Henry slipped into the passenger seat of her car, slightly out of breath from his mad dash through the light rain. Water spots darkened his sage green shirt and his brown hair stood up in wet spikes where he had dragged his fingers through it, accentuating the flecks of silver at his temples. 'Ten o'clock in the morning is a bit early for lunch, don't you think?'

'But, if I waited until lunchtime, someone would be sure to see us.'

'Good point,' he said. He leaned over to cup her face in his damp palm and give her a kiss. 'And I am getting hungry. It's been weeks since I had your luscious body against me.'

Charlotte inched up her skirt to bare an expanse of stocking-clad thigh. 'Would you like to see what's on the menu today?'

Henry loosened his tie. 'Oh, I think I'll just have the special.'

She angled over the gearstick and into his lap. It was no small feat, given the length of her skirt and the tight fit of the narrow bucket seat but, within moments, she was straddling him, her skirt hiked up around her hips.

'This would be better with me on the bottom,' she said. 'But I don't think it would work.'

Henry slid his hands under her bunched skirt and fingered the lace tops of her sheer black stockings. 'You could probably get me to do anything you want right now,' he said, stroking the bare skin above the lacy bands of nylon. 'You look like the clichéd sexy librarian. Nice touch. Just for me?'

She leaned over and nibbled his neck above his collar,

breathing in the spicy scent of his aftershave. 'Of course. All for you, darling.'

He moved his hand to the juncture of her thighs. She squirmed against him, silently urging him to touch her. 'This is my favourite magical spot,' he said as his fingers found her wetness. 'You're already excited, bad girl. Have you been thinking about me?'

She smirked. If only he knew. Wriggling against his rain-chilled fingers, she gasped, 'I could barely keep from touching myself before you got here.'

He cupped her pussy in his hand, his thumb stroking her swollen clit in slow, lazy circles. 'Really?'

She kissed him, sucking his bottom lip into her mouth. It wasn't the most comfortable position to be in, but she was too aroused to care. 'Mmm-hmm.'

His fingers delved deeper, parting her silken wetness as his thumb kept moving on her clit. 'Well, I'm sorry for keeping you waiting then.'

'You're here now,' she murmured against his mouth. 'That's all that matters to me.'

Tangling her fingers in his damp hair, she moved against his hand, showing him the rhythm. He groaned into her mouth as he played with her, driving her to the edge of any rational thought. It would be better if she came while he was inside her, but he was just too good with his hands. Now all she could think about was getting off.

She slid up on his lap a couple of inches to give him some more room, enough so that the top of her head was now above him and her breasts were in his face. With his free hand, he undid the ties of her pale yellow wrap blouse. His mouth found one of her hard nipples through the fabric of her bra and he sucked the tender bit of flesh in the same rhythm he stroked her clit. Charlotte pressed her breast to his mouth, every muscle taut as she clutched the car seat behind his head.

'Oh. Oh yes,' she moaned as he moved his mouth to the other nipple. He suckled it hard through the fabric until it stood in rigid attention. Her bra was wet now with his sucking, but she didn't care. 'I can feel that in my pussy.'

He murmured his pleasure as he slid a finger inside her. Her skin had warmed his fingers and she moaned softly, eyes closed, giving herself over to the feeling. Her nostrils flared, smelling not only Henry's aftershave now, but also her own arousal. It was an intoxicating scent and, as he pushed a second finger inside her, she felt her body tighten. He slid his fingers in deep, then slowly withdrew them to her opening before pushing inside her once more. He curved them forwards, finding her G-spot, and did it again.

The feeling was so intense she nearly told him to stop. But she knew that, if she could just take it for a few more strokes, he would make her come. So, instead of pulling back, she made little thrusting motions with her hips, giving him what he was after. She bit her bottom lip, feeling her orgasm like a knot inside her, slowly loosening. Warmth coursed through her, starting low in her belly and spreading outwards.

'Oh, God,' she whimpered, tightening her pussy around his fingers.

Henry kept up his steady rhythm, using his fingers to coax her towards that elusive orgasm. She went still on him, straining towards inevitable release. As if sensing how close she was, Henry rolled her clit under his thumb as he stroked her sweet spot. She cried out, oblivious to her surroundings, feeling a gush of liquid as her orgasm washed over her.

'Yes, that's it,' he murmured against the swell of her breast. 'Come for me.'

And she did. Wet heat radiated outwards from her swollen

clit, drowning her in sensations as she rocked her hips on Henry's fingers. She bent her head over him, pressing his hand between their bodies as her body throbbed with her release.

'Yes, yes,' Henry whispered. 'You are so beautiful when you come.'

'Inside me,' she managed to gasp as she struggled to undo his belt in the tight confines of the car seat. 'I want you inside me. Now!'

Henry withdrew his fingers from her still throbbing pussy and assisted her in her quest. He winced as she dragged his zipper down. 'Damn, love, try not to rip it off or it won't be any use to either of us.'

A fit of giggles hit her then, the incongruity of the situation striking her as funny. 'Oh, don't worry, I always have a spare handy.'

'What?'

'Just a joke,' she said. 'Fuck me.'

Aftershocks of her orgasm still rippled through her as Henry finally freed his erection from his trousers and angled it inside her. Suddenly, there was nothing humorous at all about her situation. She gasped, instinctively tilting her hips to accommodate his length. He was all the way inside her and there was no need to go slowly because she was already so very wet.

'Oh, God,' he groaned, giving a short quick thrust. 'You feel so damned good.'

She pushed back against him, feeling his cock go so deep it almost hurt. She felt full and swollen, as wet as she had ever been. Being on top gave her the control of their rhythm and she went slowly, enjoying the fullness and how she could feel every inch of him gliding inside her. She leaned back in his lap, letting him slide out a bit, then forwards, pressing her breasts to his face. He clutched at her hips like a man overboard, seeking solid land.

'Oh, love,' he moaned against her breasts. 'You're driving me out of my mind.'

She'd already had one orgasm, but she could feel a second one building. His fingers had felt nice, but this sensation of engorgement couldn't be caused by anything but his cock. She thrust a little harder against him, her clit rubbing against his pelvic bone. She was so wet and her range of motion was limited; it didn't seem as if there could be enough friction for Henry to reach orgasm. But a few more thrusts and he was gripping her ass in his hands, guiding her faster on his rigid length. She tightened her pussy around him and he sucked in his breath, his cock twitching in instant response.

'Come inside me,' she whispered in his ear. 'I want to feel you coming deep inside me.'

His cock felt impossibly large as she thrust down on him. She could tell he was close to finishing by the way he went still against her. She rotated her hips on him and he all-but-roared as he started to come, jerking against her so hard she bumped her head on the roof of the car.

She had been so caught up in making him come that she hadn't realised just how close she was to her own orgasm. She kept up those little thrusting motions, dragging her aroused clit over the patch of hair above his cock until she was pushed over the edge into her own climax. She rode him like that until her sensitive clit couldn't take any more.

Collapsing on top of him, her arms hanging down the back of the seat, she gasped and giggled as her pussy clenched around his slowly shrinking erection.

'Holy hell,' she whimpered. 'Who would have thought doing it in the car would be so hot?'

Her breasts muffled his reply. 'No kidding.'

Suddenly conscious that they were in the faculty parking lot and the car windows were completely fogged, she reluctantly slid back into her seat. There was so much wetness between her thighs and on his lower stomach, she didn't know who had made a bigger mess. She suspected it was her.

'Hand me my panties,' she said. 'They're in the glove box.'

He chuckled as he handed her the black lace thong. 'You're just going to make a mess of them.'

'Better them than the back of my skirt,' she said ruefully as she shimmied into her panties and smoothed her wrinkled skirt into place. She looked over at Henry sprawled in the car seat with a satisfied smile on his face and his flaccid cock glistening against his pale stomach. He was an even bigger mess than she was, and she frowned. 'You can't go inside like that.'

He looked down. 'No mistaking what I've been up to, is there?'

'There should be tissues in there, too,' she said.

He fumbled through the glove box until he found the packet of travel tissues and cleaned himself up as best he could. Moments later, shirt tucked in and pants fastened, he still looked like the cat that ate the cream. The noticeable wet spot on the front of his pants didn't help matters at all.

'Don't worry,' he said, following the direction of her gaze. 'I have a spare pair in the office.'

'Keep extra clothes at work, do you?'

He grinned. 'You never know when a beautiful young woman is going to offer herself up in exchange for an A.'

'Always prepared.' She smiled at him. 'You're quite the Boy Scout.'

He stroked a hand through her mussed hair. 'You're not bad yourself, love. I'm wiped out.'

'Hmm. Well, don't think I'm letting you off the hook that easily,' she said with mock sternness. 'You never know when I'll be wanting a repeat performance.'

'Sounds promising.' He retied his tie and adjusted the collar, using the vanity mirror to guide him. 'Not that this wasn't a nice surprise, but when can we spend a little more time together?'

'I'll give you a call later.' Though she was completely satiated, Charlotte couldn't help but give him a teasing smile. 'Tennis tomorrow, maybe? I'll make you sweat to get me into bed.'

'I love a challenge,' he said, leaning over to press a kiss to her forehead before he slipped out of the car.

She laughed as she watched him sprint across the parking lot. At some point during their lovemaking, the sun had broken through the clouds and the squirrels had returned to their frolicking. She waited until he was gone from sight before she pulled out of the lot and headed back to the library. She was going to need an energy drink before the day was over.

'I need you,' Ian growled.

'That's sweet, but I'm going out with the girls tonight,' Charlotte said as she drove through the heavy downtown traffic. 'Remember?'

'Ah, right, I forgot it was girls' night,' Ian said. 'I'm on call this weekend, but, as long as there isn't a five-alarm fire, maybe we can do something tomorrow?'

Charlotte hesitated. 'Well, I told Henry I'd play tennis with him tomorrow. I haven't seen him in weeks.'

'Fine, fine, far be it for me to come between you and your old professor. How is grandpa, anyway?'

Charlotte found a parking spot on the street and manoeuvred into it one-handed. 'Don't be mean. Henry is barely fifty and he's in great shape.'

'But I want my girl to myself,' Ian said. 'I guess I'll have you on Sunday.'

'You're a darling,' Charlotte said, and meant it. 'Why don't you stay over tonight? I'll be in late, but I'll wake you when I get home and you can *have* me then.'

'Oh, really.' Ian's voice reflected his interest. 'It's that time, hmm?'

Charlotte checked her lipstick in the vanity mirror and smiled at her reflection. She looked happy. She *was* happy – and hopeful. 'Well, yes, but I'd still want you to stay over.'

'Uh-huh,' Ian said, not sounding at all convinced. 'Well, then, have a good time with the girls and hurry home.'

Charlotte disconnected and smoothed her skirt before leaving the car. Henry wasn't the only one who kept a change of clothes at work. She now wore a shimmery silver blouse with a red skirt. Red was Terrence's favourite colour.

Melissa and Wendy were already waiting at the bar for her inside the trendy bar Fringe. The décor was disco-chic and Charlotte's silver blouse glinted in the light reflected by the mirrored tiles embedded in the walls.

Melissa handed her a dirty martini and leaned in close to be heard over the house music. 'I didn't think you were going to make it. Is Ian peeved?'

'Oh no,' Charlotte said, scanning the growing crowd in the club. 'He's staying over and I promised to wake him up when I get home.'

'You've got that man wrapped around your little finger.'

Wendy laughed. 'He's not the only one.' She tilted her head towards the opposite side of the club. 'Here comes your little boy toy.'

Charlotte followed the direction of her friend's gaze and felt her pulse jump. At six-foot four, with a body of lean planes and sculpted muscle, Terrence was hardly little – nor was he anyone's boy toy. He was, however, barely out of college, a fact that held more appeal than Charlotte could ever explain. She had met him when he'd come to the library to do research for his senior thesis. He had kept coming back after graduation. He was a lazy, but brilliant, music student with hands that could play her like a finely tuned instrument. As he strolled across the room, oblivious to the predatory looks he was getting from women of all ages, a shiver went up her spine.

'Hey, babe,' he whispered in her ear as he pulled her into a tight hug. 'Long time no see.'

'I suspect you've been staying busy.'

'I do all right,' he said with a careless shrug. 'But I've missed you.'

Wendy and Melissa made themselves scarce, giggling behind their hands as they left the two alone. Terrence knew the effect he had on women, with his exotic features and often insolent expression. It amused him to turn women into quivering, stuttering schoolgirls. Charlotte let him think she could take him or leave him – which she could – and that made her attractive to him.

'Want to get out of here?' There was no subterfuge with Terrence, no hidden agenda. It was one of things she liked best about him.

'Impatient, sweetie?'

He threw an arm around her shoulders and leaned in. 'Impatient to be inside you,' he said. 'I told you. I've missed you.'

A naughty thought took hold in her imagination. She took Terrence's hand and pulled him towards a dark hallway. She led him into the women's restroom off the kitchen area where harried kitchen staff put together heavy appetisers to complement the cocktails.

'What are you up to?'

Charlotte closed and locked the door behind him before turning on the light. 'What do you think?'

She didn't give him a chance to respond. Pressing him up against the door, she wrapped her arms around his neck and pulled his head down for a fierce kiss. She parted his lips with the tip of her tongue, deepening the kiss with the intention of distracting him from their surroundings. He tasted of tequila, and the sharp tang taste reminded her of other things. She knew she had him when she hooked her leg around his hip and rubbed against him. He groaned softly, gripping her ass in his hands as he pulled her up hard against him. She could feel him beginning to stiffen and whimpered low in her throat.

He pulled back, a little breathless from their kissing. 'You are wicked.'

She fumbled with his belt, laughing softly. 'Let me show you just how wicked I can be.'

'I really don't think this is a good idea.'

Having managed to get his belt unbuckled, Charlotte was not about to stop now. She proceeded to unfasten his trousers, noticing Terrence's cock did not share his doubt about her naughty intentions. His cock was shaped like his beautiful fingers – long and smooth. She felt her own body respond to his arousal and clenched her thighs together.

'Maybe I can change your mind,' she said, thankful for her thigh-high stockings as she slipped to her knees on the dirty tile floor.

Above her, Terrence's dark eyes went wide. 'What are you up to?'

She pulled his cock free from his pants and underwear and kissed the engorged tip. 'What does it look like?'

'It looks like you're a very nasty girl.'

Wrapping her hand around the length of him, she looked up into his eyes. 'Oh, you have no idea.'

She held his cock in her hand and licked his shaft from the tip to the base and back again. His sharp intake of breath turned her on, made her want to tease him long and slow.

Unfortunately, she knew they didn't have that kind of time before someone came knocking on the door to use the restroom, but that didn't mean she couldn't tease him a little bit.

Looking up at him, she licked the ridge of his cock again. He threw his head back against the door and closed his eyes as she took him inside her mouth, cradling the broad head in the hollow of her tongue. He groaned softly, tangling his fingers in her long dark hair. She didn't move, didn't suck, just held him there in her mouth as she looked up at him. Finally, his eyes opened and he looked down at her, his gaze unfocused.

'Please, babe,' he said hoarsely.

That was all she needed. She took him deeper into her mouth, sucking him to the back of her throat before sliding off him. She went back down again, as far as she could, sucking him in rhythm to the muffled throb of the music beyond the door. When he was slick with her saliva, she used her hands to stroke his shaft as she sucked, slow and steady until he was reflexively pumping into her mouth.

Reaching under his cock, she cupped his velvety balls in one hand. When she gave them a gentle tug, he gasped and bumped his head against the door.

'Oh hell, Char.' His fingers clutched at her hair. 'You're driving me out of my mind.'

She swirled her tongue around the head of his cock, tasting his arousal, before pulling away. Much as she would have liked to finish him with her mouth, that wasn't in her plan tonight. She couldn't help but smile at his grumble of disappointment when she stood up. She stroked his cock as she reached up to kiss him.

'I need you,' she said. 'Please.'

He kissed her hard, thrusting against the palm of her hand. 'Anything you want, babe.'

A sense of urgency came over her, not only because they

were in the public restroom and she could hear voices not far away, but because she ached to feel him inside her. She pulled up her skirt and turned to face the counter. Thrusting her bottom out, she looked at him over her shoulder.

'Fuck me, Terrence. Fuck me hard.'

He didn't hesitate. Pulling her cherry-red panties to the side, he was balls-deep inside her in one smooth motion. She arched her back and whimpered, biting her lip to keep from screaming at the sudden, shocking fullness.

Guiding her hip with one hand, he caught her long hair up in the other hand. She met his lust-filled gaze in the mirror as he pulled her hair hard enough to make her arch her neck. They were both a little out of control now. She knew it and knew the risks – and she didn't care.

'Yes, yes, yes,' she gasped as she met his steady thrusts. She closed her eyes, lost in the intense feeling of him deep inside her.

'Open your eyes,' he said roughly. 'Look at me.'

She did as he said, staring at him in the mirror as he drove into her. This was her favourite sexual position, being taken from behind, because his cock hit her G-spot in just the right way to give her mind-blowing orgasms. She liked the feeling of his lean body covering hers, the way he pulled her hair that sent shivers down her spine. The tables were turned now. She wasn't the dominant older woman any longer; she felt feminine and helpless, completely at his mercy. But now, the mirror seemed to add another layer of intimacy to their lovemaking.

She couldn't hide behind her curtain of hair, couldn't escape his dark, knowing gaze as he moved his hand up to tweak her nipple through her flimsy blouse. She tried to tuck her chin against her chest, feeling incredibly vulnerable all of a sudden, but Terrence gave her hair another tug so that she had no choice but to look up.

'Watch me, babe,' he said, his voice low as he thrust into her wetness. 'Watch me while I'm inside you.'

What had started out as a playful, seductive game had become something else. She felt out of control, wanting him to be rougher with her, to pinch her nipples harder, to drive his cock into her until she screamed. She knew they didn't have much time, but she wanted to strip off her clothes and let him fuck her senseless. She gripped the edge of the sink and tried not to cry out as he withdrew his cock to the tip and then slammed into her. Over and over again, bumping against that sensitive spot inside her, he fucked her until she could feel her juices trickling down the insides of her thighs.

She whimpered softly, biting the inside of her mouth because the temptation to scream was almost unbearable. Not that anyone would hear her over the club music, of course. Terrence was silent and stoic, only his heavy-lidded eyes giving away his arousal. He had been so turned on by her going down on him she expected him to finish inside her at any moment, but now he seemed capable of going on like this for hours. If only they had hours.

'I'm not coming until you do,' he said, as if reading her mind.

She whimpered again, clenching her pussy around his cock. She wanted to come, but she was distracted by the sound of the voices and music, and Terrence's penetrating stare. She closed her eyes once more, feeling like she needed to close off one sense so she could concentrate on what he was doing to her body. She focused on the sensation of his cock gliding into her, the way her body clung to him as he slowly withdrew before pushing back inside. She arched her back a little more, feeling his cock angle down.

'Right there,' she gasped.

He thrust into her, faster now, pulling her hair taut until

she felt like a bowstring humming with tension. She reached the breaking point as he curved over her, whispering in her ear, 'Come for me, babe.'

She couldn't help it, she let out a loud, lingering moan as her orgasm washed over her. She opened her eyes, meeting his in the mirror so he could see what he had done to her. He watched her as he continued to fuck her through her orgasm, sweat glistening at his fine-boned temple.

'Yes. Oh, God,' she gasped, feeling as if she was being turned inside out. 'Terrence!'

Terrence made a sound low in his throat and went still against her. Her pussy rippled along the length of his engorged cock, and with one hard thrust that elicited another soft moan from her, he was coming too. Eyes closed, he pumped into her a few times before going still again. He leaned over her back, his damp forehead against her cheek when she turned her head.

'Oh my. That was nice,' was all she could manage to say.

She felt, rather than heard, his rumble of laughter. 'That's one way to describe it,' he said, nipping her ear lobe. 'You really *are* wicked.'

'Yes, I am,' she whispered.

Still feeling the lingering tremors of her orgasm, she became acutely aware of their risky position. Reluctantly, she shifted beneath him. His cock slid out of her and she felt empty. Wetness streaked down her inner thighs and she met his gaze in the mirror, smiling contritely.

'I need to clean up,' she said. 'Think you can sneak out while I make myself presentable?'

Terrence's laugh was pure masculine satisfaction. 'You are perfectly presentable. You just look as if you've been well fucked.'

She shifted her gaze to her own face and realised he was right.

Her hair was mussed and her cheeks were flushed. Her dark-red lipstick was smeared and she was fairly certain she'd left some behind on Terrence's cock. Her eyes sparkled in a way that suggested she had a very delicious secret – which she did. She shook her head.

'Well, I'll do the best I can.'

Terrence straightened his clothes and tucked his still-damp cock back into his trousers. 'I don't think it'll be a late night for me. I'm wiped.'

'Oh, poor baby,' she said. 'Every woman in the club will be disappointed to see you go.'

Terrence gave her a tired, teasing grin. 'I only care about the woman who just came on my cock.'

She didn't really believe that, of course, but it was sweet of him to say so. Terrence was still young and wild and unlikely to settle for one woman when he could have three, but he had good manners. 'That was lovely, darling.'

He listened at the door before turning the lock. 'Give me a call, babe. It's been too long and I'd like to do this properly sometime soon.'

'I will. Promise.'

Charlotte smiled as he slipped out, giving her a rakish wink as he went. She locked the door behind him and met her own smudged eyes in the mirror. 'See you in four weeks, darling boy,' she whispered as she set about taming her hair back into place. 'Maybe.'

Charlotte awoke at dawn, naked and cuddled against Ian's warm, bare chest. She felt a pleasant kind of soreness through her entire body that seemed to radiate from between her thighs. Sighing contentedly, she tucked in close to Ian and breathed in his clean, masculine scent.

Just as she started to drift off again, she felt his hand shift from her hip to between her thighs. She squirmed, thinking he was still asleep by the sound of his steady breathing. Then his fingers began a gentle probing that let her know he was awake – and wanting her.

Silently she shifted until she was lying on her back, still nestled against his muscular shoulder. He touched her gently, parting the lips of her pussy with his fingers. She wasn't aroused yet, but she knew his soft touches would get her there fast. Sighing, she spread her thighs so he could continue his exploration.

He rested one finger at her opening as he cupped her mound in his warm palm. He gently squeezed her, letting just the tip of his finger slip inside her. She gasped at the dual sensations and pushed her pelvis up to meet his touch.

Sunlight streamed through the half-closed blinds, casting dappled light across their bed and making his reddish-blond hair look like spun gold. The quiet was soothing, with only the soft sounds of her sighs and the rustle of the bed linens. Charlotte could feel her thigh muscles tensing in anticipation of his touch and she forced herself to relax and breathe slowly. She had all the time in the world to enjoy this. Neither of them had to go to work, no one was in the next room, there was no pressing need to leave the bedroom until hunger drove them out of bed.

Still, she couldn't help but wiggle against his hand, silently urging him to push his finger deep inside her. He resisted, keeping it just inside her pussy and making small circles. She sighed, impatient for more.

'You got in awfully late last night,' he said, his voice still gravelly with sleep. 'I missed you.'

She could feel his cock, thick and hard, pressing against her hip. She'd been so focused on his gentle, teasing touch, she hadn't noticed he was already fully aroused.

'Sorry. You know how the girls are,' she said. 'But I missed you too. You looked so sweet when I got home.'

'Why didn't you wake me?' He kissed the top of her head as he continued to stroke her.

She sighed sleepily. 'I was so tired by the time I took a shower I just wanted to curl up and go to sleep.'

He stroked her pussy gently. 'I would have helped you get to sleep.'

'This is so much better than sleeping,' she whispered, covering his hand with her own. 'That feels good.'

'Want more?'

She nodded against his shoulder. 'Yes, please.'

Slowly, he pushed his finger inside her. 'You're getting wet.'

'Imagine that.'

He kept up his slow circles, teasing her with his warm touch. 'Naughty girl.'

Charlotte hooked her leg over his, spreading herself even wider for his touch. 'Oh, yes,' she said, ending on a sigh as his finger slid deeper. 'I think I want more.'

He added a second finger inside of her. 'Like that?'

She moaned, arching off the bed to take his fingers inside her. 'Just like that.'

He stroked her slowly, her wetness coating his fingers. She could hear the liquid sounds her pussy made as he stroked her. The noise was as arousing as this slow build-up of tension. She squirmed against his hand, eager for more but willing to let him set the pace.

She reached down and fondled his cock just as slowly as he was touching her. He made a soft sound of approval and pushed against her hip. She smiled, sure she could hold out at this languid pace longer than he could.

He apparently didn't want her to think she had the upper

hand because he upped the ante by pressing his thumb to her swollen clit. She jumped as if shocked and clamped her thighs around his hand.

Ian chuckled. 'I wanted to make sure you were awake.'

She harrumphed as she swirled her thumb over the tip of his cock, catching a bead of wetness along the way. 'I'm as *awake* as you are, sweetheart.'

'Excellent.'

His fingers glided into her, curving upwards to stroke the inside of her pussy. She was still tender from the previous day, but she was getting wetter as he touched her. A familiar ache began to build inside her and she felt her nipples pucker in response to her growing arousal. Ian's arm was beneath her neck and he reached down to stroke the swell of her breast, the dark edge of her hard nipple. His fingers, callused from years of handling fire equipment, felt rough against her tender flesh. The sensation sent chills through her and she inhaled sharply.

'Mmm, nice,' she whispered.

'You're ready for me.'

She nodded again. 'Oh, yes.'

He shifted his arm from under her and moved to kneel between her spread thighs. As he lifted her legs over his broad shoulders, she expected him to push his cock into her. He surprised her by cupping her ass in his large hands and raising her up until her pussy was beneath his mouth. Back arched, she stared down between her legs and watched as he licked her swollen clit.

She whimpered at the zing of pleasure that accompanied that one swift stroke. Squirming for more, she was rewarded by his tongue parting the lips of her pussy and swirling around her opening the way his fingers had earlier. She pushed her hips towards his mouth, grasping at his shaggy mop of tousled golden curls, aching to feel his tongue inside her. He pulled back, teasing her.

'You do seem to want me.'

'Yes!'

He lowered his mouth between her thighs, the day-old growth of his beard scratching her sensitive thighs. 'You smell like heaven. Taste like it too.'

'Lick me!'

Finally, he gave her what she wanted and slid his tongue inside her. She whimpered low in her throat as he lapped at her with the flat of his tongue, drawing her own wetness up over her sensitive clit. She clutched at him, pulling his head into her and rubbing against his mouth shamelessly. Her orgasm was quick and explosive, catching her by surprise. She held his head between her thighs, riding out the long, rolling waves of her climax as he devoured her with his mouth. Then, just when she thought she couldn't take any more, he lowered her down to the bed and guided his thick cock into her.

With tremors of her orgasm still rippling along the walls of her pussy, he felt huge inside her. She wrapped her legs around his strong back, arching up to meet his slow, deep thrusts. He reached under her to hold her ass, anchoring her to him as he rocked into her. She nibbled his neck, licking the salty moisture from his skin as her whole body quivered against him.

His thigh muscles trembled as he came, still moving so slowly inside her as her pussy squeezed the length of his shaft. His orgasm seemed to last as long as hers, every short thrust followed by a deep groan. She held him to her, hands soothing the bunched muscles of his back and down to his clenched ass. Finally he relaxed against her, his solid weight both sensual and comforting.

'Think we did it?' he murmured, tucking his head against her neck.

She stroked his hair, a private smile curving her lips. She was suddenly sleepy again. 'Maybe. But the doctor said the more times I make love around ovulation, the more likely I am to get pregnant.'

'Give me an hour and I'll see what I can do to increase our chances.'

She giggled. 'Lovely, but don't forget I'm playing tennis with Henry at ten.'

'Girls' night out, tennis with Henry. My girlfriend is in high demand.' Ian moved off her, pulling her over on her side and into his arms, where she settled with a contented sigh. 'At least until you get knocked up. Then you're all mine.'

'Exactly the way I want,' she said, stretching like a well-fed cat. 'Maybe this month is my month.'

'Well, if it doesn't happen this time, we'll just have to try again next month,' Ian said. 'It's all about the timing, right?'

'All in the timing,' she agreed.

Kristina Wrights' 'The Rancher's Wife' can be found in the Black Lace *Seduction* anthology.

Archeogasms

K D Grace

Mac was saying something about Gemma's nipples and ripe redcurrants. Gemma shot a surreptitious glance at Allegra. She always pretended that she didn't notice Allegra sitting at the booth in the corner pretending not to watch the two of them get more and more bold in their gropings. Though Allegra was the archaeologist in charge of the dig – maybe because she was the archaeologist in charge, and a woman – Gemma liked to push the boundaries. And Allegra was embarrassed to admit that she let her get away with it because Allegra was a bit of a voyeur, and a little escapism after a hard day's digging was just what she needed. She knew if she came to the pub every night at this time, Gemma and Mac would be here. And either they got off on the idea of her watching them, or they truly were so in to each other they hadn't noticed. Since Allegra hadn't had a good shag, or even a bad one, in longer than she cared to remember, either way was fine with her.

Allegra could tell from the way Gemma shifted and slumped in her seat that Mac's hand was in her knickers or very close. She accidentally dropped her biro, as she often did, and ducked under the table to find it, catching the expected glimpse of Mac's hand, fingers thrusting and circling between Gemma's spread legs. Just imagining what Gemma was experiencing, Allegra felt the wetness grow in her own panties. She was pretty sure when they finally decided to find some place more private to do the deed, she'd be treated, as was usually the case, to a view of Mac's 'Big Mac', as he called it, struggling hard to be free from the tight shorts he always wore. They left little to the imagination where his package was concerned. Mac's cock was sizeable, and he liked to make sure it was well displayed whenever possible.

Allegra flipped the page in the journal she'd been pretending to read. It was always like this. When Gemma started squirming at the table, and Mac no longer minded who saw him kneading her tits, Allegra pretended harder to be immersed in the fascinating scholarship of her fellow archaeologists. What she was really doing was memorising every move the two nymphos made. Then, later that night, alone in her bed, Allegra planned to use her observations for her own fantasy purposes, substituting herself for Gemma, and whichever hunk suited her fancy for Mac, while she let her own imagination enhance and rearrange the evening's events until she made herself come.

On the nights when the couple were really amorous and even bolder than usual she could make herself come while just watching the two of them, and tonight was looking like it was going to be one of those nights. Under the table, out of sight, Allegra opened her legs and leaned forwards, rocking against the hard wood of the chair, enjoying the combined pressure of her clenching quinny with the rubbing of the seam of the tight jeans she'd worn deliberately as a masturbatory aid. She knew if she went into the bathroom and slipped her fingers into her panties, she'd be slick and swollen and ready to come. In fact, a few times she had done just that and not even made it back to her room.

Above the edge of the journal, she watched Mac stroking Gemma's nipples until she was sure they'd poke holes through the woman's silk blouse. She imagined what it would be like to move over next to them and offer her nipples for his tactile pleasure, or for Gemma's. That would be OK too. She was imagining whose hand would be doing what, while manoeuvring as unobtrusively as possible under the table to get the crotch of her jeans where it would do the most good between the lips of her pout, when she was interrupted.

'Excuse me, but are you Dr Allegra Thorn?'

She jumped and slammed the journal shut as though it contained photos of what was going on in her dirty little mind. Irritated, she looked up.

But the man standing before her was gorgeous. He had a swimmer's shoulders and his jeans displayed an arse so perfect you could bounce a penny off it. As he sat down, uninvited, Allegra could smell the heady scent of night air permeating the anorak folded over his muscular arm. His broad chest was well displayed in the white polo, which snugly caressed the hard slope of his belly.

'I'm Dan Martin. I work for the *Daily Update*.' He spoke with an American accent; she guessed he was from somewhere on the West Coast. In the subdued pub lighting, she caught sight of ice-blue eyes beneath a fringe of sun-bleached hair in need of a cut. 'I'd like to interview you about your new discovery.' He shot the two lovers a knowing glance and smiled. 'That is, if you're not too busy.'

Just then Gemma moaned something about Mac's loaded balls, and no matter how hard Allegra pretended not to hear, the colour burning in her face was a dead give-away.

Dan Martin glanced over at the two and smiled. Gemma actually blushed. Allegra was sure that was a first. Then he turned his attention back to her. He sat his pint on the table and leaned in closer, holding her gaze, bringing the scent of the outdoors with him. 'I'd like to do an article about your site and the archaeologist who discovered it. I promise I'll be good, and I won't take up too much of your time. I've read it might possibly be the underground temple of a fertility cult.' He glanced again at Gemma and Mac, who had gone back to behaving like they were the only two people in the pub. 'Who wouldn't want to know more about such a discovery?'

Allegra had nothing else to do that evening. And, for the first time in a long time, there was something in the pub more interesting than Gemma and Mac. In fact, Gemma and Mac had long since adjourned to a more private place before the interview came to an end. When at last there was a lull in the conversation, Allegra finished off her pint and smiled up at him. 'Is there anything else you need?'

'There is.' The look on his face told her that he liked her choice of words. Though he managed to keep his eyes on hers, she suddenly felt as though he was imagining her naked, or maybe it was just the result of watching Mac and Gemma every night after digging all day in an ancient fertility site. He glanced down at his watch. 'Wow! We've been sitting here for nearly three hours. I hadn't planned to take up so much of your time. I hope you don't mind.'

She didn't. She didn't mind at all. In fact, what had started out as an interview for some newspaper she'd never even heard of had turned into a very interesting evening. She had expected stupid questions like 'What's it like to be an archaeologist?' and 'How did you feel when you discovered the site?' But the man had actually done his homework and was amazingly familiar with the neolithic period, unlike a lot of people who thought Stonehenge was built by Celts.

Dan closed his notepad and finished his pint. 'Can you show me the site tomorrow?'

Allegra looked at the white polo shirt stretched over an impressive chest. 'You do have to crawl on your stomach to get inside, you know?'

'Doc –' the cheeky buzzard had started calling her Doc almost immediately, and she found she rather liked it '– I'm willing to do whatever it takes to get inside.'

Allegra leaned over the table. 'Then how about a little experiment?'

'What do you have in mind?' The sparkle in his eyes told her he was up for anything.

'We're only one day away from summer solstice. My suspicion is that the entrance of the chamber is aligned with the setting sun on summer solstice. With the days being long, we could go up tomorrow evening just before the sun sets and check out my theory.'

'You and me alone in a possible fertility site at summer solstice?'

She nodded.

'Wild horses couldn't keep me away.'

Allegra thought the next day would drag by as she waited for her rendezvous with Dan. She had kicked herself for not inviting him back to the cottage for a drink. Was she really so out of practice with men? She'd had to settle for a solo session between the sheets in which, for the first time in a long time, Gemma and Mac played no role, but a certain journalist with an interest in archaeology took centre stage in her fantasies.

That day, as she worked along the back wall of the cave, she noticed a feeling of light-headed euphoria. As she excavated several stone tools that she could only think looked like dildoes, she found herself wanting to grab the arse of the young assistant working next to her. For some reason, his bare shoulders seemed broader, more inviting, and he seemed to be labouring around an erection that tented the front of his shorts. Surely it was just her imagination. But when he brushed by her to exit, he touched her arm in a near-caress – something he would never have been bold enough to do. In fact, there seemed to be an inordinate amount of touching and feeling among the troops that day. Or perhaps the anticipation of her meeting with Dan Martin was playing tricks with her perception? It was hard to say.

At lunchtime, she sought privacy. She needed to come, and the need wasn't going to wait for her journalist. She stepped back into a stand of oak trees at the foot of the hill, surrounded by a hawthorn thicket, and was already undoing her jeans when she stopped suddenly and held her breath. There before her stood Mac, leaning against a tree, fly open, his pole fully extended in his stroking hand. His grunts and moans told her he was enjoying himself too much to notice her. She should have left, but she didn't. Instead, desperate for some relief of her own, she stepped back into the thicket and watched. It wouldn't take her long to come, then she'd go back to the site as though nothing had happened.

'Looks like this place is making us all horny.' Before Allegra could even jump, she felt a soft whisper against her ear. 'Sssh. Don't surprise him. Let's watch, and we can all come together.'

Allegra recognised Gemma's voice just as she felt the other woman's arms slip around her from behind, one hand sliding brazenly up to cup and caress her breasts, the other sliding down her stomach into her open jeans. 'Let me help you with that. Open your legs a little wider. There, that's it. Mmm you feel so nice, and slippery.' She didn't give Allegra a chance to argue. Her fingers found their way between her swollen lips to dip into her moisture and circle her straining clit while she rubbed her own pubis against Allegra's arse. 'How many times have I fantasised about making you come? Both Mac and I get off on you watching us.' She licked and nipped a wet, nibbly path down Allegra's neck. 'You should join us.'

Allegra said nothing. She wasn't sure she remembered how to speak. She just watched Mac thrusting against his hand while she rode Gemma's fingers, which slipped deeper and deeper in and out of her wet grip.

'Mac's about to come,' Gemma gasped, 'and so are we.' She lifted the back of Allegra's shirt and pressed her hard, bare nipples against her spine. Was she topless, or had she just lifted her own shirt? Allegra's pussy clenched as Gemma inserted a second, then a third finger into her slick opening. She was close, and she could tell by the thrusting of Gemma's hips against her and her accelerated breathing that she wasn't the only one.

Just then Mac grunted and bucked and shot three, four, five spurts that arced into the air like a fountain. Allegra just had time to wonder how he could be so full when he fucked Gemma every night, before her pussy contracted in her first spasm, and Gemma nearly knocked her off her feet with her thrusting as her own orgasm hit and the smell of female heat filled the hawthorn thicket. They both watched as Mac wiped his penis on a handkerchief, manoeuvred his tool back into his shorts and walked away. Then they were buttoning, straightening, tucking and giggling like a couple of teenagers. Before she turned to go, Gemma caught Allegra's face in her hands and kissed her with a deep tongue probe of a kiss. She pulled away, smiling. 'Thanks. I've wanted to do that for a long time.' Then she disappeared into the thicket.

When Dan arrived that evening they took his Jeep as far as they could, then walked the last quarter of a mile to the entrance. Allegra tossed a couple of sandwiches and a bottle of wine into a rucksack, along with torches, a Swiss Army knife, a trowel and other essentials she always carried with her to the site. Dan had his own rucksack, which she assumed was filled with his journalist's toys. When they reached the top of the hill, he let out a low whistle at the slitlike entrance of the chamber set between worked sandstone monoliths. 'Wow! It looks like a ...'

'Like a vulva, I know.' She looked over her shoulder at the setting sun. 'Come on, we have to be inside when the sun sets. If I'm right, the light should come right through the entrance and shine on the back wall.' She had already dropped to her knees, rucksack pushed ahead of her. As she squeezed through the narrow entrance, she could hear him crawling behind her. Once inside, where the passage widened out, she stood in a cruciform chamber with a corbelled roof.

Dan was soon standing at her side. 'I've never seen anything like this before.' His voice was breathless against the back of her neck as he regained his footing and looked around.

'Neither have we. In fact the entrance and the shape of the chamber isn't like anything we've found before. These things are always a puzzle without a written record to fill us in. Come on. It's almost time.' She grabbed his hand and scrambled to the back wall of the cave where she sat down. He sat next to her. 'Should be any minute now. Switch off your torch.'

They waited in almost total darkness, able to make out only a greying in the direction of the entrance. His breathing came fast and heavy.

'Are you all right?'

'I don't like not being able to see. A bit claustrophobic maybe.'

She slid closer to him, her hand settling on his thigh closer to his groin than she had intended. She heard him catch his breath.

'Sorry.' She started to pull away.

'It's all right.' He laid his hand over hers. 'Leave it there. I need all the reassurance I can get.' He shifted against the wall behind them and slid an arm around her. 'I didn't think about it being so dark in here.'

'Relax, and breathe deeply. The claustrophobia will pass. If you want the full experience, this is a part of it – the experience of the darkness of the womb. Well, at least that's one theory.'

Just then it began. The first ray of sunlight sparked against the entrance of the passage, then ignited into a starburst of brilliance nearly blinding them as it hit their light-deprived eyes. It moved along the passage, over the wall, and Dan Martin was suddenly bathed in flame-red light. They both gasped.

He pulled her close and whispered, 'I think we have penetration.' His breathing accelerated.

'You're not still claustrophobic, are you?'

'Don't you feel that?' His hand kneaded hers where it lay close to his dick. 'If this site was used for fertility rites, isn't it possible they put strong spells on this place? Because something here feels really amazing.' He lifted his face to the light, and from where she sat still bathed in darkness, she could make out the pulse in his throat, the expansion of his chest and the press of nipples through the now dusty polo shirt. Suddenly her own nipples ached as her eyes followed the line of his body to a defined erection, scant millimetres from her palm.

'We've been feeling strange all day, all of us.' She thought about her encounter with Gemma and could no longer ignore the moist pulsations against the crotch of her jeans.

'Then I'm not imagining it.' He placed his hand on top of hers and slid it onto his erection.

'Not unless I am too. I feel horny every time I'm down here.'

'Is that why you brought me then?'

'I brought you because you asked.' She guided his hand to cup her breast. He fumbled with the top few buttons of her shirt and slid his hand inside to stroke a nipple through her bra.

'Ever do anything about it? Before now, I mean.' She could feel his hips rocking forwards and backwards against her stroking hand.

'I've taken to bringing vegetables for lunch.'

He pushed the bra strap off her shoulder and slid a hand inside to cup her and thumb her distended nipple and areola. 'Other than being good for your health, how's that helpful?' His other hand found its way between her legs.

'Carrots, cucumbers, courgettes.' She spoke between efforts to breathe and to open her legs so his fingers, now stroking a path against the crotch seam of her jeans, could get closer to her growing moist spot. 'I don't work alone, you know, and vibrators are noisy. They might attract attention.'

'Good point. Though I think some of your colleagues might not mind much, at least if last night was any indication.'

'Very good point,' she said, as she opened his fly and wriggled her hand inside. 'What's this? No undies? You naughty boy.'

'Never wear the things,' he grunted. 'They're too confining. Maybe my cock's claustrophobic too.'

She ran her fingers along the smooth length of his shaft and extended her palm to cup his balls where they rested in a nest of soft curls. He groaned and lifted his arse completely off the ground to get closer to her hand. 'It'll certainly make my job easier.' She was already slipping his trousers over his hips, lingering for a nice feel of his tight arse on the way, and breathing in the humid male scent in sharp contrast to the dusty confines of the cave.

'Wait. Best not let crotches control brains here just yet. We have a theory to test, remember?' He stood, nearly bumping his head on an outcropping of rock, and stepped out of his trousers. Before she could catch more than an admiring glance of his greatly expanded package in the dazzling light, he knelt next to her and went to work on her jeans, pausing only momentarily to give her hard pallet a good tonguing before he pealed her as though she were a piece of ripe fruit. He lingered long enough to stroke the small triangle of fabric at the front of her zebra-print thong, and it was her turn to lift her arse off the ground as he hurried them down her thighs, then he sat back on his bare haunches. 'Now.' He looked over his shoulder to the shaft of light, which still hadn't quite fully reached Allegra, than he shifted her slightly to the left. 'That looks about right.' He checked the light again, then slid a palm between her thighs and opened her wide to the cool air. She slumped against the wall, legs splayed in anticipation, feeling as though her cunt was as swollen and inviting as the opening to the chamber.

'Now we're ready.' He sat back next to her and slipped his polo shirt over his head.

She started to take off her top.

'Don't move. You'll lose the position.' He looked back over his shoulder at the encroaching light. Kneeling again, with his erection bobbing deliciously against her cleavage, he slid her blouse over her head, popping a couple of buttons, which bounced off the stone wall with a ping and went rolling down the passage. Then he reached behind her and unhooked her bra, lingering for a quick caress as he removed the troublesome garment. Another glance over his shoulder, and he positioned himself sitting at her side. He turned towards her with his eyes locked on her exposed sex. 'Here it comes,' he whispered breathlessly. He pulled her left thigh open a little more just to be sure, and she shifted her hips forwards towards the beam of light. They both watched as the rays of the setting sun snaked low along the wall, between Allegra's legs and onto her pussy. Just at the right moment, he slid his fingers down over her pubic curls, parted her labia and whispered against her ear, 'Looks like your hypothesis was right.'

With his fingers still exposing her to the light, he turned and rummaged in his rucksack. For a second she was slightly miffed that he could allow himself to be distracted from something as amazing as this, but when he turned back to her, she understood why. With his free hand, he now held a digital camera. 'No doubt, you'll want to see this too. I figured I'd be taking photos inside the chamber, so the camera's equipped for low light.' He adjusted her thighs again and moved in so his face was close, but not blocking the sunlight. 'I certainly hadn't planned for anything as dramatic as this.' He took the first image.

'These had better not appear in your article.'

He chuckled. 'These are for private use only.'

Allegra squirmed, lifting her arse and moving closer to the path of impossible warmth that she was no longer sure came from the shaft of tangerine light, or from Dan's hand, the fingers stroking the sunlit parts of her that beaded with moisture. Each time he snapped the shutter, he moved his fingers away from her in order not to obscure the shot. And each time he did so, he licked his wet fingertips like a child tasting the cake batter. And each time he returned his fingers to stroke her parted lips she was wetter.

She watched in fascination, straining to see between her breasts and over her stomach, wishing desperately that she had a mirror. Suddenly, the light was momentarily shadowed as Dan laid the camera aside and repositioned himself so his tongue could lap at the single remaining sunbeam slipping across her swollen landscape, which she guessed strongly resembled the cleft entrance to the cave. She arched and braced herself, feeling the rough sandstone from the wall at her back abrading her shoulder blades and the wet warmth of his tongue at her pussy. She curled her fingers in his hair, ground her heels into the hard-packed earth and, while trying to remember to breathe occasionally, she rode his face.

He nibbled and tongued his way up over her clitoris and pubic mound and onto her navel, where he lingered, nipping and probing, offering succulent intimations of what was still to come. From there, he worked his way upwards, spreading her salty sweet female scent over her belly and breasts and neck just before his penis followed the path of the shaft of light with a grunt and a deep upwards thrust.

He felt megalithic inside her and, in her mind's eye, the symbolism of all the standing stones she'd studied and admired and hypothesised about over the years became clear, as did the cleft opening to the passage they'd entered together only minutes before. While they pushed and shoved and groaned, Allegra watched the shaft of sunlight trail down Dan's spine and over the hillocks of his bottom to recede down the corridor and back through the entrance, bathing them once again in close-fitting darkness.

But they were far too busy to feel claustrophobic. The passing of the light seemed to have heightened their other senses. Suddenly it was as though her vagina had conformed completely to the anxious, insistent press of his penis, and behind her closed eyelids she could see every detail as though her insides had vision. Suddenly it was as though they covered each other, absorbing and transmitting the intimate geography of breast and penis, vulva and buttocks. The line between arousal and release thinned and stretched with each thrust. They rode it until the chain reaction began and exploded outwards, filling the cruciform passages and echoing around the corbelled chamber as they both offered their raucous salute to the summer solstice. At that exact moment a section of the wall gave way behind them in a shower of dust and pebbles.

Coughing and sputtering, with his penis still buried inside her, they covered their faces and waited until the dust settled. Dan shifted slightly to one side and a thin shaft of light sliced through the dusty blackness. 'Jesus. What happened?' The wild beam of his torch shot past her ear into the void behind her head. Her heart raced as she scrambled from under him and found her own torch.

'Holy shit, Doc! You're not going to believe this!'

She couldn't tell from the sound of his voice if he were scared or excited but, as her torch flared and joined his own, she understood immediately and was soon scrambling over the remains of the wall, wearing only a heavy coating of dust and a torch. 'We could have never foreseen this,' she gasped. 'It's like nothing we've ever found.'

Beyond the collapse was another chamber, the walls of which were covered with carvings and paintings, spirals and dancing figures, which writhed and swayed in the torchlight. In the dry, cool space, the colours looked as though the ancient painters had simply walked away from their work for a quick cup of tea.

'What are they doing? Are they hunters?'

She directed the beam of her torch at the wall next to Dan's. 'Look, there are deer and wild boar. All kinds of animals. Wait a minute.' She moved closer and squinted at the wall. 'The animals ... they're all ...'

'They're all fucking, and the people too.'

As they moved the beams of their torches along the painted wall and ceiling, the artwork became more stylised. There were orgiastic groupings of figures with exaggerated genitalia in every sexual position imaginable and in some that Allegra was pretty sure were humanly impossible. She couldn't keep from wondering if all of this prehistoric porn was doing to Dan what it was doing to her. Still, her arousal was tempered by her curiosity as she bent closer to the wall. 'What are they doing here?'

She pointed to a small circle of people, one looking possibly priestly and offering a bowl to a couple with overly developed genitals.

'Some kind of ceremony.' Dan squinted at the group on which Allegra had shone her torch.

'This is brilliant. We can learn so much from these paintings. It's the next best thing to a written record. How could we have got so lucky? Hand me your camera.'

He scrambled over the rubble and returned with the camera. 'It really does seem to be some sort of ancient fertility ritual.'

'Who'd have thought?'

They hurriedly slipped back into their clothes and for the next few hours, they took photos: photos of animals in full rut; photos of couples in every sexual position imaginable; photos of groups joined in orgiastic pleasure. Allegra thought it was a testimony to both of them as professionals that they managed to get the photos without dropping to the floor and joining in the orgy again. But the effort to stay focused when the paintings were so arousing, and the company even more so, finally took its toll.

'Come on, Doc, we've got to get out of here. I need some air.' Dan practically shoved her back out of the entrance of the cave, falling on top of her a couple of times, and each time lingering for a good grope. Outside in the light of the now-full moon, he took her by the elbow and guided her hurriedly back towards the Jeep. He spun gravel taking off, then swung wildly into a deserted farm track half a mile up the road and stopped. He was out of the seat belt before he had the handbrake set and, before she could ask what was going on, he pulled her to him with such force that she felt joints crack. Then it was time for some serious mouth to mouth.

He guided her hand to his lap. 'I need to fuck, and you do too, but I want you up here in the moonlight, under the stars where I can see you. That place has some kind of powerful spell on it. I'm convinced. So who are we to fight it?' He held her hand tight and shifted his hips so she could feel the hard evidence behind his theory.

'I'm sure it must be dangerous to fight magic,' she said. He stopped any further conversation with a tonsil-deep kiss.

Her shirt was the first article of clothing to go – not too difficult with several buttons missing from their first encounter. He slid it off her shoulders and sat back long enough to admire her breasts beneath the lace of her bra. He suckled her through the cups until the lace was wet and cool against her straining nipples. Then he deftly unfastened the hooks and released her aching breasts to his kneading fingers. They both watched in amazement as he brought her nipples to new heights beneath the rough stroking of his thumbs. By the time he lowered his mouth to suckle again, her knickers were wet through to her jeans, and she was already riding the edge of orgasm. Until this afternoon, it had been far too long since she'd come with an actual person, and the thought that it was about to happen three times in the last twelve hours was almost enough to make her cry out with excitement.

While his mouth worked her breasts, he teased and stroked her pussy through her jeans until she could stand it no more and yanked them down over her hips. He didn't wait around for further invitation. He pushed her sideways in the seat until she was slumped against the door. When he had her arranged the way he wanted her, he opened her legs to the summer night air and negotiated the gearstick until his hands cupped and kneaded her arse. His amazing thumbs massaged the outer edges of her cunt, and the blend of their rough skin and her moisture made the friction along her lips maddening. As she arched her back and lifted her bum upwards to create more friction, he went down, tongue first. Snaking about the slick valley of her pussy, dipping in deep, then circling her distended clit with a tongue that was surely prehensile, he made her come hard; he made her cry out and buck in the seat until the whole Jeep rocked.

He pulled back enough to breathe and wiped his wet face on his shirt-tail before ripping it off over his head. He dragged his jeans down and wrestled his straining erection free. 'Stand up,' he commanded.

She did what he asked.

'In the seat,' he gasped. 'Stand up in the seat. That's it. Now turn around and grab the roll bar – tight.'

She held on as he fingered her slippery opening and tweaked her clit with his thumb. She shoved back against his hand, pussy raised for his inspection like a thoroughbred in heat. He pressed the head of his penis between her cunt lips, teasing her open, before inching his thickness into her, stretching her. Gently at first, though she could feel his need to thrust like electricity humming along high-tension wire. And when he was sure that she could comfortably accommodate his cock, he began to pound against her, holding first her hips, then moving up to cup and knead her tits, which bounced enthusiastically each time he thrust.

'I can't take much more of this.' His breath came hot against the back of her neck. 'My balls are about to burst.'

He hammered into her with all his strength until he was nothing more than muscle. His grip on her hips was near bruising, and she hung on to the roll bar for dear life as he pounded her, straining back against him, making sure his cock went as deep as possible with each thrust. And when he cried out and convulsed against her, she screamed out from her own intense pleasure as the explosion of her orgasm impacted all the way up to her head.

With some effort, they managed to make it back to the cottage where Allegra's crew was staying. They arrived, already anticipating round three. As they quick-stepped each other past the lounge between gropes and kisses, they startled Gemma and Mac from the sofa in front of the television doing a little groping of their own. Allegra couldn't help feeling a superior satisfaction that at least for tonight she wouldn't have to rely on voyeurism for her kicks.

'Happy Solstice,' Gemma called after them as they headed up the stairs already undoing buttons and zippers.

Allegra's crew arrived the next morning to a big surprise. There were a few uncomfortable moments while she tried to explain just exactly how she 'stumbled on to' this amazing discovery, but she was the archaeologist in charge.

Dan's article won him several journalism awards, and the discovery secured grant money for Allegra and her team. Dan flew off the next day to do a story on a Mayan temple in Guatemala, but before he left, he gave her a large manila envelope and a brown paper bag. The envelope contained copies of the photos he had taken of their little experiment, starring her pussy and the sun god. The bag contained a courgette, which curiously resembled Dan's cock. Taped to it was a note:

Congratulations, Doc,
I can't remember the last time I've had so much fun on assignment. As a token of my appreciation, lunch is on me.
Dan Martin

'Archeogasms' is K D Grace's first short story for Black Lace.

Wednesdays and Tuesdays

Sommer Marsden

The waiting room is packed. Mobbed. Insane. Between the coughing and bored-looking patients, they sit. Well-groomed, healthy, glowing reps. Pharmaceutical representatives armed with suits and laptops, samples and magnets. They have pens and smiles that say, Try our latest and greatest. Have a mug, have a key chain. Try my stuff, buy my stuff, would you like some samples, doctor?

I glance around the room, expectant eyes on me. Patients who look half dead, half angry. And then the expectant handsome young man in the charcoal pinstriped suit. His dark hair is slicked back off his baby face with honest-to-God product and his shoulders are broad. I don't know his name, so I point to him and give him the 'Come on back' motion. An audible groan goes up in the room. I am the belle of the ball. I am the one who cracks the whip. I have seen six patients. It's time for a break. And I'm not really that far behind, which is a fucking miracle.

'You can come on back to my office,' I say, my heels tip-tapping gently on the grey industrial carpet.

'Thank you, Doctor. I promise I'll be quick.'

'God, I hope not,' I mutter, picking up my pace.

'Come again?'

'What?' I say, playing the game. If he heard me, then he had a clue of what was to come. If he didn't, he can wait. I liked to toy with them. Wednesday is my favourite day of the week.

'Sorry. I thought you said something. Anyway, my name is Branden. Today, I want to talk to you about nasal spray.'

I pick up my speed, make a left, dart through the door to my office. Branden, all six foot three of him has to do a little race walking just to keep up with me. I am almost six foot, eye to eye with him in my heels. I cut my teeth, so to speak, on late nights at the hospital, in the ER, in Intensive Care. Walking fast is a side effect of the business. Show me a man or a woman who speed-walks through life, I'll show you a doctor.

'Shut the door, Branden,' I say, and lean back against my desk. I stretch my long legs out in front of me and cross them at the ankle. This move pulls up my professional knee-length skirt enough and in the right way to expose the garters that hold up my hosiery. I know this for a fact, because I have practised and I am nothing if not a perfectionist.

'Dr Martin?' But there is that glow in his eyes. That sparkle that says, deep down under his boy-next-door blushing façade, he knows he is about to get fucked blue by yours truly. I have become a bit of an urban legend in my area. I play the game the right way. People talk, but it seems speculative and almost admiring.

I like it. I like the talk, the confusion, and the boys. And, to be blunt, I really don't care. I am a busy woman with a reputation. I walk the tightrope between rumour and fact and I like my pretty young men. A strange hard cock at least once a week, and bit of adrenaline followed by a good toe curling orgasm.

'Take off your pants, Branden,' I say, and tap the seat of my visitor's chair with the pointy toe of my Jimmy Choo's. 'Go on, take them off like a good boy and have a seat. I think we need to examine a few things before I can let you continue.'

His blush grows, turning his creamy white complexion a charming peach. He dips his head and laughs. A single lock of chocolate hair falls across his forehead. My heart stutter steps and my cunt grows even wetter. The adrenaline is zipping and buzzing under my skin. My God, he is beautiful.

'Doctor, I . . .' His cock is hard. I can see that from where I am perched. I didn't graduate from medical school for nothing. I can spot a hard-on from a mile away. I laugh.

'Listen, my waiting room is packed. My day is packed. If you can't give me the sample I want – the sample I *need* – then I can pick another flower from the garden.' I smile at him, but I'm dead fucking serious. I have twenty minutes and I need to get laid. Fast, hard, and by a pretty, pretty man.

'Oh no, I . . .' He drops his bag and he wrestles with his belt. And now he is grinning *and* blushing. His slacks slide down and he stands there, fisting his hand, unsure of what to do. I like their discomfort. Their excitement and fear and worry. It's intoxicating.

He's standing there in his blue boxers and his cock has formed the most perfect tent. I take the tip of my shoe and I push at the waistband, I push down the boxers until his lovely rosy cock is showing. 'Sit down, Branden,' I say and he drops into the seat like his legs are boneless.

The chairs are wide and generous. Dark chocolate brown with no arms. I always consider my more corpulent patients. My job is to make them less so but nothing is more embarrassing than not fitting in your doctor's office chairs. 'Oh, Doctor.'

That's it. *Oh, Doctor.* It sounds like a porno and that makes me laugh out loud. 'Have you heard stories about me?' He nods and smiles. His teeth are super white and his lips are so rosy red they almost look feminine. 'What kind of stories?'

'That you're sexy. That you're hot. That you're an animal when it comes to –' He catches himself and shuts his eyes. His cock bobs a bit like a tuning fork when I get near it with the toe of my shoe. I rub the magenta leather up his dick and he gasps like a young girl.

'An animal when it comes to fucking? Sex? Seduction? Blow jobs?'

More nodding and he is keeping his eyes shut tight like I'm a dream and, if he opens his eyes, I will *poof!* disappear. I pull down my skirt and step out of it. Here I am in my blouse and garters and hosiery. Expensive shoes and my lab coat. No panties. I can smell my own moisture and it makes the want worse. Nothing smells better than arousal in my humble opinion. I drop to my knees but don't slide – that will rip my stockings. I take him into my mouth and he makes a sound like he's crying.

Branden is a gorgeous specimen. His cock is long and thick. His hips buck up under me with an eagerness that shows more in the younger reps. The older they are, the more control they have. Today I'm in the mood for someone I can make frantic. Crazy. I suck him until he has forgotten himself and is pulling my hair, fucking my face. I take it until my pussy is so wet the insides of my thighs are drenched. 'Stop,' I say and, after one more desperate buck, he stills. His breath is ripping in and out of him and, when I sit up, his eyes are shiny. Glazed blue eyes that say, *what now?*

I stand and say not a word. I step to him and his mouth falls on me like he's dying of thirst and I can save him. His tongue is everywhere at once. No finesse, just a goal, make the good doctor come. And that is a lovely agenda. I spread my legs a bit further, teetering on my heels now. The pleasure is spreading fast, making me warm and loosening my tension. So very, very nice. His tongue is snake-quick and lovely on my clit and my hood. He parts me and suckles, covers my clit, sucks. Moving so very fast I can barely register one feeling before the next one comes. His fingers slide up my thighs with the rasp of calluses on silken hosiery. I spread my legs further, sink my hands into his hair, let my head fall back.

This. This is what I need.

I let him press and push against my G-spot until I am loose and warm from head to toe. And then I give him what he seeks. I give him my orgasm and I hold on for the ride. My fingernails are petal-pink against his dark-grey suit jacket. Branden looks up with a drugged expression that makes me feel suddenly and painfully attached to him.

I climb onto his lap, impale myself on his hard cock that has not lost any of its urgency. I take him in, my cunt stretching for him; inch by inch I let him in. I have my eyes locked with his. He appears both startled and feverish, until his eyes slide shut and his head falls back. This time, instead of 'Oh, Doctor,' it is, 'Oh, God.'

When I move it is slowly. When I breathe it is measured. When I lean in and drag the tip of my tongue along his neck to taste him, I do it inch by measured inch. He tastes like salt and sweet and some sort of spice I can't quite finger. He smells like cotton and leather and pepper. I bury my nose at the base of his throat. I inhale deeply, lick, then I bite him right above his collar and he jumps under me with a soft pained sound. 'Good, good boy.' I bite him again and he jumps. When he jerks, his cock thrusts deeper into me, pushing against the sacred places I want it the most.

The clock is not my friend and I can see that Branden is hanging onto his own body by sheer force of will. 'Please,' he says and just that word is enough to tighten my pussy and push me that tiny bit too far.

'Come for me, Branden. I'm a busy woman. I have patients waiting. Don't you think they're wondering what we're doing? I mean, people do talk. The other reps are out there wondering right now. Will it smell like sex in here when we're done? Will it smell like sperm and cunt and coupling?' I'm rambling in his ear so that he'll tip. I want to break him and make him dance under me without thought or any shred of pride.

'I don't know. I don't know.' He looks a little panicked and he looks like, if he breathed just a bit too deeply, he'd empty into me. His hips are slamming up out of my visitor's chair. It's like being on top of an electrocution victim. 'God, I don't know.'

I lean in and trap his ear between my teeth, I hover over him before plunging down again and he's pushing up under me mindlessly. 'It's a pity we don't have more time,' I breathe in his ear and he squeaks. He squeaks! Like a child's toy, he lets out a desperate high sound that makes me crazy. 'If we had more time, Branden, then I'd let you fuck me up the ass. I really get off on that. And I do appreciate you. You're new around here and very, very pretty. And I bet you're really good at your job because you're really good at this.'

Branden is nodding over and over again as if I am spewing the Gospel and he's gripping me so hard it hurts. 'I am. I am really, really good, Doctor. Good. Good, good, good ... Doctor Martin, I ... Ohhh.'

'Please call me Karen,' I laugh. 'And please come before you explode.' And that sneaky little instinctive fuck bends and bites my nipple through my blouse. It is a sharp fast white pain that drags me into an orgasm that dims my vision. 'Oh, Branden. You are a clever boy.'

I am bucking my hips. I am mindless. I am an animal. He is panting in my ear and together we are both a little wild and a little less than human.

He unclenches his fingers and stares at me, his eyes wide and realisation sinking in. He just fucked the doctor. Now what? What will happen? I'm still straddling his naked lap, his cock softening deep inside me. My pulse is slamming in my throat and chest and pussy. I clench up around him and his eyes roll back a little. I straighten his tie and kiss him for the first time ever. 'I like you. Come back next Wednesday.'

'Can I bring you something, Doc?' There is a sudden and unmistakable glint of mischief in his gaze. Big, big blue eyes and sharp high cheekbones, all topped off by a boyish grin.

I never ever take gifts. From reps or patients or other physicians. Never. It is part of my own code of ethics. But I'm intrigued. 'I'll make an exception,' I say. 'But just for you and just this once.'

He nods, looking excited and pleased. And then Branden and I are a flurry of zippers and skirts and swishing fabric as we reassemble our professional selves, leaving our baser selves in our memories for the time being. He pulls me in, startling me, and kisses me hard. It is a long, demanding kiss of a much more aggressive man than the one I just fucked. It rattles me a little. Was I really in charge? 'See you soon, Doc,' he says against my mouth and turns to leave.

'Oh, Branden?' I sing-song.

'Yeah?' He is halfway out the door, still glowing from the sex. I smile at him. 'Leave your samples on the table right outside the door.'

'Got it.' And then he is gone and my pussy is thumping. Greedy for more. Wishing I could have him again. I'll have to take care of things when I get home.

I make the boring (this time) walk down the hall and open the door. I consult my clipboard. 'Ah, Mr Storm. Albert Storm.'

Mr Storm stands up and with a look of near-jubilation, follows me back to tell me about his boil.

'Ah, there she is. You must be such a whore for the free stuff.'

I start for a minute and then see that Doug is kidding. And by 'free stuff' he does not mean sex. He means samples. My loving husband thinks that I love Wednesdays because I get free sticky notes, pens and coffee mugs. I let him think that. It's better this way.

'Oh, I'm just a whore in general,' I say, stirring my vegetables. I have stirred them approximately three hundred times in the past five minutes. My mind is not a thousand miles away. My mind is in my office, straddling Branden the new pharmaceuticals rep and fucking him dry. Fucking him and biting him and listening to him ramble like he's caught in a fever dream.

My nipples are hard, my body warm and ready to be fucked all over again. I have not had a shower and, God help me, when my husband comes up behind me and wraps his arms around my waist, I nearly come. I can tell by the way his hands splay over my skin and his fingertips trace the low waistband of my leggings that he wants to get laid. It's warm in the kitchen, but when his lips touch the spot between my shoulder blades above the lace of my tank top, it's downright hot.

'Doug, let's eat. Let me take a shower.' See me trying to be the good guy? Let me clean up. I still smell like man. I still smell like sex. Sex that did not involve man and wife but doctor and boy. Pretty boys with free samples and stars in their eyes.

'How about we put that on the back burner and we do this first. No shower. You're dirty. I like you dirty.' He moves the wok off the flame and pushes me against the oven. My hands spread wide on the turquoise enamel to steady myself. Doug pushes my legs apart like he's at work and he's frisking me. He slides his hands up the inside of my leggings and I feel that steady beat in my cunt increase. He's so close to touching me and being right where another man's cock was a few hours before. And he has no idea.

My face floods with heat as I blush at my own taboo arousal. I moan and he laughs and the kitchen is that much hotter. This is not the first time I have let my husband take me on a Wednesday. More than once I've wondered if I give off some odour or pheromone or vibe that is calling him in. *I'm ripe. I'm ready. I want it. Fuck me.*

My professional hairdo has been scrapped for my evening ponytail. I hang my head down and my ponytail sways, brushing over the oven top. I sigh as his hand finds me, touches me and his fingers slide along the seam of my pussy. The thin cotton spandex leggings offer very little defence against his excitement. 'Christ, baby, you are so wet. Your pants are soaked. You want this. Don't you? You're such a slut.'

My husband would never call me names normally. But he knows me. In this context, so close to penetration, the worse things he says, the more I like it. I am a complex woman.

'I am,' I say and, in my mind, I have pretty Branden between my thighs, eating me. I see the dark top of his head. His broad shoulders. I can feel his tongue on me and hear the noises of his lips on my pussy.

'Say it,' Doug says.

'I am a slut,' I gasp and he shoves his hands into my workout pants. He pushes his big thick fingers inside me and I grip the oven like I might fall down. 'I am a filthy cunt,' I say again. He fucks me with his fingers and the kitchen grows warmer still.

'I think there's enough juice for two dicks in you,' he laughs in my ear and I moan. Now in my mind there are two. There is pretty new Branden and I am on top. There is handsome faithful Doug and he's behind me. One in the cunt. One in the ass. I can't breathe.

I should feel guilty. I feel excited.

Doug shoves my leggings down. He drops to his knees, bites my ass. Hard, the way I like it. Until I make a noise of pain and my hip bone bangs the oven door painfully hard. I see stars and I skate along that paper edge of coming. 'God,' I say.

'God has turned his head for the moment,' Doug teases and

licks down between my cheeks. He pushes his fingers deeper, deeper and I can smell myself. I imagine I can smell the scent of me and Branden, but my husband seems just fine. 'Come for me, Karen. If you don't come for me, I won't fuck you. And I want to fuck you. Hard and fast. Dirty little slut.'

I come for him.

At the office, I am all orders and demands. Drill-sergeant barks and pushing Branden's buttons. Here, in my cosy, yellow kitchen, I am more placid, docile, soft like pulled taffy.

'Bend over,' says Doug and I bend.

He moves me to the counter, positions me like a doll and pins my wrists behind my back. He pushes his big leg between my knees and spreads my stance. Doug is a cop and he's treating me roughly, like a criminal. I hear his zipper and he squeezes me just a bit too hard with his hand. My wrist bones grind together and I let out a sigh of pain. I like the pain and he knows it. I rest my forehead against the cool marble and I can feel my pulse in my forehead. The head of his cock pushes at me, forces in me and I still. I can hear my blood in my ears.

Maybe I like his roughness because I am paying my dues. Paying my penance. I nod when my husband slides into me roughly, banging me from behind so hard that my hips are wrapping against the lip of the counter. 'What are you nodding at? What are you thinking? That you're a complete slut?'

I nod again and he grips me harder. His fingers are biting my skin, pushing against flesh that has already been gripped by another man. His cock is hitting places that have already been hit. He is fucking a pussy that has already been fucked. It is almost like having two men in me at once and I feel my body grow tight around him.

'God, you are so tight,' he moans and pushes his hands against my shoulders. Holding me flat and pinning me down and fucking me faster. I can smell hot oil from the wok and hear the faucet dripping and I remember the feel of Branden's teeth on my nipple when he bit me. A gentle purple bruise has sprung up over the rose-coloured disc. A nipple that is now mashed flat against cool grey marble.

A stinging smack snaps against my ass and I gasp. Heat floods that place and I feel the tingling burn of a welt rising up. My cunt flexes again and when that happens, Doug smacks the other side. I like it when he hits me. 'Whore,' he says. And I come again.

Dinner is decent. We didn't ruin it. After wine, I take a shower. I am hesitant to wash the two men off of me, but I do. And I start the countdown of my days at midnight. Thursday, Friday, Saturday will pass. On Sunday we will be busy with a christening and the afterparty. Monday I start my work week. Tuesday I will grow antsy and be snappy at my staff. I will tell a handful of patients they are obese and not be kind about it. Wednesday morning, I will be glowing and smiling and ready.

'Good night, love,' Doug says to me when I turn the lights out. He pulls me in and holds me tight. All of his aggression left behind. For the act of sex, for fucking. When it comes to man and wife stuff, he is my caretaker, he is gentle and kind. I fall asleep, extremely peaceful.

'Doctor?'

I glance up at my assistant, Cheryl; she looks unsure. I'm busy and a bit grumpy. The only thing getting me through the day is that tomorrow is Wednesday. 'What is it?' I try to temper my voice because Cheryl is skittish and sensitive.

'There's a young man out front. His name is . . .' She glances at a business card. 'Branden Johnson. He said he can't come tomorrow. The normal rep day?' She says this as if she is asking me a question and it makes me nuts. But I cannot fixate on my pet peeve because my heart is racing and my body has been thrown into chaos.

'Oh.'

Cheryl blinks at me. She is unused to me being tongue-tied. 'So, he asked if I would ask you if he could possibly have a few minutes of your time today.' On her cheeks are two flaming spots. She looks so nervous she could pee her pants and suddenly this is highly amusing to me. My mood has shifted.

'Of course. Show him back. I'll just finish this up.' I am trying so hard to seem in control. And I'm sure I appear to be just that. Only I can feel the flutter in my belly. I press my knees together and it only serves to heighten the lovely feeling in my pussy.

She is gone in a blink and I fluff my hair. I'm a little bit nervous and I like that feeling. That jittery anxious feeling is a high like no other. I close my eyes, calling up the feel of him from the week before. The slide of his dick into my depths. The smell of him and the taste of his lips. His dark hair and his big blue eyes. And the dip of his head where he looks boyish and shy.

A soft knock sounds and I glance up. I smile because there is handsome beautiful Branden. Then I blink and my heart sinks. Behind him is another man. A slightly shorter, thinner blond man. Handsome in a surfer boy way. Probably about my height. Skin and hair kissed by the sun.

'Doctor Martin,' Brandens says, grinning. 'This is Tad. I'm training him. I thought you two might like to meet.'

My heart speeds up again because now I am remembering that Branden asked if he could bring me something. It appears he has brought me something rather lovely. 'Come on in, gentlemen,' I say and cross my legs under my desk. The small bit of friction is almost enough to make me come I'm so aroused.

'Tad is a rep in training. He's a good guy. And I have –' Branden looks me dead in the eye and says, 'told him all about you.'

About me. That makes me light-headed. *I've told him all about you.*

'Oh. OK.' My voice is soft. Not the dominant boisterous voice from our last meeting. 'I . . .'

Tad steps forwards and shakes my hand. He squeezes my hand a bit too hard and sparkles of excitement run over my skin. 'Ah, Doctor. See, Branden says you're a bad ass. A hard case. I told him, "Hey, I bet I could take her."' He pulls my hand towards him and I rise. He wants me to stand. So I do. 'Do you? Do you think I could take you, Doc?'

He *is* a surfer. Or an athlete of some kind. The skin of his hands is dried just a bit from the salt water. He is lean but I can tell from his grip that it's all muscle. There is not a spare ounce of fat on him. I swallow hard and see Branden watching me. Grinning. He is loving this. The good doctor put in her place. My confusion is instantaneous and I can feel the crotch of my silk panties soaked by my own juices. 'I, um . . .'

It is my turn to blush and drop my head. God, I cannot breathe. Tad pulls me harder and I come out from behind my desk. He stoops a bit, sets down his briefcase, runs his hands up my thighs. Today, my legs are bare. The weather has warmed. I shiver, though my office is not cold. I hear Branden lock the door. Tad's hands go higher and I want to slap him or fuck him, or both at once.

'See, usually under a tough exterior is a woman waiting to be taught a little discipline,' he says right into my ear. A blanket of goose bumps roll over my skin and my nipples go tight. I swallow again. My throat is full of cotton and my heart is full of fear. I love the fearful feeling. The wondering about the outcome.

Branden laughs softly and I hear his zipper. Tad hooks my panties with his fingers and drags them down. When they are around my knees he stops, spins me like a dance partner. I go, feeling dizzy but eager. 'Bend over, Karen,' he says.

Not *Doctor. Karen.*

He plants me on my desk and I watch the lights flash and dance on my phone. My busy office buzzes around me. Patients come and go and wait and wonder. While this happens a strange man is running his callused palms over my suddenly bare ass while another man watches.

More fluid leaks from me. My heart jumps abruptly. I clench my cunt around nothing and wish for something to fill me. Something. One of them.

'Maybe she needs a spanking?' Branden suggests. He sounds hopeful.

Tad makes a tsking sound like an upset teacher. Maybe he is a teacher. Maybe he is showing Branden how to handle demanding women. 'No. No, a spanking won't do. Too loud. We don't need the staff wondering what's going on. It's going to be hard enough to keep her quiet soon anyway.'

I almost cry. Instead I say, 'Please. Something. Please.'

Tad shoves his finger into my pussy almost casually. My body goes haywire, clenching around him as he continues his explanation. 'I'm thinking a bit of silent pain. You know? Hand me my case.'

I hear movement and rustling but stay prone on the desk. Spectacular in my subservience. Not in charge but being controlled. Then the pain erupts. Bright wonderful bites of pain along my flanks. Up my spine. Over my shoulder. Tad is whistling while he works. I want to ask what he is using but I bite my tongue and sob softly instead.

'Who knew binder clips could be so pretty?' Branden says and answers my unspoken question. He steps forwards and his face is level with me. His olive drab slacks right in front of my face. Tad plucks at one of the clips and I writhe on my nice authoritative mahogany desk.

'Go on, try her out.'

I open my mouth without being asked. How odd and wonderful for Branden to have seen both sides of the coin. The fierce me and the meek me. I suck his cock with a drunken kind of excitement. My head is muddy and slow but I'm hearing another zipper and my pulse is not.

'Such a good, good girl,' Tad praises. I glow for him. Pleased with myself, embracing my shame. He pushes the head of his cock to my cunt and I do my best not to force myself back onto him like a slut. He stops, his fingers shove into me and then they are gone too. Confusion sweeps through me until he slides into me and his fingers penetrate my ass. Swift and sharp. I moan and take Branden deeper. He's not shy this week. He fists my hair and fucks my mouth and says some magical words. 'Dirty cocksucker.'

I come. It's as easy as sneezing.

'She is a dirty cocksucker. She just came. Didn't you, Doc? You just came.'

The trash talk is a lovely soundtrack to the debauchery. It will play in my head for days. They have given me the one thing I have been too timid to seek out.

'Come on around here, man. And you, up with you.' My new master pulls me up by my wrists, the clips biting my skin as it stretches and moves. My tears are very real but so is my thrill and the pleasure. Tad sinks onto my big chair and yanks me so I straddle him. I watch, transfixed, as his big, red cock disappears into my pussy. He's long and thick and I watch my body take him in and hide him. The small triangle of hair at my sex is ginger-brown and his is reddish-blond. I am mesmerised. Until he says, 'She's pretty worked back there. Go for it.'

And there it is. *Back there.* I let my head fall onto Tad's broad shoulder like I'm praying. Like I'm thankful. Because I am.

Branden sinks to his knees. Which puts him level with me. His presence behind me, where I am the most vulnerable, is looming. Hulking and dangerous where I sit impaled on Tad's cock. Tad is thrusting up from under me, his teeth marking my shoulder as he plucks the binder clips one by one. He removes the first and the blood rushes in and I see stars. Branden presses against the stubborn pucker of my anus and I hold my breath.

The head of Branden's cock is in and Tad is fucking me from underneath. His upward thrusts tricking my clitoris into a buzzing joy that fills my womb and makes my head feel swimmy. 'Oh, Jesus,' I breathe. I clutch the back of the chair like it can save me from my shame and my pleasure. The pinching pain sings up my spine and I let my head roll back. I let my sounds loose. Greedy, eager, ugly, transcendent sounds fill the room and Tad laughs. He covers my mouth with his callused palm and Branden pushes hard and is in. I hiccup, sob, moan.

My body is a swirl of pain and pleasure as he fucks my ass, two cocks rubbing, sinister and close, on the thin membrane of my flesh that separates them. 'Yes, yes, yes,' has joined my sounds. I'm not sure what I'm saying but I can hear my own voice. I sound breathless and raw.

'She likes it.'

'She's a slut. A gorgeous slut.'

A binder clip is removed and the blood rushing back to my flesh is damn near orgasmic.

'Greedy little slut. One cock isn't enough.' There is a grunt. I am gone from them. I cannot completely tell who is saying what. Front or back, up or down. My cunt is all I can feel and the fun house effect is maddening, but freeing at the same time.

'She needs two. Doctors are usually hard cases.'

There goes another clip and I come. Bright blips of pleasure curl through me and I feel my pussy milking at the cock that fills it. The fullness in my ass heightens it all. One of them groans and I echo the sound.

There is a knock on the door but I'm still crying. My voice is a mess. Tears are streaking my face. There goes a binder clip. Blood flows to flesh. I am babbling. 'Not now, I'm busy. I'll be done soon. Soon. Come back. I'm coming soon . . .'

Tad laughs again. A dark malicious laugh. His cruelty tightens me up on the inside and I am back to the cusp of orgasm again. What if someone were to open the door? What if they found out? What if Doug found out? The anxiety only makes the feelings that much better.

Tad's pinching my nipples. Hard. Over and over again as Branden releases the skin of my back from its bonds. The nerve endings compete and I twist. Impaled. Two cocks move inside me. Sometimes in tandem, sometimes opposing. I am pushed and pulled and tugged and stretched and full. So very fucking full. I watch my pink fingernails bite into the brown fabric behind Tad's head. I hold on and pray. Pray I will come again. Pray it won't end. Pray that this is not the only time. And I wonder about myself and Doug and wonder again why there is no guilt.

My G-spot is bumped and prodded from both angles and I clench up, coming without warning, as my phone blips and bleeps impatiently.

'You're in demand, Doc,' Tad says.

'Can't you see why?' Branden jokes.

Both men laugh. I am an object. A cunt. A slut. A whore. I come again. How many is this? I have lost track. At home I am a doctor, a lover, a friend. A mate. I have meaning. Right now I have no meaning. I am the pleasure and the pain and I am free. 'Dirty little slut,' I say.

They still for a moment. 'Dirty little slut,' Tad says almost tenderly and locks eyes with me as he fucks me. When Branden runs his hands down my back, now devoid of clips, it is a softer touch.

'I'm done, man,' he then says. 'You've such a sweet ass.' Then he's clutching at me, tugging me, coming with a stifled groan that sends another thrill through me.

Tad bares a breast and nips me with his teeth. Hard. Little sharp bites. I am so very close but don't think I can manage. Until he grips me and slams up into me. Angling me back a bit so he is hitting new and virginal nerves. Branden is still buried in my ass and I think of their cocks rubbing together. How they can feel each other. How they are both in me at once. Bright white sparks ignite in my vision and I come again.

Tad is right there with me. I slump onto him as he empties into me. 'Such a dirty little cocksucker,' he says. He kisses me and wipes my tears.

'You look pretty happy for a Tuesday. To look at you, you'd think it was Wednesday,' Doug says, as I kiss him hello.

He has a steak on the grill and his handcuffs and Glock are on the table. He's still in uniform but for his Kevlar vest and white shirt. He smells nice and looks better. I kiss him harder. I love how he looks in his uniform. He is the law. In charge. Striking. Strong.

I am used and bruised and boneless. Such spectacular pain fills my body. And the thumping aftershocks of pleasure race through me. Next Wednesday I may pick a new rep. I may not. I have a week to decide. I have considered pencilling my new boys in on Tuesdays. Earlier in the week. But I want to keep my options open.

'You in there?'

'Sorry. Wool-gathering. What?'

'I said, you look pretty happy for a Tuesday,' he laughs and smooths my hair back off my forehead.

'I'm thinking Tuesdays can be good too,' I say and kiss him again.

Short stories by Sommer Marsden are included in the Black Lace collections *Lust at First Bite* and *Seduction*.

The Woodsman

Charlotte Stein

He lives in a caravan in the woods somewhere, I know he does. No matter what time of year I come up to my little cottage in the middle of nowhere, he's around. So it follows that he must live here, doing God knows what. He's probably a pervert or a mental patient; I've always known that I'll wake up one night to find he's killed a squirrel and left it in my kitchen.

Or worse than that. I think about *Deliverance* and *Straw Dogs* often.

And yet I'm not scared at all when I wake up one morning and he's standing in the doorway of my shadow dusky bedroom. I have no idea why I'm not – I should at the very least be startled – but instead I just turn off my stomach so that I can see him better, and rub my sleep-furred eyes.

He looks immense in the doorway, shoulders broad and almost touching the frame on either side, as tall as a tomb. He looks like a caveman, most of his face obscured by hair, thick and shaggy and black. The hands that sprout out from the unbuttoned cuffs of his checked lumberjack's shirt are like bear paws.

But I'm not afraid. It seems I was right not to be, because then he just turns and walks away again, and when I roam around looking for evidence of him, there is none.

I've never told anyone about him – about the woodsman, I mean. Francie says things like: 'Did you have a nice holiday in your hermit's hole?' And I reply that I did, that it was great, I got loads done and I saw seven squirrels, but I never tell her that some hairy maniac lives in a caravan nearby.

I'll never tell her about what happened, either, even though it's an actual event worthy of telling. *He just stood there in the doorway of my bedroom, looking at me with his great still eyes.* They looked very pale amidst all that black hair. Like pools of water set into his granite face.

I know all of this because he does the same thing the next time I'm up there, and I get more of a chance to study him. This time I sit up in bed, and stare right back into his pale water eyes. This time I'm not just unafraid, I'm the opposite. Come in then, I think. Come right in and do or say whatever you want to do or say.

But he doesn't, and I should be glad because they're mad and dangerous thoughts to have. Though, then again, it's not like what he's doing isn't mad and dangerous. What if I did actually believe that he was a maniac, and had a can of Mace under my pillow? Or a crossbow?

That would almost certainly get a reaction out of his stone-monolith-self – pointing a crossbow at his chest. *Then* he'd have something to say, like: 'You've got a gas leak.'

Because that's obviously what it will be. Something boring and mundane and that he couldn't quite voice because he's mentally impaired in some way, or mute. It probably isn't the former because that gleam of sharpness in his eyes is obvious, but it could be the latter.

Or maybe he thinks I'm a stupid townie, and deserve to die in a massive gas explosion.

Or maybe I'm just an idiot, and he's waiting for me to ask something of him, like: 'Can I help you at all?' He's probably just recently knocked himself unconscious and is still dazed with concussion, and needs me to help him to a hospital.

Which seems very, very reasonable to a person who doesn't really believe in the things that happen in a movie called *The Woodsman Has Perverted Sex With Some Townie*. Porn music would certainly start up in the movie version of him standing in my bedroom doorway, but this is my real, boring life. It's not going to happen now, I can promise you. I don't even want something like that to happen, because that's insane.

So I'm totally *not* wanking at 7.28 the next morning, two minutes before he usually turns up. That's what he is now: usually. He's become as regular as a stripper's gyrations when I put my coin into the slot; I've hit play on the DVD and here he is. Fantasy number two-eight-zero: vaguely threatening rugged hunk wanting sex with you sort of against your will.

Only it isn't against my will at all, and that's even better. I've never been the sort for rough-housing in the bedroom, but I've always been the sort, apparently, for a mysterious woodsman hungry with lust for my soft pale curves. He probably saw me in my underwear through the window one day, and couldn't take his eyes off all my womanly flesh the likes of which his hungry hermit eyes hadn't seen in years and, oh, Christ, my clit is diamond-hard and I think I could come just because he's suddenly there.

And he is. There, I mean. Watching me with my hand beneath the waistband of my shorts, the sheets covering some things but certainly not all. It isn't him watching me rub one out that embarrasses me, though – it's the fact that I moan, I think. I moan loudly and uninhibitedly and twist my face into the pillow.

I'm embarrassed, but I don't stop rubbing my aching clit. I don't stop doing anything until the bed dips and I feel his hands on my thighs, and I only stop then because I want to touch him instead. He doesn't let me, though. He takes my wrists in one hand and puts them above my head, and then grabs the waistband of my shorts with the other.

I've never seen anyone remove an item of clothing so effectively. They whoosh off my body and then it's just me, a stranger, and my naked pussy. I squirm on the bed thinking that he's going to fuck me now, only he doesn't. Well, I suppose he *does*, sort of, but it's not in the way I expect. He gives me this one last long glittering hungry look, and then he spreads my legs with the clinical precision of someone who is not a caveman hermit, and puts his face in the space in between.

The first thing I think is: I've never been eaten out by a man with a beard. The second thought is somewhat less coherent. It's sort of somewhere between an 'oh' and a 'yes', but never quite fulfilling the jobs of either.

I don't even know what he smells like or what he looks like naked or, for God's sake, what his *name* is, and he's kissed my cunt before he's kissed my mouth. His name's something like Butch, I think, and then I giggle; then the giggle dissolves into another sound that is neither something nor another thing when his apparently long tongue effortlessly parts the lips he *has* kissed.

It doesn't take long. He can't have lived in the woods forever; at some point he must have learnt how to give a girl head, because he's good at it. Quick little laps with just the tip of his tongue and then slow circles and then back again until I'm sure I can feel my heart pounding in my clit. Buzz-saws of sensation thrill from the core of my cunt to the tips of my toes, and they get louder every time I see his great work-roughened hands on my smooth townie thighs.

God, he makes me feel smooth, I think, crazily, and then I come and come in great jerking heaving spasms, groaning and hissing like a porn star, wishing that I knew his name so I could give him the personal praise he deserves.

Woodsman, I think. Thank God for you, Woodsman.

He never says anything, so I'm sure he must be mute. The first few times I don't say anything to him, either, so he can be forgiven and I can assume. But the fourth time, as he's getting up to leave, I say to him: 'Don't you want anything in return?'

It's a stupid thing to say, but then it's a stupid thing we're doing. He comes in every morning, licks my pussy like some sort of pussy expert, and then gets up and leaves. It's sort of like wham, bam, thank you ma'am, only without the wham bam. And the thank you. What has he got to thank me for? I never do anything except lie there and get tongue-fucked into oblivion.

Of course, it varies. Sometimes he plays with my tits while mouthing and licking my pussy. He'll pluck and rub my ever erect nipples until I'm half mental, or else he'll cup my breasts with both hands, test them out, check them for consistency.

Occasionally he'll slide two thick fingers into me and twist until I go incoherent, or run them up my slit then follow the path they've made with his tongue. Sometimes I'll feel just the edge of his teeth, and then he'll suck my clit into his mouth as though to soothe the pain he didn't actually create.

There's never any pain. He's never rough with me. As I said, he never even wants anything in return, like sudden rough butt sex. Even when I ask, stupidly, he doesn't reply. He just looks back from the doorway and half smiles. I think. It's hard to tell, beneath all that hair.

I'm dying for his cock. Who would have thought it? All any man needed to do to make me hungry for cock was give me five or six fuck-tastic orgasms with his mouth. Though it's not really that much of a surprise – usually it's the other way around. Too much cock, not enough head. Or there is, just not any head aimed in my direction.

But, God, I want his cock. I've never even seen the fucking thing! He probably doesn't even have one.

Only he does, because I've seen it making a tent out of his thick muddy green trousers. So clearly this whole bizarre scenario excites him, and he's capable of being excited, it's just that he's fucked up inside, possibly, and can't have me polluting his sacred phallus with my whore's pussy. Or something.

But I bet his sacred phallus is amazing. Smooth and long and thick, like his fingers, with a gleaming slippery head that feels the way they always do, like running your tongue over the almost not-there soft skin of the insides of your mouth. That soft hardness all at the same time yielding to and resisting the pressure of my mouth – oh God, oh God. I want to give him what he gives me. Not even Patrick Connelly gave me what he gives me, and he had a degree in biology.

But I don't reach for him, or really say anything to him, or do anything at all but lie there and think of England. An England in which people constantly have hot, hot sex.

It's truly like it isn't allowed. This is some sort of mad game in which the rules are: he can touch you and make you come, but you're not allowed to do anything to him. They're not even unspoken rules, exactly, because I feel as though he's said them. It's that clear.

So when I put my hand into his curly black hair as he feasts on me for the eight thousandth time and he doesn't push it away, it feels like a minor triumph. I've won the battleground of your hair, I think, and am more excited by the feel of it – not at all greasy, as I sort of expect, but soft and thick and fine – than I am by what he's doing between my legs.

However, I think I am then sent some sort of message. It's not that he stops me, or even seems irritated by my touching of him, but he does stop the oral assault. He kneels up, just keeping two fingers inside me, and I think I moan or twitter or urge my hips up at him because he then smiles this odd smile. It's not cruel, exactly, but it is hard. Hard, and ... triumphant, I want to say. His eyes gleam in a way that makes me not want to give him the satisfaction, but I *do*, because I can't help myself.

He fucks me hard with those fingers, twisting and rolling them in my slick greedy cunt, and I'm shocked by the intensity of the feeling it provokes. I spread my legs wider, and urge him to go faster with my jerking hips, and only half hate myself, because it's not like he's lording it over me exactly. I have no idea what he actually is doing, but, good Christ, it's hot.

By the end I'm panting and my eyes are closed and I'm thinking, I've never come like this before but I'm absolutely going to. Still, it surprises me when my pussy contracts around his fingers and strange brutal pleasure gathers itself in me and then crashes back out again. So much so that I blurt out: 'Oh, God, I'm aching for your cock!'

I can almost feel him grabbing me, and fucking me, and the image is so good that once isn't enough, and I put my hand between my legs. I'm so wet that my fingers glide and my thighs are slick, and I'm so turned on that I don't care what he thinks. Nor do I care when he puts his fingers into my mouth and I can taste myself on them; I lick and suck and pull on them until all of me is gone and I can only taste him. I show him how well I could suck his cock, and then just the thought of it sends me off again. My clit pulses against my fingers and my pussy grasps hungrily at nothing as I shiver and moan around the not-a-cock in my mouth.

And then I collapse in a soggy, wicked heap.

When he gets up to leave, this time he's trembling.

It's all disturbing my life. I mean, that's not a shock, or anything, but still. The disturbance is there and I should definitely do something about it. Like going to my hermit's hole every single weekend instead of just once a month, so that I can unravel the mystery of my Woodsman.

I don't even know his name. His name is so unknown to me that I've started capitalising Woodsman. Of course it's probably not an appropriate name – he's probably more of a Criminal, or a Caravan Man, or a Gypsy – but it sticks anyway, and he's just going to have to live with it.

I wonder if he knows my name. I wonder so many things about him that I go insane and write him notes that I can't give him, and walk out in the middle of the night to see if I can see his caravan, and write little plot outlines for his plot-less life. He has no life; he is no one. He is a cipher, a nothing, a symbol.

Just a symbol of my own unfulfilled lusts.

Of course then I start to really worry that I'm going crazy. I consider telling Francie about him so that she can tell me how likely it is that he's real. I think up stupid plans to help prove my own sanity, like taking a secret picture of him while he sleeps.

Only he never sleeps, so I suppose that idea is right out. Or at least he never sleeps around me.

Though I'm sure he must sleep somewhere.

Which is probably how I end up investigating this whole sleeping business. All these questions in my head make me. One Friday night, after my drive down here, they make me go down to where his caravan might be and search out his dark secrets.

Of course, I have no idea if he'll be there or not. But the hour-long car journey filled my head with non-sensible thoughts, and few of them were about what would happen if he catches me. They were only concerned with him and his lack of reality.

So I creep through the woods as dusk sets in, following the ominous smell of something burning, and feel like Little Red Riding Hood. Halfway through the tilting and more-gnarled-than-they-had-seemed-before trees, I curse myself for not bringing a basket of goodies.

How do you keep off the wolf with nothing to bargain with?

Or maybe I do have a chip to bargain with, and it's something far dirtier than I'm thinking of. He's going to ask me for my maidenhood by the light of the first full moon. He's going to drink my virgin's blood at the winter solstice. He's going to sacrifice me to Fenrir, the wolf god.

And all of these thoughts keep me walking, terrifyingly, rather than stopping me. Not even the thought of my actual lack of virginity can stop me creeping towards the smell of smoke and burning flesh by the light of the rising moon.

I'm on the verge of being sure that I am lost when I get to a clearing in the woods. To what is, in fact, a caravan. His caravan, looking so squat and hunched that it could almost be the sort of thing that's in all my bloody Other obsessed thoughts. The gnarled cottage in the heart of the forest, with the dark stranger waiting inside.

There is a little fire trailing smoke before this tiny home, and over the fire there is a crude grill with a haunch of something cooking on it. Less on the nose things hang about the place, like a T-shirt or two on a half-heartedly strung washing line. A line of his tattered boots by the steps that lead to the cracked open door. Lettering on the caravan, almost washed away: *Ace.*

But I am still all darkness on the inside. That bloodied darkness that lies in the hearts of all women. Or, at least, all women like me. Grimm fairy-tale addled, subtext searching, always waiting for the dark Other to come and –

I doubt any of this is helping my need to claw back to reality.

I walk up to his door and almost chicken out at the last second, but then, after a long moment of him not springing out at me, I regain my courage. I put my hand to the barely there door handle. It's one of those spring-loaded snapping sorts of things, somewhat rusted over and reluctant to move.

Luckily, the door is open anyway. All I have to do is ease it all the way and mind the creaking and groaning of the hinges.

And then I take one step up. And another until I am inside.

Inside, it doesn't smell like cooking meat, or must, or anything else I expect. It's as dark as it had seemed from the outside, however, and I can barely see my way. The door closes to that three-quarter mark again, too, so that the darkness is made even thicker.

I try to refrain from putting my hands out in front of me, but end up doing it anyway.

And yet, when it comes to me that there are things to touch, somehow I don't want to do it. I can see a little sink, and on either side there are shelves filled with all sorts of things that my eyes can't make out. My hands don't want to make them out either, and, instead, they flutter over the impressions of things made in the black. A jar of this, a tin can of that. A sudden burst of the blue glinting colour on something made of glass.

Tiny slivers of light spread through the chinks in possible-curtains and reveal swirling patterns of dust and tender shapes in the gloom, but little else. There are just the impressions of things: the humps of a couple of worn chairs surrounding a table; the soft spread of an old shirt over something. And at the end of the short and narrow passage through his home, a bunk in which he obviously sleeps.

Obviously, because he is sleeping in it.

I jump a little suddenly to see him there. I think I jump more because I wasn't aware when I first came in that he was in here. That I didn't even feel or sense his presence in some way knocks at me, and forces me to be startled. Despite the fact that I've never been the sort of person to know when someone's creeping up on me.

I manage to recapture my breath and stop clutching at myself, and then I look on him just lying there, stretched out as much as the narrow confines will allow, lost in sleep. Though the fact that he is lost and oblivious doesn't make him look any less intimidating. The dark hair on his face seems to bleed into the shadows, and the heavy roundness of his shoulders intrudes on the small space.

I think he is naked beneath that rough-looking blanket. His chest is certainly naked. I can see all the rough coarse hair spread over his pale skin, an image that thrills me if only because I've never been privy to it before. He has never shown me himself unclothed, and this little glimpse is like prying into his secret diary.

At last, I know something more about him!

The new knowledge bolsters my probably insane confidence, and I inch towards his supine form. I know I shouldn't. I know he's probably about to leap up and devour me. But what can I say? I want him to.

I want to touch him. I want to so much that I get as close to him as I did to all of his glass jars and tin cans – fingers ghosting oh-so-close – but then his eyes open and all of my nerve dissolves.

I think part of my stomach dissolves with it. Something definitely drops. I think about running immediately, but his pale, pale eyes catch me and hold me in place. They glint and gleam and tell me *gotcha*, while I try to think of what on earth possessed me.

He's real, all right. He's as real as I am, my strange, rough Woodsman.

I think I expect him to say something then. At the very least I'm sure he will accuse me of something, grow angry, grasp my wrist. But instead he only lays his eyes on me, and remains unmoving and quiet.

It's too much just the same. I run.

I almost go back to the city thinking about his eyes pressing into me. God knows what they were pressing me to do, but I don't think I want anything to do with it.

Only they can't have been really pressing me to do something as he never seems to expect me to do anything at all. He just does things to me instead. I should be glad. I shouldn't be frightened.

Though it's entirely possible that I should change my mind on the latter when I wake up in the morning and my wrists are strapped to the bedpost.

Even worse, my first thoughts are not about my own personal safety. I struggle a little, and test the leather belt that's tangled around my wrists, but no urgency wells up in me. I know what I'm being punished for.

And, of course, I also know that if I pull hard, I could get free quite easily.

Though I don't let this thought spoil the punishment of me, the wicked girl who invaded his space. I trespassed in the dark stranger's lair and need to be taught a lesson.

Good girls get head. Bad girls get strapped to the bed.

Oh, how I wish he'd speak and tell me something like that! Instead, he just fills the doorway, glimmers beneath the dark hair on his face, and waits, and waits. I can't imagine what he's waiting for, but then that's part of his allure. I can't imagine anything about him. Nothing he does makes any sense – unless it's all rewritten into a terrible fairy-tale in which I've done the one thing I promised the beast I wouldn't.

I promised I'd never trespass and never try to touch him, and I've broken all of one and half of the other. Now I have to pay the price: to live with him forever, as his love slave. Forever getting my pussy licked and my body caressed until he gives in one day and fucks and fucks and fucks me.

I don't think I could write a better fairy-tale if I lived to be a thousand.

'Please,' I say, and squirm against my bonds. 'Please.'

Begging him is like paring myself down to the quick, but there's no real pain in doing so.

I'm not sure why. It could be something to do with the fact that he never speaks, and never shows anything but that glinting edge of lust in his eyes, and all of this cuts the tether from around the neck of my imagination. My imagination is free to see him in any way it sees fit.

He could be anything, or anyone, or filled with any thoughts at all, and I want to guess all of them and make him give in to me.

'Please,' I say, and then try out all the other things that might possibly persuade him. Is he the kind of man who gets off on the helpless victim? He must be, he must be.

'Please don't hurt me. Don't touch my soft, wet little pussy. Don't, don't!'

But his expression doesn't change to see me beg like that. The glint in his eyes doesn't sharpen to anything stronger, and he doesn't come any closer. I have to make him come closer.

I twist restlessly on the bed, kicking up the duvet and making my breasts jiggle. I spread my legs, letting it look involuntary, but completely aware of the view he must get. I'm one step away from resisting now, and into doing something more ... grasping.

His gaze flicks to the ripe wet split that I reveal to him and, when said gaze crawls back up my body, it's definitely heavier with lust. He takes a slow step towards me and his hand passes over the hilly duvet.

Oh so *very* close to my leg.

So I take another step away from resistant.

'What do you want to do?' I ask. 'Do you want to touch me?'

My voice sounds silvery and seductive, even to my ears.

'All I wanted was to touch you.'

He glimmers at that. He gleams. Oh, I've got him now. Another step is needed.

'Touch my pussy – see how wet I am for you? Make me wetter, make me hotter, I'll do anything you want.'

Another step.

'Don't you want me to suck your cock? Don't you want me to bite you, and fuck you, and rub my juicy cunt all over your body? Oh, I want that. Set me free and I'll do it.'

I feel as though there are magic words I have to say. There's a riddle I have to solve. If I get it exactly right, he will grant me the pleasure I so crave. He'll give me not only his mouth on my pussy, but his cock, his body, himself.

I arch up on the bed, the tips of my tits standing out proud and swollen, my sex spread, and demand what I want from him.

'Kiss me,' I say, and somehow I know it will be the right thing before the words are even out of my mouth.

His eyes flash over to hungry, and something that could be a smile shifts beneath all that hair.

Then he spreads his body over mine and covers my mouth with his.

He kisses my lips as hungrily as he did my pussy, pushing me until my jaw aches and urging his tongue against mine. I am crushed and devoured and triumphant all at the same time, and my feelings jumble up together and mix with the slight pain of the leather cutting into my pulling wrists. I am overloaded by it all.

I think it's the overload that makes me wrench my head to one side and fuck my hips up at his body.

'Just do me,' I tell him. 'Just take me. Just turn me inside out.'

And then I shove at him again, and this time when he lifts a little I manage to get my legs completely open and around him. Once I'm there in this most-longed-for position, I squeeze my thighs tight against him. I bite into his flesh with them.

And then I watch through heavily hooded eyes as his lips part in an obvious moan. It's soundless, but it's no less a moan for it. So I moan back at him, and rub my nipples against the rough hair on his chest, and urge my molten pussy over whatever it's pressing into.

I'm sure I briefly feel the long slide of his cock through my creamy slit, but then he gets himself up on poled arms, and my legs lose my grip on him, and it's gone. My clit jerks and aches at the loss, but he is in command.

Even if he isn't in command.

He's obviously trying to resist himself in some way, but I'm sure I know how to crack that riddle now that he's here and over me. There are so many things that I can reach with the parts of me that are free, and I take full advantage.

I run my tongue over the fur at his jaw, and then down, down, as far as I can reach. I nuzzle my face against his and manage to get to his ear lobe, which I capture between my lips and suck on. His cock deserves to know what it's missing after all.

It has the intended effect too. His breathing grows harsh, and he insinuates the side of his face against my searching, probing tongue. I feel his cock bob and pat my belly, still somewhat wet from the glide between my pussy lips.

'Give in,' I purr, and rub myself against him. 'Don't you want to feel this slick pussy around your cock?'

I pull on the straps, almost at the point where I'm just going to break out. There may well be many parts that I can reach tied up, but there's nothing like free hands and the ability to roam around with your mouth to really make a man fuck you.

Even if the riddle would then label me a cheater and disqualify me. If I break free, I lose him forever and have to wander for a thousand years in the desert. Being tied like this is part of the deal; I have to persuade him with just the wiles he gives me.

And I'm not sure if that's a better fairy-tale than the one I guessed at before, or an achingly worse one. I try to think of what persuaded him to lie down on top of me, but the logic of this thing seems fuzzy and unapproachable.

'Come all over me,' I say. 'Spurt your come on my tits and let me lick it off your still jerking cock. Fuck my tight slippery pussy until I moan and clench around your big stiff rod.'

All the dirtiest stuff I can think of spills out of me, and some of it definitely has an effect. Occasionally he'll shiver, and sigh, and flick his tongue over my lips or my throat. I tell him to blindfold and gag me, and keep me as his slave, and fuck my ass and my mouth and my pussy until I am sticky and slick with his come. I tell him that I'll stroke my clit for him, and fuck myself with whatever comes to hand, and ride his face until I cream.

But none of those suggestions push him any further.

I try to be practical and tell him about the condoms in the drawer next to the bed, and say that we can take it slow or fast and that we don't have to, if he really doesn't feel like it. I try sweet and innocent, and ask him to deflower me. My virgin quim aches for him, and I have all these feelings warming my insides, and won't he please have mercy?

But he has no mercy. He gets me to the point where I wouldn't even mind if he'd just go down on me again. Anything will do. How could I have been bothered that oral sex was all he seemed to want to do?

I'm not bothered now. All I'm concerned by is the tender swollen place between my legs, my tingling tight nipples and the hovering edge of orgasm always too far away. Sometimes I'm sure that just his hot breath brushing over the slopes of my breasts is about to be enough, but it never is.

Nothing is enough, and I choke it out into the side of his throat.

'Please,' I say. 'Please make love to me.'

I had no idea he'd be corny enough to take that as the answer to the riddle. But I suppose even dark hairy strangers need love too.

When he kisses me again, and presses his body down on mine, I liquidise. However, before I can get my legs around him again and really cross my ankles and never let him go, he leaves me. I almost crack and cry out to feel nothing but air painting over my body, before I realise what he's doing.

I'm glad I mentioned the condoms now.

And, oh then, then, he stretches out on top of me again, and in the same motion smoothes his cock into my hungry, aching pussy. I jerk at the sensation and my body warms all over; even better is the simmering relief of his fingers working between us to press down on my swollen clit.

I pant out his name – the only one I know – as I burst into a huge climax, and he gives me that glimmering look, near enough to smiling for me a second time. He does it again once he's wrung me out on my back; he turns me over and fucks me with my ass in the air until I gasp that name and see him over my shoulder, darkly watching me.

Each time I say it he seems more satisfied, as though I am drilling the word into him and that is who he will forever be: my Woodsman. In return he writes the name he knows is mine across my bare chest with one trailing tender finger, and that becomes forever me.

We make love until it gets dark, and the moon shines in through the partly opened curtains. After, my body still hums from the things we have done, but it's a relaxing sort of feeling. It's a relief to just lie here and doze and breathe him in, and think over everything that I've done that previously didn't seem like me.

I suppose it might not have been him either.

I wonder as I lie there why he tied me up at all. But then I suppose, if he hadn't, I wouldn't have dared break the spell and talk to him the way I did, and beg him, and ask him to beg me. I would have run away as I did when he caught me in the caravan, and then where would we be?

Somewhere far away from here, and not so magical.

Charlotte Stein has contributed stories to the Black Lace collections *Lust at First Bite* and *Seduction*. Her first single-author collection, *The Things That Make Me Give In*, is published in October 2009.

Glamour

Carrie Williams

Marta thinks Jacob must be someone very important indeed to be staying – living, one might say, given the length of time he's been here – in this largest and most prestigious of suites at the Pimlico Grand, with its splendid Thames views. Marta's never seen Jacob, but sometimes she thinks she almost knows him. Every day she's in here, bringing back his freshly laundered clothes and hanging them in his wardrobe, changing his bed linen. Hoovering and polishing and tidying. Sometimes she goes so far as to imagine she's his wife, getting everything shipshape for his return. Only she's not there at the end of the day when he gets home. By then she's long gone, back to Elephant & Castle where, from her high-rise bedsit, she watches the planes float down over the city, loaded with busy people whose lives are so much more interesting than hers, flying in from impossibly exotic places to which she has never been, and will in all likelihood never go.

Jacob has been here since Marta got the job of chambermaid, which came about when her cousin, a housekeeper at a sister hotel, put in a good word for her. Not that there's any shortage of hotel jobs in London – quite the contrary. But Marta had no experience, no references. She was fresh out of college in Poland, with a classical music degree she was at a loss as to how to make a living from. Violinists are ten a penny over there. So here she is, cleaning rooms for a living, albeit rather wonderful rooms complete with marble bathrooms and monsoon showers, and planning, on her days off – which are rare – to busk in the Underground.

Marta hangs Jacob's shirts carefully, almost lovingly. There's a smell particular to them – not just the posh lavender-based washing liquid they use in the housekeeping department, but something manly, as if the machine couldn't quite eradicate the scent of Jacob in them. She sniffs them, not for the first time feeling slightly ashamed of this guilty pleasure. Then she tells herself that it doesn't matter: no one's to know that she does this, or about the frisson it gives her.

Marta really doesn't know Jacob at all, beyond his smell, and his dirty coffee cups, and the used cut-throat razor in the bathroom, still limed with luscious-smelling foam from his morning shave. Beyond the little notes he leaves, some mornings, and that she's come to look forward to, perfunctory as they are:

Dear Maid,
Please could you leave a few extra English Breakfast teabags this morning?
Thanks, JT.

Good Morning,
Please don't remove the Sunday papers as I haven't finished with them yet.
Many thanks, JT.

Hello Again,
I'm terribly sorry but I broke the cafetière in a fit of clumsiness. Please could you replace it and add the cost to my bill?
Yours, Jacob T.

She doesn't know what 'T' stands for, nor whether Jacob is British or something else – German, perhaps. There's an Englishness, though, to his idiom – or so it seems to her. Something almost aristocratic even. Whoever he is, he oozes money and status.

She keeps the notes, takes them home to her bedsit, where she puts them on her dressing table. Often she sits in front of the mirror, staring at herself for a long time, trying to figure out how she got so lonely. She was popular in Poland, had successive boyfriends at university, lots of friends. But they're still there and she's here, in this ridiculously huge city she can't work out how to find her way around. All those people, and none of them know her. There's her cousin, of course, but she's married with small kids and has no time for socialising. Sometimes Marta goes over to her flat for lunch, but then, when she comes home to her empty bedsit, she only feels worse. She's made desultory attempts to make friends with the other girls who work at the hotel, but they don't seem interested – they just want to get in and out, do their job, get their money and get back to their families. Short of going to bars and accosting strangers, she's at a loss for ideas.

She knows she's attractive, beautiful even, and she has a notion that, if Jacob could only meet her, he'd fall in love with her. But he's never there when she arrives at his suite and, no matter how much time she spends there, inventing things to do, he's never back by the time she leaves. He's obviously a busy man.

It didn't take her long to work out that, since each room or suite in this hotel was serviced by one girl alone, there was no one to say how long it should take to get through her daily round. If anyone were to ask, she'd simply exaggerate the amount of work she had to do in Jacob's suite. After all, it was the biggest one in the hotel. She had ready in her head a list of the things she could plausibly have to do each day: scrub the bath out; mop and polish the bathroom floor; shampoo the carpet. In reality, she rarely if ever has to do any of those things. Jacob is very low maintenance, as hotel guests go.

In reality, Marta indulges herself. Marta likes pretending to be rich, that she's the kind of woman utterly at ease with staying in a hotel like this, in a suite like this. She kicks off her shoes, mixes herself a drink from the minibar – she restocks it herself, so the odd discrepancy won't be noticed – and sits in the big comfy leather armchair in front of the flat-screen TV, watching movies on one of the satellite channels. She loves escapist stuff and romantic weepies. If there's nothing on she fancies, she might flick through *Vogue*, *Tatler* or one of the other magazines provided in the room. These, like the films, take her to another world.

Lately, though, she's got a bit more daring, a bit cheekier. One day, having given the bathroom a quick once-over, she starts eyeing up the big deep bathtub and, before she can talk herself out of it, she has run it to the brim and jumped in, soaking in luxuriant sandalwood and geranium-scented bubbles. As she lies there, she starts thinking about Jacob and before she knows it her hand has crept down between her legs and she's rubbing at the hard little bead of her clit. There's been no sex since she's been in London – more than six weeks now – and, while she'd thought she wasn't missing it, she's suddenly hot for it, in violent need of relief. And so, looping her legs over the side of the bath, she plunges the fingers of her free hand inside herself, continues the pressure on her clit and brings herself to a juddering, gasping, aquatic climax. Water slops over the edges onto the floor but she can soak it up before she goes.

Afterwards, she dozes on Jacob's bed, in Jacob's bathrobe, and revels in the odour of this man she thinks she is falling in love with without ever having met. There's something rich and woody to him, almost chocolatey. With a hint of cinnamon, maybe. Something very male and comforting. She can't pinpoint it, but it takes her very far back, into the depths of her childhood.

From that day on, she has a routine – bath and then bed. She wanks every day, sometimes graduating from the bath or the bed to the armchair, or the thick fluffy rug in front of the hearth, for a second orgasm. She wears items of Jacob's clothes that she finds discarded in the laundry basket – shirts, boxers, all positively reeking of him in a way that gets her so horny she could die. She might seek out his shaving brush, teasing her lips and clit with its fine badger hair, then turning it around and pushing its ridged barrel handle inside herself and thrusting ever harder, stimulated by the dangerous thought that the ivory-hued ceramic might crack or shatter, pricking her. She doesn't want to be damaged as such. She's not into self-harm. She just wants to feel again. She wants to be away from the numbness of her bedsit, in an intense world of sensation and emotion and pleasure and … yes, even pain would be preferable to this feeling of being as good as dead.

After a while, she even forgets about Jacob as an actual person. He is such a distant figure, always absent despite his worn clothes, his creamy razor blade, the odd sandy-coloured hair in the shower, that she comes to believe that he doesn't really exist. This is her room, her domain, at least for the space of a morning or afternoon. Here she is queen, and no one can tell her otherwise. One day she brings her new vibrator with her and, after a couple of weeks, thinking it's pointless to carry it about in her handbag, even starts keeping it in the suite, tucked away in the back of the safe that Jacob never seems to use.

The months go by and, if she isn't happy, Marta isn't

miserable either. She thinks often of Poland, however, and thinks she will probably go back there if things don't get any better. She'll give it just one more month or two. Or maybe she'll give it to the end of the year. She doesn't have to decide right away. Things are OK as they are. She can bear it.

Summer arrives and Marta takes to lying out on Jacob's balcony, beside the Thames that glitters like diamonds in the sunlight. The planes, on their flight path over the river, don't taunt her so much any more, offering visions of what she doesn't have. She brings her bikini and takes in some rays, letting the warmth of the sun infuse her long pale limbs. Or, if she forgets it, she sunbathes naked. She wanks with her eyes closed against the glaring light.

It has to happen, though. She's on borrowed time. And just as she thinks that she's over Jacob, that she's accepted that he's a fantasy figure and no more, one afternoon when she's lying on his bed, legs akimbo, naked save a used pair of his boxers, the door swipe pings and she hears a voice. She's up on the bed like a defensive cat, back arched, panicking, and then she grabs her clothes from the end of the bed and makes a dash for the walk-in wardrobe.

Inside, struggling to control the breath coming in ragged spurts out of her, she squirrels herself away right at the back, behind Jacob's laundered shirts and suits, and listens. Her heart's thudding so hard she's sure he must hear it. But, no, he's talking to someone else. For a minute she thinks he must be on the phone, but then she catches another voice, a female voice, and she has a horrible feeling that she's going to be trapped in here for a while. She shifts a little from side to side, trying to get more comfortable, pulling on her clothes, inch by careful inch. Jacob's scent reassures her with its familiarity.

A moan startles her more than it should. She stiffens, feeling traitorous to be listening in but knowing she can't very well come out now without finding herself in serious trouble – the kind of trouble that leads to one losing one's job. So she keeps breathing, softly, steadily, trying not to hear and yet unable to close her ears to what's happening out there, to this insight into Jacob and who he really is.

The moan was a man's, and it's reiterated several times over, coming longer and louder each time, until it seems it's going to knit together in one continuous chain. The woman, she is sure of it, is going down on him. Involuntarily, Marta reaches down, parts the panels of her housekeeping dress and slips one hand into her knickers to find herself wet. She bites down on the other hand to stop herself from echoing Jacob's moans, at the same time sliding her legs apart in the wardrobe, using the walls of the partition in which she finds herself to support herself as she gains greater purchase, weaving her fingers through her pubic fronds and into her moist hole, strumming at her clit with her thumb. Leaning her head back, she closes her eyes, and it seems to her that her climax is mounting parallel to Jacob's, as if they really are making love together. She comes, mouth open in a rictus.

Jacob doesn't. She keeps listening, but either he has climaxed extraordinarily quietly, or something else is going on out there. Perhaps the woman wasn't giving him a blow job. If not, then what are they doing together?

She hopes, whatever is happening, that it will soon be done with. Sated, she wants to go now, to be home in her barren but familiar bedsit. Suddenly this place in which she spends so much time is strange to her, a little threatening. She knows she's for it if she gets caught, and she wants out. But the silence from outside the wardrobe continues for several long minutes. Finally she can't take it any more and inches forwards to peep through the slit of the wardrobe door.

Jacob is on his back, the woman astride him. She's wearing a black underbust corset that leaves her magnificent breasts bare, and below it a black thong and suspenders, and patent black leather stiletto ankle boots. A blaze of raven hair unfurls down over her shoulders to the small of her back. She looks Asian – perhaps Japanese. Beside her, Marta feels utterly ordinary.

She holds her breath, waiting for the woman to mount Jacob. His cock is hard, questing for the woman swaying over him – and who can blame him? Marta is surprised that, though she does feel envious, her primary reaction is one of excitement: she would love to be the woman, so beautiful, so brazen, so charged with eroticism. But more than that – and this is what stuns her most – she would like to be involved. Part of her just wants to step out of the wardrobe and show herself, in the hope that they will let her into their strange and magical realm.

It's a world Marta fears will always remain out of reach. Though she's had her fair share of lovers in Poland, there was never really very much beyond conventional sex on the agenda. She lacked imagination, perhaps. She didn't think of what there might be out there, for those who dared to reach out. Certainly, she'd never even considered a threesome, or being with a woman. But here she is, admiring this gorgeous, almost otherworldly, creature, wishing to be close to her, with her, *inside* her.

And Jacob? What of this man of whom she has constructed so many fantasies? Does he live up to them? In truth, she can see very little of him where he lies, in an attitude of surrender, beneath the woman – just one side of his head, the line of a jawbone, visible past the curve of the woman's arm, ivory-pale as a statue. And then the lower half of him protruding through the arch of her thighs – his muscly upper legs, his straining cock, his pointed toes, showing him to be tense in anticipation.

She's waiting for the woman to impale herself on Jacob when a gasp escapes from her own throat. Leaning forwards, the woman has swung back her hand and then brought it back against Jacob's face with a loud smack. Jacob's head turns to one side, but there's no sound from him or any outward display of surprise, and Marta could swear to the fact that he was expecting to be hit. Given that he didn't try to avoid it, could it be that he even invited it?

The woman speaks then, her voice rich as molten chocolate, with a hint of an accent that Marta can't place.

'Oh, you've been such a naughty boy,' she says. 'Such a *very* naughty boy.' And with that she slaps Jacob's head to one side again, where he's turned it to look back up at her.

Marta swallows almost painfully, her throat constricted by fear and longing mixed together in some unholy brew. She's afraid – afraid for Jacob, afraid for herself if she gives herself away. But she's incredibly turned on too. More turned on than she's ever been. And what turns her on the most is the suspicion that Jacob, despite his submissive attitude, has asked for all this.

The woman continues to look down at Jacob, imperiously, haughtily. From where she's hiding, Marta can tell that the woman in the basque has no affection for him, and with that knowledge comes another – that Jacob must be paying her to be here, paying her to humiliate him. But where Marta might have thought she'd feel revulsion, her heart opens to him, and she feels an almost maternal rush of pity and protectiveness. She wants, she thinks, to hold him to her after the woman has gone, to make it all better.

The woman leans over and reaches for something on the floor beside the bed. Marta, burning with curiosity, throat painfully dry, eases the wardrobe door open a few millimetres to get a better view. As the woman leans over, rummages around in something – a bag, Marta presumes – she gets a better view of Jacob. Still prone, he's turned his head to one side, in her direction. His eyes are firmly closed but nobody could mistake him for a sleeper – his face is taut in expectation, rigid. Marta stares, appalled, as the woman climbs back over him and cracks the whip she now has in her hand. Jacob's whole body spasms in response to the sound, but his face is hidden again, and Marta can't see his expression or find out whether he has opened his eyes.

'... so very, *very* naughty,' she hears the woman mutter, and she starts as the whip slices down through the air and lashes Jacob across one shoulder. His body jerks too, puppetlike, and he cries out. Marta's heart races. She wants so badly to go to him, but she fears the consequences. The woman is frightening. Who knows what she might do? Far from wanting to be involved, Marta now just wants out. But she's trapped.

She's about to retreat to the back of the wardrobe again, cover her ears until it's all done, when the woman commands Jacob to turn over. He obeys, and Marta can't take her eyes from his honed body, tanned and athletic, so powerful-looking and yet so utterly submissive. Buttocks presented to the woman, he hangs his head like a dog. The whip whistles as it comes down on him and, even from where she hides across the room, Marta can see the red mark it leaves across his shoulders and then, a few moments later, across one arse cheek. She bites her hand. With the other she clutches one breast, hard, so that she no longer knows where pleasure ends and pain begins, or if the two aren't actually the same thing.

The whip comes down, over and over, and Marta carries on watching, her hands digging into her own flesh, wondering when – *if* – Jacob will call out for it to stop. From what she's read about this sort of thing, which is very little, she is aware that there's supposed to be some sort of code word, a safe word they call it, telling the dom that it's time to call a halt. Because 'no' doesn't always mean 'no', not in the world of sex and desire. And, though Marta has long known that in theory, it's only now that she truly begins to understand it, within her flesh itself. Her brain is crying out 'no', wants her to rush to Jacob's aid, but her body is assenting fully. In fact, she's amazed how quickly she's coming round to it all. She's empathising so much, she can almost feel the hot sting of the whip as it flicks against Jacob's skin.

But then the woman stops, leans over the edge of the bed again, her hair trailing down past her face like dark water. Jacob remains utterly motionless, head still pendulous. It's as if everything has gone from him, all will, all fire. It's almost, thinks Marta, a form of massively intensive relaxation, a release of inner tension. She wonders what his life is like, that he needs it so badly.

'Hands behind you,' barks the mistress, and Jacob stretches his arms behind him, across his lower back. The woman clasps them, forcing them together in the middle of his back then strapping them into leather manacles. Reaching round and under him, she does something that invokes a little mew of pain from him – Marta supposes she is pinching or twisting his nipples. She does the same to her own, her mouth open in an O of near-ecstasy. She's worried she might come now, even without touching her clit or pussy.

And then the woman takes something from beside her on the bed, unfurls it slowly, like a snake that has lain dormant – a snake that one must awaken gently, lest it lose its temper and strike. Marta watches, fascinated, as she begins to bind Jacob with the rope. There's a softness now, almost a tenderness to her movements, as she loops it around his legs and then his ankles. It's an art form, Marta realises; this woman is an artist who has learnt her skills and techniques as any other artist must.

Then it's over: the woman stands, surveys her work for a moment, and then she slips on her long black overcoat, covering her dom's attire, and exits the room, without a backward glance for Jacob on the bed. Marta is stunned. She can't, seriously, be leaving him that way? She shakes her head. No, she's coming back. She'll go down to the bar for a drink, put it on Jacob's tab, and then she'll return and release him. Or she'll nip off to service another client and come back just as Jacob is beginning to squirm and sweat, wondering how he'll get out of it.

The silence is overwhelming. Outside the window, the light is falling, and the room slowly darkens, by imperceptible degrees. A long time passes, hours maybe. Marta feels the need to pee but holds it for so long that the urge disappears. Sometimes she closes her eyes, holds her breath so that she can hear his, like the susurration of the sea, proving that he's still there, within the hollowed-out figure on the bed, the almost-man that he has become.

Then, suddenly, she can't stand it. No longer can she stand to stay here and watch him hang motionless on the bed, like a cur. Not that that isn't what he's asked for, paid for even. But it's over now. He's got his money's worth, surely? What joy can he gain here alone, in the darkness, unable to move, waiting for his mistress's mercy?

She pushes the door open, causing the hinge to whine a little. Jacob cocks his head to one side, opens his eyes. She moves towards him, confident that he can see little of her in the darkness, although the curtains haven't been drawn so the room is infused with some of London's neon and nighttime sparkle. His head follows her movement across the room. She's holding her breath, walking on tiptoe; she doesn't know why.

He doesn't speak, doesn't ask her who she is. For a moment she stands over him, and then she reaches out one hand and runs her fingers lightly over his shoulder, tracing the red weal that bisects it. When he winces, she removes it, brings it down and lets it rest for a moment in the pool of his lower back. She feels the sweat that lightly films his skin, hears how shallow his breathing is, still. She moves her hands to his wrists and unclasps the manacles that bind them. They remain limp in the small of his back. Shifting down to his legs, she picks at the knots with her nails, working them loose until the ropes fall away and he is unshackled.

He still doesn't move, and she stands now, looking down at him, admiring the patterns that the rope has left imprinted on the flesh of his legs. She wants to say something, but words won't come. She doesn't know what there is to say. Instead, almost involuntarily, she brings her hands to her lips and then lowers them to the pink candy stripes across his shoulders. He moans then, low and long, as if inviting into himself the kiss that he can't possibly have seen.

Like the dom, she leaves quickly, without looking back. There's no sane explanation for her presence here, for her having been holed up in his wardrobe, and she can only hope that he didn't see enough of her face for him to be able to recognise her should they ever meet again.

Outside, the world seems surreal: all these purposive people, rushing backwards and forwards, while inside that suite time seems to have stood still, have frozen in the air like breath on an icy morning. Walking to the Tube station, she wonders what the mistress will think when she returns to find him unbound. What will he tell her? Or won't he let her enter? He's no need for her now he's free. *Unless* ... Unless he wants to start all over again. She feels a stab of jealousy at his desire, or need, for this woman.

Back home she can't sleep for thinking about him. She still, despite having seen him naked, doesn't know what he really looks like. If she saw him in the street, he would be just another anonymous face in the sea of strangers that London is to her. And yet they have lived through something intense together. A connection has been formed and, in this city with its millions of isolated souls, that counts for a lot.

Marta thinks she can't very well not go to work but, when she does, she suggests to her supervisor that she might work in another part of the hotel, get a change of scene by swapping with one of her colleagues. When the supervisor pulls a face, says that it's important to have continuity, to be familiar with one's patch, Marta feels a rush of blood to the head – fear overlaid with excitement. She'd have been disappointed, she realises, if her boss had accepted her proposal but, by putting responsibility in the hands of someone else, she can accept more readily what she had to do, can explain it away as fate. Whatever happens, it was meant to be.

Still, when she knocks twice, three times, at the suite door, checking that no one is in, her heart is pounding, and her hands shake as she swipes the room card even now she knows he's not there. She walks in, eyes the bed nervously. As always, it's unmade. Beside it, on the glass side table, is the usual used coffee cup.

She walks over to the bed, looks down at it, as if she might see the imprint of his body on the base sheet. She lays her hand on it and his scent rises from it like smoke. Inhaling it deeply, she feels fainter still and has to sit down.

For a while, Marta remains utterly still. Then she thinks she needs to get on, clean and tidy the room and get out of there as soon as possible. She mustn't be there when he returns, just in case he did get a proper look at her face. She dips back out into the corridor, takes some cleaning materials from the trolley and returns.

It's now that she sees the note, on the bureau, beside the telephone. It's in the same place as usual, on top of the pristine white pad, with the silver pen placed neatly next to it.

Was it you? it says, simply.

There's no signature, no name, today. She panics, gives the room a cursory clean and tidy, and hurries out. In the corridor, she has to sit down, she's so afraid and so excited. He must have guessed; he isn't stupid. Yet the note, short and uninformative as it was, seems to hold no threat. He's not going to complain to the management that a maid was hiding out in his wardrobe, spying on him – and not out of embarrassment because of what he was doing, or not primarily. No, she feels there's almost an invitation in there somewhere. But an invitation to what? She knows that she'll only find out by accepting.

Walking to the Tube through the rain, Marta stops at a news kiosk for a paper and a magazine full of celebrity gossip. She hates herself for reading such trash, but she knows there's a sleepless night ahead, a night of questions whirring around in her brain, and sometimes, when she's like that, only trivia of the most banal kind can distract her.

Deciding to take the bus instead, she locates the stop she needs and then opens her magazine, holding it in one hand beneath her unfolded umbrella. The rain patters against the umbrella, lulling her. Maybe, she thinks, she will sleep after all. She didn't get much last night, after releasing Jacob and returning home. She's exhausted.

She half turns where she stands to check the number of the approaching bus, and her attention is caught by a flickering bank of screens in the window of an upmarket electronics store by the bus stop. There's a man in there, on screen after screen after screen, talking, gesticulating, looking very serious and concerned. She can't hear the words but she feels he is saying something of great import. She looks back at her trash mag, then lifts her eyes, almost unwillingly, to the screens. There's something familiar about him, something that she can't put her finger on. She can't place his face, yet she feels that she knows it, in some dark part of herself. Her eyes roam down to his body, swathed in a well-cut, well-fitting suit. It's the same unusual shade of sage green that she remarked upon when she brought back Jacob's laundry yesterday, freshly washed and pressed. She swallows. The newscast ends, and the name flashes up, reminding viewers of the speaker's identity should they have missed it at the start. Jacob Tavernier, Minister of Intergovernmental Affairs.

Her eyes travel along the row, every screen relaying his image and his name back at her. In her mind's eye, inscribed over the top of them, is the note, his words. He was summoning her, she's sure of it now. He knows she's the one who can save him.

Running back to the hotel, Marta thinks that maybe an interesting life is not that big a deal after all, that one can be surrounded by people, always on the move, rolling in money, doing important, worthwhile things, and still be the loneliest person in the world.

Slipping through the back door to avoid her colleagues on reception and evade their inevitable questions, she slips through the kitchens and takes the service lift up to the eighth floor and the penthouse suite. She has her room swipe in her bag, along with her uniform, but she knocks instead. She's not sure if he'll be back yet, if the broadcast was live or used video footage.

The door opens, so slowly it feels as if her heart will burst. His face appears. He's still wearing his overcoat, collar turned up against the rain. His hair, damp, is a burnt-sugar colour. He smiles but makes a gesture of helplessness with his hands.

'I was hoping you'd come,' he says, yet it comes out like an apology.

She steps inside. Suddenly she feels powerful, charged with a sort of demonic energy that takes her beyond herself, into that realm that she thought was forever closed to her.

'Onto the bed,' she says, pointing to the other end of the room, surprised by her tone.

He bows his head, turns, but as he walks away from her he throws her a glance over his shoulder, and she sees a fire in his eyes that belies his cowed demeanour.

She strides after him and, as he climbs onto the bed, still in his outdoor clothes, she reaches into her bag, tosses him her housemaid's coat. 'Strip,' she barks, 'and then put this on. Now.'

She watches as he fumbles with the buttons of his coat, his fingers trembling. 'Faster,' she commands. 'What are you waiting for?'

He does as she bids, pulling off his coat without undoing the rest of the buttons, causing some to pop off and spin across the room like coins. Frantically he pulls off his sage suit beneath, then his matching tie and his sharp, starched white shirt. She remains still, watchful, amazed by her own sense of calm and mastery of the situation. She knows what she wants, where she's going. It feels as if she's been sleepwalking through her life until this point, and now she's suddenly awake. She feels utterly lucid and clear-sighted and in control.

'What now?' he says. His voice is pleading, pathetic. She feels like smacking him. She points at the uniform. 'That,' she says. 'Or have you forgotten?'

'Sorry, Mistress.'

'I should think so too.'

At that, all at once, laughter starts to ripple up inside her. Her mask, she realises, is slipping.

She suppresses the laughter, but he must see it in her eyes, for as soon as he has slipped the costume that she has provided over his head, his own eyes lose their desperate subservience and he reaches up to her, places a hand on her face, on her cheek. She tries to pull away but she's falling, falling, letting him pull her down onto the bed.

'Stop it,' she giggles. 'I'm the one in charge, here.'

He laughs too, and this time, as he unbuttons the housecoat to reveal his nutmeg-brown torso with its fine blond tendrils and his cock rising proudly from its nest of darker, thicker hair, his hands are sure, unfaltering.

He doesn't need saving, she knows that now. He just needed to learn how to laugh. He wasn't the only one.

She's laughing as she rolls him over, spanks him playfully on his arse cheeks as she pulls off her clothes with her free hand and tosses them to the floor beside the bed. Sitting astride his back, her pussy oozing onto on his warm and pliant flesh, she smacks him again.

'C'mon, horsey,' she titters.

He rises on all fours beneath her, and she lies forwards against his back, breasts crushed against him, reaching one arm around him. As her hand grazes his downy bollocks, his cock insinuates its way into her moist palm.

As she moves her hand up and down Jacob's taut shaft, Marta closes her eyes and lets herself dissolve into the moment, lets herself be all body, nothing but this woman here in this room with this man. For the first time in her life, Marta thinks nothing.

Carrie Williams is the author of the Black Lace novels *The Blue Guide, Chilli Heat* and *The Apprentice*. She has also contributed to numerous Black Lace short story collections as both Candy Wong and Carrie Williams.

Under the Big Top

Mae Nixon

My mother always drummed into me that I should never be tempted to hitch-hike. But when I went away to university and Mike, my boyfriend, went to another two hundred miles away I began to grow a little disobedient. Well, we were young and horny and neither of us could bear the thought of going a whole week without getting laid.

So every Friday night my friend Kelly would give me a lift to a lorry drivers' café on the A1 and, before long, I'd be on my way. And, in spite of my mother's fears, none of them ever tried it on. To tell the truth, they were mostly just glad of someone to talk to and, if that someone happened to be a young woman with long blonde hair and curves in all the right places, the journey would be just a bit more interesting.

I even got to know some of the regular drivers and, after a while, I grew used to their routines. I knew that, if I arrived by a certain time, I was guaranteed to get a lift with one or other of my driving buddies and would arrive in Durham just before the Union bar closed.

It was so easy and familiar that I more or less forgot that I'd ever worried about hitch-hiking. One Friday night I arrived at the transport café a little later than usual and all my regular pals were long gone. The place seemed deserted.

It was a cold, drizzly night but I didn't even have enough cash on me for a cup of coffee so I didn't dare shelter in the warm. I waited for ages, growing progressively colder, wetter and more depressed. I was just about to give up and ring a friend to come and get me when a huge American-style truck turned into the car park.

I watched it pull into a parking space. The driver had his hood up and his outline seemed huge and sinister, but I couldn't afford to be choosy. When he jumped down onto the Tarmac I came out of the shadows.

'Jesus,' he said, 'you look like a half-drowned angel.'

'I need a lift to Durham,' I tried to say, only I was so cold that my words came out strangled and shivery.

'You look to me as though you need something nice and warm inside you.'

'I ... er ...'

He laughed. 'Don't worry, I don't mean this ...' He handled the front of his jeans. 'I meant some nice hot soup or something. Let's go inside?'

'I haven't got any money.'

'I kind of gathered that or you wouldn't be hanging around in a freezing cold car park waiting for a lift from a stranger. Didn't your mother ever tell you hitch-hiking was dangerous?'

'All the time.'

'And she was right. Look, come on inside and I'll buy you a hot meal then give you your lift to Durham.'

'You're going to Durham?'

'That's right. I'm planning on going all the way.'

Inside it was wonderfully warm and smelt of frying bacon. I followed the driver over to a table and we sat down. He unbuttoned his duffel coat, pushed down the hood and I saw his face for the first time. He had long, dark, curly hair pulled back in a ponytail and a pencil-thin moustache. His face was all angles: chiselled cheekbones; square jaw; a long thin nose. He reminded me of a pirate, and the red bandana tied around his neck seemed to emphasise the impression.

He smiled at me and I noticed that one of his front teeth was capped with gold and his eyes were a vivid blue. He coughed theatrically and I realised I'd been staring at him.

'Sorry,' I said. I fiddled with my coat buttons to hide my embarrassment.

He shrugged his shoulders. 'I bet your mother told you it was rude to stare as well, didn't she?'

I nodded.

'So . . . do you like what you see?' He held his arms wide and looked down at his body, inviting me to look.

'Oh, yes,' I said without thinking.

He laughed out loud.

'No . . . no . . . you misunderstand. It's just that –' I stopped mid-sentence, suddenly aware how stupid I must sound. 'You see, when you got out of the van with your hood up I couldn't help being reminded of the Grim Reaper. I'm just relieved that you look so normal.'

'Normal? Never been called that before.' He stuck out his hand. 'Johnny Lee. Pleased to meet you.'

We shook hands and he held on to mine slightly longer than was necessary. I could feel hard calluses on his palm. He slid his hand slowly out of mine, trailing his fingers across my skin. A tiny shivery tingle slid along my spine. 'I'm Jo.'

I ate a bacon sandwich while Johnny tucked into a huge fry-up. After several cups of tea I finally felt warm again. We didn't speak much while we ate but, for some reason, I couldn't take my eyes off him.

He wore a denim shirt that was a little grimy around the neck and a leather waistcoat over it. When he reached out for a bottle of ketchup I saw a thick rope of old scar tissue running up the inside of his forearm.

I don't know what came over me but I couldn't resist the urge to reach out and stroke it. I caught his wrist in my hand and ran my thumb along the puckered ridge of his scar. Johnny used his other hand to unbutton his sleeve and he pushed the shirt up to his elbow revealing more of the scar. I ran my trembling fingers along it, reading it like Braille. When he finally pulled his arm away I realised I'd been holding my breath.

'How did you get that?' I asked.

He shrugged. 'Accident at work.'

Outside Johnny helped me into the lorry. The cab was huge and luxurious. The seats were broad and comfortable like armchairs and, behind us, was a curtained-off partition where the driver could sleep. Johnny took off his coat and tossed it into the back. He started the engine and it roared into life.

'It's a powerful beast, isn't it? I don't think I've ever been in such a huge one before.'

He laughed. 'You're right, it is. I didn't realise you made a habit of accepting lifts off strange lorry drivers. What's the story? Fetish for the smell of oil? Got a thing about big hairy men with dirt under their fingernails?'

'Nothing so exciting. Boyfriend at Durham University and I can't afford the train fare.'

'So that's what makes you risk your life. Hormones.' He steered the lorry out onto the road. 'We like to think we're civilised and rational but underneath the surface we're all still animals, driven by instinct and ruled by nature.' He turned to look at me and, in the half-light of the cab, all I could see clearly were his gold tooth and his glistening eyes. I looked away. Prickly fingers of excitement trailed over my scalp.

'What's in the back? Anything exciting?'

'Actually, this is a beast wagon – adapted to carry animal cages.

I'm with a circus,' he added, when he saw the confused look on my face.

'A circus? So you're a lion tamer?'

'Among other things. In a circus you have to do a bit of everything. I do some knife-throwing and blade-glomming – that's sword-swallowing to you. And I'm not bad on the trapeze. But it's the animals I really love.'

'Is that how you got the scars on your arm?'

He nodded. 'And the rest. Hazard of the job. Haven't we all got them?'

'Oh, I don't know. My dad manages a medical equipment factory. The only industrial injury he's likely to get is a paper cut.'

'Wouldn't suit me. Can't bear to be tied down.' Johnny smiled at me and his gold tooth came into view. I found myself wondering what it would feel like to run the tip of my tongue around the contour of the gleaming metal, feeling the heat of his breath on my face and slowly, slowly opening my mouth until we were kissing. He smiled again and the expression in his eyes was so direct that I could have sworn he knew what I was thinking.

In the confined space of the cab, I quickly grew warm and began to relax. I took off my coat and curled my legs under me. Sitting so close to Johnny I could smell the leather of his waistcoat and an underlying, powerful aroma that I couldn't quite place. There was the normal musky smell of man but, underneath it, something strange and feral that was as intoxicating as it was unusual.

We talked most of the way to Durham. He was funny and interesting and surprisingly well-educated for someone who'd never really been to school. He told me about his life in the circus. His dad had been a knife-thrower and his mother had done a horseback act. He'd spent his childhood travelling with them from town to town, always on the move all over Europe. He spoke half a dozen languages tolerably well and had never lived in one place for more than a month. He'd always been drawn to the animals, had got himself apprenticed to the lion tamer and had slowly learned his craft. Now he had a part-share in the circus.

And all the while he spoke I couldn't take my eyes off him. I wouldn't have called him handsome, but his angular face made him seem masculine and powerful – like the heads of those American presidents carved into the side of Mount Rushmore. I tried not to make it obvious I was staring but the way his eyes followed me I was pretty sure he knew that I was checking out his hard, wiry body as well.

His thighs were long and lean and, when he moved his foot on the accelerator, I could see the muscles tense. I tried hard not to look at the point where his long legs met but somehow I couldn't help myself. The crotch beneath his tight jeans seemed to bulge with a promise that made me blush so hard I prayed he wouldn't notice. But, when I looked up, I realised he was still staring at me.

'Where's the rest of the circus? Don't you usually travel together?' I asked to cover the silence that was growing increasingly embarrassing.

'Usually we do, yes. But one of my lionesses was sick and I didn't want to move her. I stayed on a couple of days.'

'So there are lions in the back?'

'Tigers too and a leopardess. I did tell you it was a beast wagon.'

'You did. Somehow it just didn't occur to me that we were riding along with wild animals in the back.' I shivered.

'Not just in the back.' He winked.

'Is this where you tell me you've got the heart of a lion and a python in your trousers?'

'Actually, it's probably more of an adder than a python, but no one ever complains.' He looked at me for so long that I began to worry we might crash into the vehicle ahead, but I couldn't look away.

'Didn't you tell me earlier it was rude to stare?' I asked finally. 'Get your eyes back on the road before we end up a traffic statistic.'

'Yes, ma'am.' He drove in silence for a while.

We'd left the A1 and were on the outskirts of Durham. I watched Johnny's long fingers cradling the wheel. My eyes strayed to the long scar running up the underside of his right arm and disappearing beneath his sleeve. I remembered the feel of it, shiny and hard, under my greedy fingertips and allowed myself to imagine exploring it with my lips then slowly taking off his clothes and exploring the rest of him in the same way.

I was acutely aware of my body beneath my clothes. My nipples were erect and sensitive and heat and tension pulled at the base of my belly. I looked away.

'How would you feel about a little diversion? I promise I'll drive you all the way to your boyfriend's doorstep afterwards.'

The mention of Mike should have made me feel guilty but it just served to make my secret fantasies all the more sweet. 'What have you got in mind?' I asked, trying to sound casual.

'The girls need their freedom. They get restless and agitated when they're locked up for too long. Come with me to the pitch and let me unload them. Then, I promise, I'll deliver you straight to your undeserving boyfriend.'

'What makes you think he's undeserving? He might be wonderful, for all you know.'

Johnny slowly shook his head. 'No, he's an idiot. Otherwise he'd have gone to Cambridge with you. Woman like you ... I wouldn't let you out of my sight. Any Tom, Dick or Harry could try it on with you.' He turned to look at me and a flash of someone's headlights lit up his face, making his eyes and his gold tooth gleam.

'Don't you mean Tom, Dick or Johnny? Though, personally, I think I prefer the sound of Dick ...'

He laughed. Though I hadn't actually said yes, I wasn't surprised when Johnny turned off the main road before we entered the city.

'What's it like, living on the road? Don't you miss a real home and proper plumbing?'

Johnny shook his head. 'Only a josser would say that – jossers are what circus people call the rest of you. I've got a real home; it just isn't made out of bricks and mortar. It's even got a flush toilet.' He smiled again and I wished he'd stop it. Every time he did it blood rushed to my head. And not just to my head, if I was honest.

I kept my eyes on the road after that, trying as hard as I could to keep my mind off my obvious attraction to Johnny. I thought about Mike, waiting for me at the university with a week's worth of pent-up lust and longing zipped up behind his flies, but I couldn't fool myself that my pounding heart and damp knickers had anything to do with him.

'Here we are,' said Johnny, 'up ahead in that field.'

I peered into the distance and could just make out a collection of winking lights. As we drew closer, I saw the shapes of caravans and trailers and, finally, the outline of the huge, white big top. It seemed to be lit from within and gleamed with a golden glow like a giant paper lantern. The knot of excitement that had settled beneath my ribs gripped a little tighter and was matched by a similar tight heat lower down.

'It looks ... it looks like fairyland.'

'That's the magic of the circus. The roar of the greasepaint, the smell of the crowd.'

As we approached the field someone came and opened the gate for us. Johnny expertly steered behind the big top to where a raggedy line of trucks and trailers were parked. He turned off the engine and we were surrounded by a group of people, dark shapes in the dim light. He opened his door and jumped down then came round to my side to help me down. When I reached the bottom of the truck's steps I found myself face to chest with the tallest man I had ever seen. He stuck out a hand and I shook it, trying not to grimace as his strong grip crushed my knuckles.

'This is Jim,' said Johnny. 'He's the second-tallest man in Europe.'

'Only the second? Who's the first?' Before either of them could answer I felt someone tugging at my jacket and looked down to see a man who barely reached my waist.

'Well it certainly isn't me,' he said, standing on tiptoes.

'And this is Franco,' Johnny introduced him. 'Let's get the girls unloaded and settled, everyone.' The group swung into action. Johnny unhooked the rear doors of the lorry. I heard the roar of distressed big cats and my stomach flipped from a mixture of fear and excitement. A ramp was dragged up to the back of the truck and chains attached to the cages; everyone lined up to haul them down the ramp.

In the first cage were two huge lionesses with their hackles up. They growled as their temporary home slid down the ramp. As their cage reached the ground a gust of breeze blew in my direction and the smell of the big cats reached me; my nipples instantly hardened as I recognised the feral, exhilarating aroma I had smelt on Johnny.

I watched him supervising the unloading. When he hauled on the chain or jumped down from the truck he moved with the effortless, powerful ease of man used to hard, physical work. But there was also something supple and graceful about him, like a dancer or an acrobat – which perhaps he was, for all I knew.

The crew unloaded three more cages from the truck, a huge lion, two magnificent striped tigers and a leopardess who clearly hadn't enjoyed her incarceration. She hissed and lashed out as they manhandled her cage. I watched Johnny kneel down beside her, his face so close to the bars that she could easily have ripped it off, and softly talk to her.

Even though I couldn't hear what he was saying, the soft murmur of his words and the look of total concentration and tenderness on his face sent jolts and shivers around my body like bonfire night fireworks. When the leopardess finally lay down and rolled over onto her back like a kitten eager to have her belly rubbed I felt like joining her.

One by one the cages were loaded onto wheeled trolleys and taken to a large tent beside the big top. As the last of them was rolled away Johnny came over to me. He was slightly out of breath from the effort of unloading the animals. I could see his chest heaving and sweat gleamed on his throat. I had to fight the urge to lean forwards and lick his salty skin clean. Maybe he knew what I was thinking because he smiled and held out his hand. I took it wordlessly and allowed him to lead me into the tent.

I looked around at the interior of the tent. It was obviously used for storage. Beside the cages there were sacks of animal food and bales of straw together with various pieces of circus equipment. There was a brightly painted clown car, a rack of colourful costumes and a huge cannon with flames painted around the rim of its barrel. 'What's that for?' I asked.

'Franco does a human cannonball act.' The way Johnny said it he could just as easily have been saying that Franco was a bus conductor or an accountant.

'Isn't that dangerous?'

Johnny laughed. 'It's obvious you're a josser. Of course it's dangerous. The circus is about danger. It's all part of the appeal.' He pulled on my hand and led me over to the side of the tent where a circular flat piece of equipment stood upright. He reached out and set the circle spinning. I realised it was the turntable knife-throwers use to spin their glamorous female assistants, then toss their knives just right so that they'd land between her spread limbs.

Johnny bent down and picked up a knife. He put his face right up against mine. I could feel his hot breath on my skin. His strong, animal scent was overpowering and thrilling. 'The public want danger. They like the idea that you might miss.' My legs were still trembling like mad, but I didn't think fear was the cause.

I couldn't help myself. I laid one hand against his ponytail, to pull his head closer. My mouth sought his lips but he pulled away. 'Fancy having a go?' he asked.

Without waiting for an answer he put the knife into his belt and caught my wrist. He brought it up to the turntable and fastened it with a leather strap and buckle built into the board. When I realised what he had in mind I began to panic. 'You're not serious? I might get hurt.'

He pushed me back against the board then trapped me there using the weight of his body. I couldn't move. My heart was pounding. But, in spite of my fear, my nipples were rigid. Johnny reached up and stroked my hair. Sparks of pleasure prickled all over my scalp.

He put his mouth right beside my ear and began to whisper, using exactly the same tone he had when calming the agitated leopardess. 'It'll be all right. I'll take care of you. You're perfectly safe. I'd never hurt you. All you've got to do is trust me. OK?'

I brought up my free hand and pulled his head down for a

kiss and this time he didn't resist. His mouth was hot and silky, but the contact was all too brief. He broke the kiss and stepped away, waiting for my response. I looked him straight in the eye and flattened my back against the turntable. I spread my legs, positioning my feet over the ankle cuffs, then brought up my free hand and laid my wrist inside the strap.

No more words were necessary. Johnny bent down to fasten the ankle cuffs. His head was about level with my crotch and I was acutely aware of the heat and growing moisture there.

When he stood up to fit the wrist cuff his breathing was as loud and ragged as my own and I noticed that his hands were trembling. He bent down to pick up the rest of the knives then got up and walked away. He turned round to face me and I instantly saw that he had an erection. 'Your cock's hard,' I said.

'Yes, it is. But, don't worry, it doesn't affect my aim.' He tossed a knife straight at me and it landed between my legs with a thud before I'd even had the chance to be really afraid. He threw another and it landed in the space between my arm and leg. I could feel the impact as its tip pierced the board. Adrenaline wooshed around my body like a drug rush. He tossed one knife after another, each one of them landing in the board with a loud thump that cranked my excitement up a notch.

The final knife landed high up between my spread legs, almost as high as the hem of my miniskirt. Johnny was out of breath but clearly pleased with himself, because he couldn't stop smiling. He walked over to me and collected the knives, pulling them out of the wooden board and sliding them into his belt. 'How was it for you, darling?' he asked as he extracted the final knife from between my legs.

'It was . . . incredible. Exhilarating and terrifying at the same time, if you know what I mean?' I looked at him and he nodded. 'In a funny way I felt . . . oh, I don't know . . . twice as alive. Does that make sense?'

'Oh, yes.' He ran the tip of one finger along my lower lip and my skin instantly rose into goose pimples. 'Dicing with death can do that to a person.' Johnny set the board spinning and I was instantly disorientated. The interior of the tent seemed to flash by in a series of images that my brain didn't have time to make sense of. I couldn't work out whether I was up or down and I could hear the wind gushing by as the turntable spun. My senses went into overdrive. I could smell the animals, dung, straw and, underneath it all, the earthy scent of the ground beneath us.

The board seemed to jolt for a second, making a momentary judder and I realised that Johnny had thrown a knife. I had no idea where it had landed, but I knew I wasn't hurt. The turntable juddered again and again as knife after knife hit the board. I heard the sound of splintering wood beside my head. The lion roared.

Slowly the spinning slowed and I was able to make sense of the images hurtling past me. I could see the animal cages, then the white roof of the tent billowing above us, then the higgledy-piggledy collection of circus equipment, and finally Johnny standing still and looking at me. When the board came to rest I was horizontal, my head and feet on the same level. I was breathless and trembling. 'Come and turn me the right way up,' I gasped.

'Whatever you say.' Johnny ambled over as if there was no urgency at all. He rotated the turntable until my feet were pointing at the sky.

'That's not the right way up.'

'No? Are you sure?' He carefully folded down my skirt, revealing the top of my tights. He stroked my Lycra-covered pussy with the flat of his hand, cupping it for a moment in his hot palm. I sighed. He pulled the nearest knife out of the board and used it to cut away the crotch of my tights.

'Oh, this isn't fair.' I struggled against the cuffs. All the blood had rushed to my head and I knew I had straw in my hair.

He carefully peeled the wet crotch of my knickers away from my body and used the knife to slit it. I felt the cold air against my naked pussy and, a moment later, his hot mouth. I gasped. I felt his tongue trace the length of my slit, quickly followed by his strong fingers pulling my lips apart.

I could feel his rough moustache prickling my sensitive skin and his hot slithering tongue exploring my wet cleft. It was wonderful. It was agony. I longed to be able to touch him. I struggled and the board shook noisily

He stopped licking. 'No point fighting. Those cuffs are strong . . .' He sucked my clit into his mouth and flicked his tongue over the sensitive tip. My body jolted and the back of my head cracked against the turntable. He lifted his head again. 'Relax, Jo. Relax –' he kissed my pussy '– and surrender.' Again he used the same tone as when he was calming the big cats and I tingled all over.

'OK,' I gasped between moans, 'I get the message. You're in charge. I give in.' I felt his thumbs massaging either side of my clit as the point of his tongue flicked across the tip.

'I always knew you would . . .' he murmured. Johnny lavished my pussy with loving attention. He pressed his muscular tongue up against my opening and pushed it inside. He sucked each labia in turn into his mouth and gently nibbled on it. He slowly licked the entire length of my slit from top to bottom, not forgetting to explore the wrinkled, secret rosebud of my arsehole.

My body was rigid from a mixture of excitement and the strain of my unnatural position. My nipples were erect and painful, rubbing up against the fabric of my bra every time I breathed. My crotch was on fire. Johnny's talented tongue was bringing me to a pitch. He covered my taut clit with his hot mouth and circled it hard with his tongue. He slid two fingers inside me, bending them upwards and pushing them hard against my G-spot. My whole body stiffened, banging my head against the turntable again.

'See, I told you it was dangerous,' Johnny mumbled between licks.

'You should never talk with your mouth full.' I struggled hard, trying to free my hands. 'This is torture. I can barely move and my head's full of snot. Let me down so that we can do it properly.' I kicked my heels uselessly against the wood. 'I want to suck your cock,' I begged.

'Shhh, shh . . .' he soothed. He circled his fingers inside me and went back to licking me. His fingers worked my G-spot, each gentle thrust setting off a little peak of excitement that I knew would lead, inevitably, to orgasm. He was working directly on my clit now, alternately flicking it with his tongue, then covering it with his mouth and sucking on it hard. I moaned.

Between Johnny's legs I could see the leopardess prowling backwards and forwards in her cage. She scented the air, extending her neck and sniffing. Her tail snaked.

My crotch tingled with delicious sensations. Each lap of his tongue unleashed another wave of pleasure. Excitement was building to a pitch. Sweat ran across my face and into my eyes. My hair dragged in the dirt.

He sucked on my clit again and I knew I was going to come. I thrashed against the cuffs, my body banging against the turntable. I dug my heels in, trying to move my hips and create some rhythm. Johnny wrapped his free hand around my hips and licked my clit with the flat of his tensed tongue in long, slow strokes. 'Yes . . . yes . . . yes . . .' I said with a gasp. 'Like that. Don't stop.'

My clit danced in his mouth. Heat and tension throbbed in

my belly. My nipples ached. I was groaning loudly now, responding to each divine pulse and tingle Johnny's talented mouth created. He rubbed his whole lower face against my crotch and his scratchy moustache created a wave of eye-watering pleasure.

I clenched my fists and stiffened my whole body, digging my heels into the turntable, forcing my pussy against Johnny. I was coming. Tears welled in my eyes. I trembled and shook, my body banging noisily against the wood. I moaned and sobbed. The sound seemed to fill the air like a feral cry of satisfaction and desire.

He rode it out with me, holding onto my hips as I thrashed, his mouth always moving, sucking the orgasm out of me. As I let out a final cry of pleasure and excitement I realised that the leopardess, too, was roaring, standing on her hind legs and shaking the bars of her cage as she roared into the night.

When Johnny finally unfastened my ankles and turned me upright I was dizzy and out of breath. He released my hands and I instantly dropped to my knees and began fumbling with his belt with trembling fingers. He unbuttoned his own flies and pushed his jeans and underwear down to his knees. His hard cock stood out in front of him, thick and purple-tipped and glistening. 'You told me it was only an adder,' I murmured, before taking it into my mouth and sliding all the way down until my nose was pressed into his fragrant pubes.

'I lied,' he whispered, his voice husky and soft. His cock was silky and hot. I could feel the blood pumping under the skin and taste the salty pre-come. I stroked his balls, already hard and tight inside their wrinkled sac. I slid a finger behind them and ran it around the wrinkled rim of his arsehole and was rewarded with a shudder and a long, low moan.

I bobbed my head, moving my mouth up and down his slippery cock. I could hear my own snuffling breathing mingling with the restless voice of the leopardess. Johnny's thighs had begun to tremble and his hips pumped, establishing a rhythm that I quickly followed. He reached down and stroked my hair. 'That's absolutely divine, Jo. But if you don't stop it I'm going to come pretty soon and – wonderful though that sounds – I think I'd rather come in your cunt.'

The crudity of the word made my nipples prickle and my crotch ache. I released his cock with a soft plopping sound and struggled to get to my feet. He half pushed, half led me over to some piled-up straw bales beside the animal cages. I quickly threw off my jacket then pulled off my jumper. Johnny dragged down my bra straps, uncovering my breasts.

'God, you're beautiful ...' He pushed me down on my back on one of the bales. He knelt down and spread my legs then shuffled forwards until he was positioned between them. I watched as he took his erection in his hand and pressed it up against my wet pussy. With a single slow thrust of his hips he pressed it home.

I couldn't help trembling as it slid inside me, awakening and enlivening every one of my nerve endings and making them tingle. It was hot and hard as a piece of newly forged iron and it filled me like only cock can. He held onto me and began to fuck me. I wrapped my legs around him and brought my hips up to meet him. Johnny bent his head and sucked a hard nipple into his mouth. He began to nibble and I moaned.

Beside us, the cats were restless and noisy. They moved about in their cages, growling and pacing. One of the tigers stuck its snout through the bars and roared and I felt its fiery breath on my skin.

Johnny released my nipple. Strands of his hair had escaped his ponytail and fallen in his face. His eyes were slitted, making him look mysterious and sensual. His gold tooth gleamed. His hips pumped, fucking me hard.

He pulled open his shirt. His nipples were pierced with heavy gold rings and the right side of his torso was criss-crossed by thick raised scars. My entire body quivered and shook. Blood pounded in my ears. My heart thumped.

I was on the edge again, riding that divine moment of pleasure that can tip over at any second into orgasm. I rocked my hips, meeting his thrusts. Johnny was sweating and gasping. Light gleamed on his closed eyelids. Damp hair clung to his forehead.

He gave a particularly hard, deep thrust and I started to moan. Another couple of thrusts and I'd be there. I gripped him hard with my legs and ground my crotch against his scratchy pubes.

Johnny began to grunt. His hips pistoned and his fingers dug into my skin as he held on to me. His strokes grew shorter and more urgent and I knew he was going to come. His eyes flickered and he groaned between clenched teeth. It was all I needed to push me over the edge.

Pleasure burst inside me like a bomb going off, spreading out from my crotch and rocketing down to the tips of my toes and the roots of my hair. I rocked my hips, rubbing my clit against his hairy crotch. I was trembling all over, feet locked behind him and my back arched. I was practically screaming now as each wave of pleasure overwhelmed me.

Johnny held on to me as we rode it out. His body trembled. His cock pumped out hot sperm inside me and I realised that I could no longer tell where he ended and I began.

The cages rattled and shook, the cats' agitated voices joined our own. Their roars, growls, snarls and howls filled the night air; it was a cacophony of pleasure and wild animal urges that were as old as time.

After I showered and changed my clothes in Johnny's caravan, he drove me to the university where a very horny and slightly drunk Mike was waiting for me. We fucked all night and he never suspected a thing.

I never saw Johnny again and, though I think of him often, to tell you the truth I think I preferred it that way. But, whenever the circus is in town, I remember him and the night when I was as wild and greedy as the leopardess who rattled her cage and roared, hungry for a taste of freedom that was as terrifying as it was exciting.

Mae Nixon is the author of the Black Lace novel *Wing of Madness*, and her short stories have appeared in numerous Black Lace collections. She also writes as Madeline Bastinado for Nexus.

A Stroll Down Adultery Alley

Portia Da Costa

Running footsteps behind me. 'Katie! Wait! Are you going for a walk? May I join you?'

I turn around and think, Thank you, God, what on earth did I do to deserve this? I've been fancying this guy since almost the first instant he moved in with us and here he is chasing me, not the other way around. 'Of course ... why not?' With my best smile on my face, I hope to do the best I can to impress my mother's latest lodger, Doctor Peregrine Nash, noted academic and all-round tasty morsel of hot quirky male pulchritude.

I wait for him to catch up with me, still hardly believing my luck. With my mum on guard duty there's not really been a chance to show the good doctor I've had the voracious hots for him.

The desire to ogle him is intense, but I manage to restrain myself to sneaky glances as we fall into step along the path to the common, Kissley Copse, and what the locals all call Adultery Alley.

I'm pretty nervous too. This man is brilliant. A real brainbox as well as a cutie, an eminent mathematician newly arrived at the local university. I'm not exactly thick, in fact I'm fairly sharp in my own way and I have a damn good job. But I'm not in his league where grey matter is concerned.

'Lovely day, isn't it?' he says.

He's nervous. I can tell. A shy guy, despite his academic eminence. And that *is* sexy. I've always had this thing for tutoring a less-experienced man. It's like a major fantasy of mine. And to tutor a gorgeous bloke like this, who's so used to tutoring other people, will be something of a twist. Of course, I could be imagining things and he's got available women coming out of his ears ... but somehow, my hottie-sex-radar tells me I'm right on the money. And, with any luck, we'll both learn something down the Alley.

'Smashing ... fantastic day for a walk. I like to get out of the house, you know ... I mean, my mum is great, but she watches me like the proverbial hawk. She thinks that, just because I'm not married now, I need to be kept under constant surveillance.'

Why, oh why, am I babbling and telling him all my intimate troubles? If I'm not careful I'll be telling him that I'm dying to get laid next. And also that he's the one I'd like to do the honours.

'Yes, quite,' he says, flashing me another cautious little smile, as if he's not quite sure whether he hasn't stumbled into something he really hadn't bargained for. What if he really does only want a perfectly innocent walk in the fresh air with his landlady's divorced daughter?

We reach the edge of Kissley Copse and I'm still trying to weigh him up. It's a warm evening and he slips off his denim jacket revealing a white T-shirt laundered lovingly by my mum. I must admit that he's not really a classic Adonis. He's short, for one thing. No taller than I am. And he's also ever so, ever so slightly chubby, with a rounded face and a stocky little body. But he has got 'it'. The X factor or whatever. Or, in his case, Pi factor or some other esoteric number. He's sort of dark and swarthy with a slightly hooked nose and the maddest mop of black curls. He looks like a delicious combination of sex animal and innocent naif. I could eat him alive.

We don't say anything, but I catch him sneaking the same sort of glances at me as I'm sneaking at him. Sly, discreetly assessing, but also cautious. I'm convinced he wants me but is calculating the precise theorem of a successful seduction pounce. I wish I could tell him that I'm a dead cert. Disgracefully easy in his case, although not as a rule. Well, at least not since . . .

'What are all those cars doing lined up in the lane?'

We've reached the footpath that runs parallel to the 'alley', our track separated from it by a sparse and scrubby hedge that looks as if it's been deliberately pushed through in places. Which, of course, it has. This is a prime spot for both sexual exhibitionists and doggers, and voyeurs who lurk on this side of the shrubbery watching the performers both in their cars and out of them. How to explain this to the good Doctor though?

'Well . . . um . . . this is a sort of hang-out for people who are having a bit on the side. They come here to . . . er . . . do it in their cars.'

Beautiful brown eyes widen. Brighten. And also darken at the same time as his pupils dilate. His lush mouth curves into a smile that would grace the image of the wickedest-ever sex pixie. And I like that – 'Sex Pixie' – it sums him up perfectly. My mother would go ballistic if she saw the way his eyes glint, and suddenly he licks his lips. She thinks he's a gentleman and above all that sins of the flesh lark. She thinks he's too good for me. But curiously, and conversely, that no man is actually quite good enough for me. Which means that me finding a bloke at the moment is pretty much a lose-lose situation.

She blames me squarely for my divorce and current lack of grandchild-producing potential. And she's right in some ways. It was an error of judgement on my part. But that's by the by. This is not the time to be worrying about what my old mum is thinking and how she perceives I've let her down. 'Everyone round here calls it "Adultery Alley". Because most of the people in the cars are married, but *not* to the people who are in the car with them.' This ought to bug me and make me uneasy, but it just makes me hornier than ever. I'm so screwed up.

'Indeed.' His eyes twinkle again. He's definitely up for something, I hope. 'A sort of "Liaison Lane", I presume.'

Liaison Lane. I like that too. Although it does rather over-dignify the grubbiness of these gropers and cheaters and adulterers. 'If you say so.'

Is he closer now? I never saw him move. But somehow he's in my personal space, smelling sumptuously of a rather expensive cologne. 'And ...' He hesitates and a cheeky grin spreads across his impish features. Being so dark and saturnine, he always seems to need a shave. 'Do you come here often, Katie? Do you like to observe the fornicators in their natural habitat?'

I'm gobsmacked. I never realised he was so full-on. I suspected he had a frisky rampant satyr's heart beating in his mathematician's chest, but I didn't expect the switch from polite respectful lodger to total horn-dog to be quite so sudden. Still, in for a penny, in for a pound. I take a deep breath that unconsciously, or perhaps consciously makes my breasts lift and displays them to their best advantage. I'm wearing a white T-shirt too, and my frontage is one of my most attractive features.

'Yes, I do. Is that a crime?' My chin comes up and it's like there's a clash of two sabres as our eyes meet and hold. I match his grin with one of my own. 'I like to watch. I can't deny that. And this lot are fair game if they shag in a public place.' I gesture vaguely towards the scrappy hedge and the vehicles parked beyond.

'No crime. None at all. I find your honesty refreshing and

healthy. And I must confess to snatching the opportunity to observe a fuck in progress whenever I can too.'

He chuckles. I snigger. We both simmer and gurgle and boil and then nearly collapse, trying not to howl at our own absurdity and alert the shaggers in the nearest cars to our presence just yards away.

Oh, I love his grin. His sparkling eyes. His aura of total naughtiness. He might not be a Greek god, but he makes up for any deficiencies in this newly revealed and scrumptiously open horniness. Whoever would have guessed? I was quite wrong about him. The demure Doctor Peregrine is a rampant, sexy pervert.

'Perhaps we should partake of the show that's on offer then?'

'Way to go ... um, Peregrine?' I've never called him by his first name. At home, because my mum had me in her 40s and is in her seventh decade now, we observe the proprieties and he's 'Doctor Nash' at mealtimes.

'Perry,' he says softly. 'I'd love it if you call me Perry. All my close friends do.'

And, boy, do I want to be a close friend. The closest of close kind of friend. The kind of close friend who gets to touch and fuck that cute chunky little body. The one I got a glimpse of the other day when he came rushing down to the door to collect a courier parcel, draped in a bath towel. There's a lovely little mat of dark hair on the chest that's hidden behind the snowy T-shirt.

'Righto, Perry. I'm game if you are.'

The conspiratorial smile he gives me lets me know we are in agreement.

We pad forwards, sneaking right up against the hedge. Again, more by design than accident, I trip on a root and he catches me by the arm to stop me falling. And it feels like he's just goosed me with five thousand volts; all the current goes straight to my pussy. I cling on to him, more wrong-footed by his touch than by anything else.

And he's strong too, far more powerful than his modest stature and slightly soft build suggest. He's like a rock I could hold on to forever. 'Thanks,' I whisper, reluctantly releasing my limpet-grip. He gives me an odd, sweet, complicit little smile as we edge forwards again and take up our position.

Here among this section of the scrubby bushes, tucked up against a drystone wall, we're higher than Liaison Lane, and we have a perfect view into the light-blue Japanese saloon car below. Where a middle-aged couple are already going at it.

And they're really bold. They've stripped off completely. She's sitting astride him in the back seat, her heavy breasts bouncing as she pounds up and down upon him. I can't see as much of his body as hers, but the tangly mat of dark hair on his chest reminds me of Perry's delightful pelt. Unable to stop myself, I glance to the side instead of at the raunchy goings-on in the car.

Perry's looking at me. As if my reaction, and my response to the illicit shaggers, is far more interesting and arousing to him than they are. He gives me that devil–cherub smile of his again and waggles his dark brows before nodding towards the car.

Oh, God, I barely care what they're doing now. I just want to grab him, roll down into the dip behind us, and climb on board him just the way the bouncing woman in the Honda is astride her bloke. But Perry gives me a strangely commanding look and nods again to the cavorting couple in the car.

The woman is really putting on a show, lifting and grinding and shimmying. The man's holding her hips, but she's in charge, and she's all about her own pleasure, not his. She's tweaking one of her nipples as she jogs up and down, and her other hand is down between her body and his, obviously rubbing at her clitoris in the nest of her pubic hair.

I want to touch myself down there. Oh, hell, I really, really do. And I want to do it with delicious Doctor Perry watching me do it. My mind more or less blanks out the Honda adulterers or whatever they are and presents a picture, in high definition, of me and him in the back of that car. We're both naked, as they are, but to me we're a much more attractive proposition, our physical shortcomings notwithstanding.

If it were us, I'd be looking down into his chocolatey brown eyes as I twist and gallop, getting off on the wicked smile in them just as much as his cock in my pussy. And instead of holding my hips and just using me as some kind of masturbation aid, as the guy in the car is, he'd be touching me in lovely ways as I fuck him.

Talking of touching, as the woman ups her pace to a frantic thrash and the man shouts 'Oh fuck' so loud it echoes out into the copse we're lurking in, I feel a warm sure hand settle on my back, urging me forwards to lean against the wall.

The touch is light, but there's a definite sense of command about it. I comply, spreading my arms out across the uneven surface of the top layer of stones. My breasts press against the hard lumpy blocks and I nearly yelp because they're so tender and sensitised, the nipples like swollen foci of sensation. Perry's fingers slide slowly up and down my back, stroking me gently through the cotton of my T-shirt, in a way that's as reassuring as it is intensely arousing. I shimmy – my appreciation expressing itself automatically – and, before I can bite my lip, a little moan escapes from my mouth.

I'm lost. I'm burning. If a simple, almost-chaste caress through the fabric of my T-shirt can send me soaring, how the hell am I going to be if he *really* touches me?

In the car, the man suddenly seems to take control too.

He says something harsh that I can't quite make out, and his fingers gouge the hips of his paramour. He holds her hard and he holds her still. She's obviously rushing towards her climax, but he wants her to go slow so he can hold out a bit longer, make it last.

My ex was a bit that way. It was all 'do that', 'do this', 'slow down', 'speed up' with him. All about his experience, rather than mine – the selfish git.

But, without knowing why, I know it wouldn't be like that with Perry. With him, it would be all about my pleasure. As I acknowledge that, it's like he's heard my thoughts, and the stroking of my back takes on a different quality. His fingers dip lower, and slide beneath the waistband of my jeans. They just probe and flutter, working in the confined space then, a moment later, he reaches around the front, undoes the button and eases down the zip.

Oh, God. Oh, God. Oh, God.

All that fantasising and now something's really going to happen. My pussy flutters wildly, even though he's nowhere actually near it yet. A gush of lubrication oozes out and anoints my panties. I literally sob I'm so turned on, so full of desire. My eyes close but, as they do, Perry whispers in my ear, 'Watch them, Katie. There's a good girl.'

I moan again, my clit throbbing as if his words had actually touched it.

The woman in the car is still now, her face tense where I can see it from this angle. I bet my face is tense too, but it's the tension of yearning and excitement and a sudden inexplicable adoration of the man who's standing behind me.

I watch as the woman submits to being handled, the man's hands roving over her now like those of a greedy boy grabbing at sweet things in a candy store. He snatches at her nipples and twists them this way and that in a way that looks quite cruel, although somehow I sense his partner really gets off on it. I send up a silent prayer that Perry isn't *too* gentle when he gets to mine. Something that might well happen soon as he's plucking at the hem of my T-shirt now.

The feel of his fingers against my bare skin is like a spiritual communion. I wonder if the woman in the car feels like this? I doubt it, but I could be wrong. Why should Perry and I be the only ones who can go transcendental?

But I love the way his hand sneaks up my back, then slides round to cup my breast through my simple cotton bra. He just holds me, as if weighing the flesh, then lightly squeezes. Then he abandons my tit and I somehow sense that he likes playing below the waist much better. Or at least that's what he's in the mood for right now.

While the woman in the car continues to get manhandled, I get some of that too, but with considerably more finesse. Moving his hands inside my jeans, Perry slides them down my thighs and then pushes them right down to my ankles. Briefly he embraces the rounds of my bottom through my panties, then they follow, sliding right down the whole length of my legs to settle on the denim bunch of my jeans.

I bite my lip. I adjust the position of my arms on the wall so I can cram my fist against my mouth and stop myself groaning out loud at the sheer, raw, weakening vulnerability of being so completely exposed like this. It's a form of shaming, yet at the same time an exaltation. I've never experienced anything quite like it in my life before.

'Let's watch them come,' breathes Perry in my ear as he takes his position against the wall at my side.

I want to moan and sob I'm so excited. And I can barely breathe. My pussy feels swollen with blood and it seems to bloom like a flower. Another thick slithery rush of silky juice pours out of it and starts to slide down the insides of both my thighs. I'm saturated and my intimate flesh screams for contact, while Perry the Perverse quietly ignores it and watches another show.

Or does he? When I sneak another glance to the side, trying not to plead with my eyes, he's looking at me again. He gives me an odd enigmatic little smile and then indicates that I should watch the other show too.

They're bouncing again, going at each other wildly, the woman back in the ascendant, getting her own way. Distracted as I am, I still notice that the man's face looks fiery and red in one particular spot. What's happened? Has she slapped some sense into him to make him toe the line and think of her pleasure?

But as I watch them lurch up and down and slam on and into each other, thinking becomes something that's slightly beyond me. And Perry doesn't need telling or slapping, that's for certain.

I'm staring at the car but, as his hand slithers between my legs, I'm not seeing it. I seem to see the two of us from the outside. Me leaning on the wall with my bottom on show, and him, leaning in, his face intent, his eyes dark as he fondles me.

His fingertips comb their way through my pubic hair and swoop into the swamp of my pussy. He finds my clit unerringly, and starts to run circles round it, brushing it lightly, first to one side, then the other, but not going in for the direct heavy manipulation. Which drives me crazy. Of their own accord my hips too begin to circle and weave; my clit follows his pattern as if magnetised and tries to get more action. Things get worse – or better, depending on how you look at it – when Perry starts to play with my bottom from behind, feathering up and down my anal crease with the fingers of his other hand.

He's working me like some infernal puppeteer, using not strings but the electric zones of my pussy. I moan behind my own fist, my pelvis weaving like that of some kind of exotic dancer. I've never felt like this before. Never known I could be such a wanton lust-crazed trollop. But I'm glad I've found out now, because Perry seems to really, really like it.

He starts murmuring in my ear, using just those words – 'trollop', 'slut', 'horny little raver' – and the words sound doubly, trebly, quadruply arousing in his beautifully enunciated, Oxbridge-educated tones.

As if from a huge distance and through a veil of fuzz, I watch the couple in the car finally climax. It's not a pretty sight. Their faces contort and their movements are jolting and ungainly; the woman's breasts jiggle up and down in a way that's hypnotically ugly. But, who cares? They're getting off, and that's what I want too.

'Please,' I whimper, my hips still following Perry's plaguesome fingers. I don't know whether I want him to fuck me or bring me off manually and I don't much care. I just want an orgasm. Right now or I think I'll die.

'Please what?' he purrs in my ear, his mouth close to my skin. In fact, all of him is close. I can feel his heat. I can smell his really nice cologne all mixed up with a touch of foxy male perspiration that's just as much of a turn-on. 'Please what?' he repeats when I'm too far gone in frustration to be able to form the English words to answer him.

I'm a vortex of frustration and confusion. Part of me wants to whine for pleasure at his hand. Part of me thinks, Who the fuck do you think you are, mister? Just give me what I want. Now. Because I want it. I think the woman in the car turning the tables has inspired me. 'You know what I want, Doctor. Just get me off!'

He laughs, but it's a merry sort of sound, and when I look over my shoulder at him he looks pleased, and excited, and even slightly awed. 'Your wish is my command, Madam Katie.

Nothing would give me more pleasure …' He pauses. 'Well, I know a few things, but first things first.'

He reconfigures his hold on me, adjusting the position of his hands and his digits until they're in exactly the right places to give me pleasure. Then he goes to it, as if it's a science. Maybe it *is* to him? But I don't care. He's just too good!

Swirling, pressing, squeezing and teasing, he assaults my clit, and with his other hand he plays around my entire pussy, stroking and exploring. And as he does this with tender skill, he also kisses me, covering the back of my neck and my shoulder with peppering little pecks, then more elaborate caresses with his lips and tongue.

Pleasure gathers, glowing between my legs like an expanding sphere of heat, like a science-fiction star globe of energy and intensity. I start to wiggle and wriggle again, but he doesn't miss a beat. He just goes on touching me, and basting me with delightful kisses. And it's that which tips me over. The kissing as much as the touching. Despite the raunchy, naughty nature of what we're doing together, it's the fugitive quality of tenderness that turns just sex into the unforgettable.

I almost scream when I come, but at the last millisecond I remember that, if we can hear the couple in the car, they'll be able to hear me if I howl and shout. So, as I nearly faint, I stifle my cries with my fist.

My pussy clenches, my sex ripples, my knees turn to water and I slump against the wall. Perry persists and drives me through the barrier again and again, still kissing, and also whispering much sweeter nothings into my ear this time. I'm not sure what he says, but I've a feeling that, when I regain the use of my brain, I'll be surprised.

The next thing I do perceive clearly, and completely compos mentis, is him and me sitting in the grass by the wall, cuddling.

My pants and jeans are still around my ankles but it doesn't seem to matter.

At least it doesn't at first and then, suddenly, real life kicks in, as opposed to some sort of sexual fantasy state, and I'm thinking, Oh, God, Oh, God, what have I done? And experiencing an overpowering compulsion to cover myself up.

I start dragging at my knickers and jeans and manage to get myself in total twisted muddle with them. To my horror, tears of embarrassment and frustration – the bad kind – spring to my eyes. I can't look at Perry but, before I know what's happening, he's helping me in a gentle, careful manner. Working as a team, we manage to get me decent again.

I still can't look at him. 'God, you must think I'm a nightmarish slut. We barely know each other and not only do I lead you to the most notorious place in Kissley, but I let you get my knickers off me without as much as a murmur of protest.' I fish in my pocket for a tissue, but Perry beats me to it, handing me a white handkerchief perfectly laundered by my mother. That makes me feel even worse. I'm just the worthless, no-good trollop I often fear Mother thinks I am. I know she loves me, but I've also 'let her down'.

'Of course you're not a slut. Far from it.'

I wish I could believe he meant it. 'But you said I was one ... when you were touching me. You said I was all sorts of dirty things.'

He slides his arm around me in an almost fraternal way and gives my shoulders a squeeze. 'But that was just sex talk, Katie. Just fun. A game. Part of the pleasure. For both of us.'

Speaking of his pleasure, I note that the bulge in his jeans is very much at odds with his current mode of brotherly solicitousness. Which makes me feel even more guilty.

'Never mind that,' he says almost casually, as if his own body and its reactions are of no consequence. He takes me by the shoulders, his grip firm yet compassionate and he makes me look into his eyes not at his groin.

'You shouldn't be ashamed of being sexy, Katie. Why would anyone think any less of you because you're a beautiful desirable woman? I don't. I like you and I respect you.' He leans in and kisses me softly on the lips. I nearly swoon it's so sweet, and as longed for as the caresses and the orgasms. 'I'd like us to be friends. Spend time together. Go out, you know?'

I can't speak.

'What's wrong, Katie? What have I said?'

I give myself a little shake, but still he holds me. I like his strength and, amazingly, I feel desire begin to stir all over again. 'Nothing. Nothing wrong at all. It's just me, I'm a bit screwed up at the moment.'

He takes a deep breath, then reaches to brush my hair out of my eyes. 'Tell me about it. What can I do? How can I help?'

I shimmer on the edge of tears again, and it's all mixed up with that new rush of lust.

'It's all mixed up, and crap. I did something, well, a bit questionable and now my mum's disappointed in me. She's old school, she had me late in life, and she believes in traditional values and stuff.'

Perry's expression is almost serene. He seems like a therapist more than a mathematician. He's waiting, apparently without judgement to listen to my woes. Why the hell does that make me want him more?

'I split from my husband.'

'Is that so bad?'

'Well, I was unhappy, I went with another bloke. I didn't even like him all that much, but it gave my husband grounds for divorce.' I drag in breath, and let it out gustily, trying not to start crying again. 'And now my mum is so disappointed with me. But, while I'm saving for a place of my own, she still offered me a home back with her.'

I lose the fight against tears and collapse even deeper into Perry's comforting arms. I've been holding this in for so long, holding it from myself in a way, and even to let some of it out now is so sweet a relief.

He makes a lot of quiet, soothing sounds and mutterings, along with pattings and strokings of my back. The voice is the same one that called me a 'naughty slut' and all that and, in its way, just as exciting. I feel a great rush of something more than desire, but also tangled up with it. A sort of momentum towards Perry from my heart. I barely know the man but I feel a glimmering of something special, or maybe just the potential of it. Which is enough for now.

Patting and stroking gently morphs into hugging and rocking against each other, and kisses. Actual kisses this time, our mouths pressing, savouring, opening, so our tongues can explore. It's sexy and still naughty, I suppose, to be snogging and making out with my mother's lodger in the undergrowth down the side of Adultery Alley but, somehow, it also feels clean and healthy and right, even though we're rolling about in the grass and dust in a hedgerow.

When Perry slides his hand beneath my T-shirt again, it feels as if he's sweeping away the bad and replacing it with the good. I respond by rocking against him, smiling in the kiss. When I reach down and cup his groin, he laughs in his throat, the sound raw and happy.

'I haven't got a condom with me, you know,' he mutters against my lips, but he doesn't sound too worried about it.

I am worried, though, and I pull back to look at him. I so dearly want to fuck this sweet imp of a man and this is a serious obstacle.

He touches my cheek. 'Don't worry, sweetheart.' He gives me

the quirkiest little smile that sets my pussy fluttering without it even being touched. 'There are plenty of nice things to do without penetration. And I know you like being fondled, don't you?'

Fondle? What a word. Sort of old-fashioned, but I like it.

'But what about you?'

He shrugs. 'Oh, a little spurt into the bushes will do me, as long as you have a hand in it.'

'Or on it.'

'Exactly.'

Perry slides his hand right under my top this time, and flips my bra off my breasts with a suspicious deftness. He's certainly done this plenty of times before, but who cares? Who cares when his fingertip is so light and clever in the way it circles first one nipple then the other, 'fondling' them both to stiffness, to a new sensitivity. He pays them extended attention, stroking and playing, the pressure there a perfect conduit to the even-more-responsive zone between my legs.

After ten minutes of this I'm beside myself, pushing my crotch against his thigh. It feels solid and warm and perfect to rock against. I set up a rhythm and Perry helps, cupping my bottom, adding momentum, increasing the pressure.

I want him to touch my pussy, but he keeps rocking me, sliding against me in a syncopated dance, arousing me through my clothes and his. Heat and wetness and excitement gather and gather and gather until critical mass is reached.

I climax furiously, burying my face in his shoulder, my head full of his cologne and his foxy male sweat as he holds my bottom and my back, clasping him close. I want to cry out, but I just sob against his T-shirt. The car we were watching drove away some time ago, but who knows who else might be around and listening.

Shuddering, I come down again, a bit weepy, but happy with

it. I have good feelings about this. Better than I've ever had, even in the first days of my marriage.

With a sigh, Perry kisses me, as if setting a seal on my thoughts and my hopes. 'You're beautiful,' he whispers, still holding me. 'So beautiful ... I love to see you come.'

I look up into his warm brown eyes, and I know he means it. And I also know, when my hands rove to his crotch, that he needs to come too.

His eyebrows shoot up when I unfasten his jeans and get him out, but then his smile widens and goes sort of smug, and very, very male.

He's a nice size. A very nice size. It's a great shame we can't put Tab A into Slot B on this occasion, but I resolve to rectify that situation sooner rather than later. Next time we come out for a walk, I'll have condoms. Lots of them.

I begin to rub him and he cups his hand around mine, guiding my strokes. I don't mind this. I want to please him. I want to give him exactly the kind of wank that he prefers, because, God knows, he got his fondling of me spot on.

We slip and slide, using the silky fluid that flows from his tip as a lubricant. He mutters and whispers, praising my technique and also letting out some far less cogent utterances. It doesn't take long because he doesn't hold back and, pretty soon, he's arching and snarling silently, his penis jerking and jetting out his cream.

I kiss him as he comes, just as he kissed me while I came. And, as promised, his come *does* end up in the bushes.

On the way home, I don't quite know what to say to him, and I find myself worrying about what lies ahead for us. Or for me, because, despite my hopes, there might not be an 'us'. He'll be getting a flat or a house soon, and he'll move away, and out of my circle. My job and his university are miles and poles apart.

Perry's hand slips into mine and gently but firmly jerks me to a stop. 'Why the frown?'

It's hard to explain. I still want him. But I want more. And it's awkward. To him this was probably just a frolic, an illicit 'liaison', nothing more. I bite my lip and, just as I'm about to summon up some kind of explanation, not the real reason, but something acceptable and not too embarrassing for both of us, his impish, stubbly face settles into very firm and professorial lines. 'Katie, what sort of man do you think I am?'

I shrug. 'I don't know. I barely know you at all. That's the problem. You must think I'm awfully cheap and easy and slutty.'

'Please, don't go there again. I don't think that at all. Except only in the nicest, sexiest way.' He pulls me to him, and gives me a very chaste kiss on the tip of the nose. 'Now we've broken the ice, I'd like to go back to the beginning, and do things differently. Properly.'

My heart thuds. 'What do you mean?'

'How would you feel about dinner? A trip to the theatre? A stroll that doesn't involve Adultery Alley?'

I'm speechless.

'In fact, I think it would be nice if we took your mother out somewhere for dinner too some time. So she can get used to us as a couple, if you know what I mean?'

'That'd be lovely.'

He smiles. 'I want her to think that I'm above board, and worthy of her daughter.' He gives me a wink. 'So that when I get my own place and you stay overnight, she won't be too cross with me.'

'I can't wait.' I throw my arms around him and give him a hug, my heart lighter than it's been in a long time. 'But do you think we can still pop down to the Alley now and again as well? I'd still like to be naughty on occasion. And I still like to watch.'

He laughs and shakes his head. 'Oh, don't you worry. We'll still be naughty too.' He slides his arm around my waist, then lets his hand rest on my bottom. 'We'll be incredibly naughty. Naughtier than you can possibly imagine.' My pussy ripples again in anticipation. 'But I think we'd probably best not tell your mother about that.'

'Yeah, probably not.' I kiss him, and the future suddenly looks incredibly bright.

Portia Da Costa is the author of the Black Lace novels *Continuum, Entertaining Mr Stone, Gemini Heat, Gothic Blue, Hotbed, Shadowplay, Suite Seventeen, The Devil Inside, The Stranger, The Tutor, In Too Deep* and *Kiss It Better.* Her paranormal novellas are included in the Black Lace collections *Lust Bites* and *Magic and Desire.*

Visit the Black Lace website at
www.blacklace.co.uk

LOOK OUT FOR THE ALL-NEW BLACK LACE BOOKS – AVAILABLE NOW!

All books priced £7.99 in the UK. Please note publication dates apply to the UK only. For other territories, please contact your retailer.

To be published in May 2009

CASSANDRA'S CHATEAU
Fredrica Alleyn
ISBN 978 0 352 34523 3

Cassandra has been living with Baron Dieter von Ritter in his sumptuous Loire valley chateau for eighteen months when their already bizarre relationship takes an unexpected turn. The arrival of a friend's daughter provides the Baron with ample opportunity to indulge his fancy for playing darkly erotic games with strangers. Cassandra knows that if the newcomer learns how to satisfy his taste for pleasure and perversity, her days at the chateau may well be numbered, something she can hardly bear to contemplate. But help may be at hand from an unlikely source.

HIGHLAND FLING
Jane Justine
ISBN 978 0 352 34522 6

Writer Charlotte Harvey is researching the mysterious legend of the Highland Ruby pendant for an antiques magazine. Her quest leads her to a remote Scottish island where the pendant's owner, the dark and charismatic Andrew Alexander, is keen to test its powers on his guest. Alexander has a reputation for wild and – some say – decadent behaviour. In this rugged environment Charlotte discovers the truth – the hard way.

To be published in June 2009

KISS IT BETTER
Portia Da Costa
ISBN 978 0 352 34521 9

Sandy Jackson knows a certain magic is missing from her life. And her dreams are filled with heated images of a Prince Charming she once encountered, a man who thrilled her with a breathtaking touch. Jay Bentley is also haunted by erotic visions starring a woman from his youth. But as the past is so often an illusion, and the present fraught with obstacles, can two lovers reconcile their differences and slake the burning hunger for each other in a wild and daring liaison?

DARK OBSESSION
Fredrica Alleyn
ISBN 978 0 352 33281 3

Ambitious young interior designer Annabel Moss is delighted when a new assignment takes her to Leyton Hall – home of the very wealthy Lord and Lady Corbett-Wynne. But the grandeur of the house and the impeccable family credentials are a façade for some shockingly salacious practices.

Lord James is spending an unusual amount of time in the stables while his idle son shows little interest in anything save his stepsister, Tania. Meanwhile, Lady Marina is harbouring dark secrets of her own. Annabel is drawn into a world of decadence where anything is allowed as long as a respectable appearance prevails. In an atmosphere of intensity and sexual secrecy, she becomes involved in a variety of interesting situations.

DOCTOR'S ORDERS
Deanna Ashford
ISBN 978 0 352 33453 4

Helen Dawson is a dedicated doctor who has taken a short-term assignment at an exclusive private hospital that caters for every need of its rich and famous clients. The matron, Sandra Pope, ensures this includes their most curious sexual fantasies. When Helen forms a risky affair with a famous actor, she is drawn deeper into the hedonistic lifestyle of the clinic. But will she risk her own privileges when she uncovers the dubious activities of Sandra and her team?

To be published in July 2009

SARAH'S EDUCATION
Madeline Moore
ISBN 978 0 352 34539 4

Nineteen year old Sarah is an ordinary but beautiful girl engaged to a wealthy fiancé, and soon to be the recipient of all the privileges and opportunities marriage into the upper class can bring. She is also a virgin but, at an exclusive party at a hotel, loses her virginity to a man who is not her fiancé. In the morning she wakes to find an envelope containing $2,500 on the bedside table; Sarah has been mistaken for a high class call-girl. Soon, she is leading a secret life in top hotels with strange and exciting men, until one of her clients turns out to be her professor from university and a man she has long had a crush on. Their nights of passion and journeys into erotic role-playing become an expensive obsession for each of them. The biggest decision of all for their future has to be made when they are both threatened with exposure. What will Sarah sacrifice for the passion of a lifetime?

GOING TOO FAR
Laura Hamilton
ISBN 978 0 352 33657 6

Spirited adventurer Bliss Van Bon sets off on a three-month tour of South America. Along the way there's no shortage of company. From flirting on the plane to being tied up in Peru; from sex on snowy mountain peaks to finding herself out of her depth will local crooks, Bliss hardly has time to draw breath. And when brawny Australians Red and Robbie are happy to share their tent and their gorgeous bodies with her, she's spoilt for choice. But Bliss soon finds herself caught between her lovers' agendas. Will she help Red and Robbie save the planet, or will she stick with Carlos, whose wealthy lifestyle has dubious origins?

THE SEVEN YEAR LIST
Zoe Le Verdier
ISBN 978 0 352 33254 7

Newspaper photographer Julia Sargent should be happy and fulfilled. But flattering minor celebrities is not her idea of a challenge, and she's also having doubts about her impending marriage to heart-throb actor David Tindall. In the midst of her uncertainty comes an invitation to a school reunion. When the group meet up, adolescent passions are rekindled – and so are bitter rivalries – as Julia flirts with old flames Nick and Steve. Julia cannot resist one last fling with Steve, but he will not let her go – not until he has achieved the final goal on his seven year list.

ALSO LOOK OUT FOR

THE NEW BLACK LACE BOOK OF WOMEN'S SEXUAL FANTASIES
Edited and compiled by Mitzi Szereto
ISBN 978 0 352 34172 3

The second anthology of detailed sexual fantasies contributed by women from all over the world. The book is a result of a year's research by an expert on erotic writing and gives a fascinating insight into the rich diversity of the female sexual imagination.

Black Lace Booklist

Information is correct at time of printing. To avoid disappointment, check availability before ordering. Go to www.blacklace.co.uk
All books are priced £7.99 unless another price is given.

BLACK LACE BOOKS WITH A CONTEMPORARY SETTING

☐ UNNATURAL SELECTION Alaine Hood ISBN 978 0 352 33963 8
☐ UP TO NO GOOD Karen Smith ISBN 978 0 352 33589 0
☐ VELVET GLOVE Emma Holly ISBN 978 0 352 34115 0
☐ VILLAGE OF SECRETS Mercedes Kelly ISBN 978 0 352 33344 5
☐ WILD BY NATURE Monica Belle ISBN 978 0 352 33915 7 £6.99
☐ WILD CARD Madeline Moore ISBN 978 0 352 34038 2
☐ WING OF MADNESS Mae Nixon ISBN 978 0 352 34099 3

BLACK LACE BOOKS WITH AN HISTORICAL SETTING

☐ A GENTLEMAN'S WAGER Madelynne Ellis ISBN 978 0 352 34173 0
☐ THE BARBARIAN GEISHA Charlotte Royal ISBN 978 0 352 33267 7
☐ BARBARIAN PRIZE Deanna Ashford ISBN 978 0 352 34017 7
☐ THE CAPTIVATION Natasha Rostova ISBN 978 0 352 33234 9
☐ DARKER THAN LOVE Kristina Lloyd ISBN 978 0 352 33279 0
☐ WILD KINGDOM Deanna Ashford ISBN 978 0 352 33549 4
☐ DIVINE TORMENT Janine Ashbless ISBN 978 0 352 33719 1
☐ FRENCH MANNERS Olivia Christie ISBN 978 0 352 33214 1
☐ LORD WRAXALL'S FANCY Anna Lieff Saxby ISBN 978 0 352 33080 2
☐ NICOLE'S REVENGE Lisette Allen ISBN 978 0 352 32984 4
☐ THE SENSES BEJEWELLED Cleo Cordell ISBN 978 0 352 32904 2 £6.99
☐ THE SOCIETY OF SIN Sian Lacey Taylder ISBN 978 0 352 34080 1
☐ TEMPLAR PRIZE Deanna Ashford ISBN 978 0 352 34137 2
☐ UNDRESSING THE DEVIL Angel Strand ISBN 978 0 352 33938 6

BLACK LACE BOOKS WITH A PARANORMAL THEME

☐ BRIGHT FIRE Maya Hess ISBN 978 0 352 34104 4
☐ BURNING BRIGHT Janine Ashbless ISBN 978 0 352 34085 6
☐ CRUEL ENCHANTMENT Janine Ashbless ISBN 978 0 352 33483 1
☐ DARK ENCHANTMENT Janine Ashbless ISBN 978 0 352 34513 4
☐ ENCHANTED Various ISBN 978 0 352 34195 2
☐ FLOOD Anna Clare ISBN 978 0 352 34094 8
☐ GOTHIC BLUE Portia Da Costa ISBN 978 0 352 33075 8
☐ GOTHIC HEAT ISBN 978 0 352 34170 9
☐ THE PASSION OF ISIS Madelynne Ellis ISBN 978 0 352 33993 4
☐ PHANTASMAGORIA Madelynne Ellis ISBN 978 0 352 34168 6
☐ THE PRIDE Edie Bingham ISBN 978 0 352 33997 3

To find out the latest information about Black Lace titles, check out the website: www.blacklace.co.uk or send for a booklist with complete synopses by writing to:

Black Lace Booklist, Virgin Books Ltd
Random House
20 Vauxhall Bridge Road
London SW1V 2SA

Please include an SAE of decent size. Please note only British stamps are valid.

Our privacy policy
We will not disclose information you supply us to any other parties. We will not disclose any information which identifies you personally to any person without your express consent.

From time to time we may send out information about Black Lace books and special offers. Please tick here if you do <u>not</u> wish to receive Black Lace information.   ❏

Please send me the books I have ticked above.

Name ....

Address ....

....

....

....

Post Code ....

Send to: Virgin Books Cash Sales, Black Lace,
Random House, 20 Vauxhall Bridge Road, London SW1V 2SA.

US customers: for prices and details of how to order
books for delivery by mail, call 888-330-8477.

Please enclose a cheque or postal order, made payable
to Virgin Books Ltd, to the value of the books you have
ordered plus postage and packing costs as follows:

UK and BFPO – £1.00 for the first book, 50p for each
subsequent book.

Overseas (including Republic of Ireland) – £2.00 for
the first book, £1.00 for each subsequent book.

If you would prefer to pay by VISA, ACCESS/MASTERCARD,
DINERS CLUB, AMEX or MAESTRO, please write your card
number and expiry date here: ....

....

Signature ....

Please allow up to 28 days for delivery.